FULL CIRCLE

Since leaving Drama School Jane has pursued two careers, one as a director of theatre and opera, and the other as a writer. For her own company, the English Chamber Theatre (President, Dame Judi Dench) she wrote and directed over 30 productions. These productions took her all over the world and she has met and worked with many fascinating people including Dame Margot Fonteyn and Robert Helpmann, Jackie Kennedy Onassis, Anthony Quinn, Sir Derek Jacobi, Jessye Norman and many others.

For 10 years she was the Artistic Director of Opera UK – and apart from directing operas and concerts, she wrote 3 English translations of opera librettos and an original libretto, The People's Passion" which was filmed for BBC 1. She also wrote the libretto for an original children's opera, Hello Mr Darwin. All Jane's productions are now under one umbrella, TJM PRODUCTIONS.

Jane is now devoting her time to writing fiction and all details of her books can be found on her website, www.janemcculloch.com

She has four children and ten grandchildren and is now based in London.

FULL CIRCLE
NATASHA'S STORY

BOOK 3 OF THE THREE LIVES TRILOGY

First Published in Great Britain

Copyright © 2016 Jane McCulloch

The right of Jane McCulloch to be identified as author
of this work has been asserted by her in accordance with the
Copyright, Designs and Patents Act 1988.

*All characters in this publication are fictitious and any
resemblance to real persons, living or dead,
is purely coincidental.*

All Rights Reserved.

No part of this publication may be reproduced, stored in a
retrieval system, or transmitted, in any form or by any means,
electronic, mechanical, photocopying, recording or otherwise,
without the prior permission of the copyright owner.

ISBN 978-1532918650

Cover Design by Gracie Carver
Typeset by Green Door Design for Publishing

For Bridget Armstrong

'What is love? There is nothing in the world, neither man nor Devil nor any thing, that I hold as suspect as love, for it penetrates the soul more than any other thing. Therefore, unless you have those weapons that subdue it, the soul plunges through love into an immense abyss.'

Umberto Eco "The Name of the Rose"

PROLOGUE
LOS ANGELES - 1994

Euan Mackay awoke with a start, opened one eye and found himself fully clothed, lying on a deserted beach. He quickly snapped his eyelid shut. But that one swift glance had been enough to ascertain that the Los Angeles early morning smog had lifted, that the sun was high in the sky and that it was now beating down on him with a terrible ferocity. He also ascertained that he was not in the best of shape. His head was pounding, his body had a limp, bruised feel and there was that faint sensation of nausea usually associated with a night of heavy indulgence. He tried to lick his lips but his tongue was dry and rough and had the texture of old cracked leather.

A few minutes passed and then he ventured to open the other eye. Gingerly lifting his head he noted that his left shoe was missing and there was a hole in his black silk sock.

A solitary child stood watching him. Euan didn't feel up to conversation so lay back and let out a faint moan.

When he next opened his eyes the child had gone and the beach had returned to its deserted state. He felt unnerved. Maybe he had imagined the child. Maybe he had DT's.

After a couple of attempts he sat up and forced his eyes back onto the dazzling sand. A little further down the beach he saw his shoe. The pounding of the surf was drastically increasing the pain in his head. Somehow he had to make an effort to move. Summoning all his strength he got to his feet, picked up the wayward shoe and limped across the sand towards the dirt track, where he found his car parked at a jaunty angle, blocking the entire roadway. With something nearing panic he searched for the car keys in his pocket, but found nothing more than a few dollar bills, a credit card, a squashed pack of cigarettes and a box of matches from the 'Zulu Club', a place he had never heard of. He lurched towards the car and to his relief found the offending keys in the ignition. Starting the engine he thanked the Gods that there was just about enough fuel to get him home. He turned the car round and slowly headed back towards Venice Beach.

By the time he reached the comfort of his leather sofa it was well past midday. He lay with his eyes shut, vainly trying to piece together the events of the night before. But his mind was an alarming blank. This was not a good scene. Not a good scene at all.

Stretching out a practised toe he hit the message button on his answering machine. After an unpleasant series of clicks and bleeps a familiar voice came on the line. It was his good friend Jack Kline.

"Boy, oh boy Euan. That was some night! Who found that Zulu Club anyway? What a dive! Remind me never to touch Tequila again."

Tequila. So that was the cause of all the trouble.

"I sure didn't think I was going to make it this morning. Those last shots did for me. Anyway, thanks for the good times. See you around."

The machine clicked and the robot-like voice spoke, "Tuesday 10.20 a.m." It clicked again into the unmistakeable Bronx whine of his agent Otto.

"Euan, baby, what are you trying to do to me? You don't visit, you don't call. Do you want to bring my ulcers back? I need that final draft. By Friday. Did you hear that Euan? By Friday. In my optimistic moments I see you working there right now which is why you aren't taking this call. Give me a break and tell me this is true."

There was a pause on the tape. He heard background office noises. Otto had obviously been distracted. But not for long.

"I hope you've remembered that Gloria Heidelburg is interviewing you today at 2? It's an important one Euan. Be there. Yer, and take a shower. Dress nicely for Gloria. She'll notice."

Another click. The robot spoke again. "Tuesday 11.25 a.m. No messages."

Euan pushed the off button with his toe and started searching his memory. Gloria Heidelburg? What sort of name was that? And who the hell was she?

He made a decided effort not to give into temptation and fall asleep for a week. Instead he staggered to the kitchen, flung open the fridge door and tried to make a decision between a Bloody Mary and a Budweiser. In the end he decided on the latter. It was too much effort to make the other. As he drained the last drop he decided he felt strong enough to take a shower. He then rang Otto.

"Just putting you through," the girl assured him. Even so it took some time and he listened to some horribly loud and cheerful music which tempted him to give up.

"I wish you wouldn't do that," he said crossly as Otto came on the line.

"Do what for Christ's sake?"

"Play that bloody awful jingle music. It gives your clients stress."

Otto chuckled. "Only you Euan baby. Only you. So what's gotten into you? Didn't you make it last night?"

"I haven't a clue what I did last night. Jack tells me we had a lot of Tequila, but that's about all I know."

"You gotta cut out the alcohol Euan. I'm serious." Otto sounded reproving. "We're all living healthy these days. No drink, no drugs and certainly no sex. The Aids thing has turned us all into clean and sober citizens. Its carrot juice and yoga classes now. You should try it."

Euan ignored this. "So what's with this Gloria Heidelburg? I don't remember you telling me about her?"

Otto's voice had a note of triumph. "You see? That's what alcohol does. It affects the memory. You don't remember things. I did tell you many times about Gloria Heidelburg. And for why? I'll tell you for why, because she's a big fish in this Movie pond. Everybody who is anybody in the Movie Business reads her. If you weren't so goddam aloof and British you would know this. More to the point this Broad has asked for you especially. She's doing an article on Brits in Hollywood and you're the token screenwriter. So be a good boy for Otto and turn on some of that Scottish charm."

Euan inwardly groaned. "All right Otto. I'll do it. But if you want the final draft by Friday I can't give her long." There was a short pause and then he asked in puzzled tones, "What day is it today?"

"Tuesday Euan, Tuesday. My God what is it with you? Are you that bad you can't even remember what day it is?"

Euan grinned. "Yes Otto. I'm that bad."

As he put the receiver down he thought of Otto's expression and for the first time since he'd woken up he felt almost cheerful.

Otto Gelb was one of Hollywood's living legends. He had arrived from the Bronx when a young man. Now in his early fifties he had more screenwriters on his list than any other agent in town. His obvious success, his prodigious work rate and his quirky sense of humour, meant that in the main his writers remained with him. Although some were brave enough to quibble at his demands, few were brave enough to disregard them, for Otto was a good agent. The best. He knew everybody. He knew all the Studio bosses and where the next project was coming from. He could be seen daily in Harry's Bar sniffing out assignments and it was taken for granted that no project with any potential was ever missed by Otto Gelb.

When Euan first met him, he thought Otto bore an uncanny resemblance to James Cagney. Later he decided he was more like Danny de Vito. Whoever he looked like, his face had that comedic, rubbery look which gave rise to expressions that would make the onlooker laugh. He chain-smoked cigars and had a characteristic way of running his hands through his receding hair when he became excited. No-one knew much about Otto's private life, if indeed he had one. There was a rumour that there was a Mrs Gelb, but nobody had ever seen her, nor did he ever refer to a spouse. It remained a mystery. His world was his office and the only appearance of a social life was that connected to his work.

Otto Gelb had been the first person Euan had met in Los Angeles. On his arrival in 1987 he had been taken by limousine straight from the airport to a meeting with his producers. It was typical of the speed with which Hollywood moved. As he went into the office Otto was in reception, waiting for him. He'd immediately walked over to Euan and introduced himself.

"Mr Mackay? Nice to meet you. The name's Gelb. Otto Gelb. I think you're gonna need an agent. Here's my card. Be in touch."

And that was more or less that. Otto Gelb had arranged and organised Euan's life from that moment on. He'd found him an apartment, a car, a lawyer, an accountant, 'female companions' and best of all, one assignment after another. In many ways Euan was the ideal client. He always met his deadlines, he worked fast and fluently and never complained about the content of the work, even though some of it was fairly trivial stuff. Euan just shrugged his shoulders and remarked that the pay was the same. This had surprised Otto. Some of his British writers, less talented than Euan, make it very clear they felt they were selling out when they came to Hollywood, that their work was somehow immediately made inferior. If Euan felt this he never said so. Nor did he throw temperaments as did many of his countrymen when asked to do re-writes, or even worse, when someone else was asked to do the re-writes for them. That's when the screaming usually started. Not so with Euan. He remained totally laid back about the whole process of writing. In fact, he was totally laid back about the whole process of life. Otto sometimes tried a minor probe in an effort to get beneath the shell. But he hadn't succeeded, even though Euan had been with him now for almost seven years. Recently he hadn't bothered. He liked the guy, he did his work and he was best left alone if that's the way he wanted it.

It certainly suited Euan. From the time he had arrived in Tinsel town, he had made a determined effort to remain uninvolved, in every way. Gone was the ambition to write something powerful, or original. Gone was the wish to have a meaningful relationship, let alone a passionate one. As long as the work kept coming in along with the money, he was happy enough. He didn't want to think, or feel, ever again. At least, that is what he told himself. But just recently he'd found his thoughts drifting back to England. Small bouts of homesickness and misery would sweep over him as he remembered the events that led up to his abrupt departure. He'd think of Natasha and then Natasha and Gerry... and then he'd climb into his car and indulge in what his friends politely referred to as 'Euan's drinking sessions' and what he less politely referred to as a 'full blown bender'. Presumably that is what he'd been doing last night although it was worrying he had absolutely no recollection of the evening whatsoever. He'd have to ring Jack Kline later and find out. With a little prompting it would probably come back to him.

He looked at his watch. It was nearly one already. The famous Gloria's arrival was imminent and he was still in a bath robe. He went into the bathroom, stared into the shaving mirror and decided designer stubble was not for her. He had promised Otto to make an effort and this he would do.

He stared again. Was it his imagination or was his skin really beginning to turn yellow? It had to be the light, or had he got liver damage already? At his age? He was only forty two. He patted on some aftershave and vowed never to drink again. In the bedroom he made a frantic search for clean clothes and then took a glance at the long mirror to make sure he had carried out Otto's instructions to the full. Even the briefest of glances revealed more lines on his face than he remembered. Women often told him he looked craggy but he wasn't entirely sure this was a compliment. Most probably they really meant he looked raddled, or even debauched. Was he going the way of Oscar Wilde and Dylan Thomas? He peered again more closely. No he wasn't quite as bad as that, yet. On closer inspection he noticed a few strands of grey ran through his hair. He hoped this gave him a distinguished look, although he was aware that male vanity in Hollywood did not allow for greying hair. Gloria would just have to accept the fact that he was British and nothing to do with the Hollywood specimens of manhood.

Gloria Heidelburg arrived on time, looking immaculate. It was all too predictable really. Long, leggy and blonde with more gleaming white teeth than anyone had a right to expect. She settled herself on the leather sofa, elegant in tailored pink linen and removed her large sunglasses. He offered her a drink. She flashed him a dazzling smile.

"I don't suppose you keep my speciality," she said with irritating archness.

Euan protested that he had practically everything in the alcoholic line.

"Oh no." She looked shocked. "Nothing alcoholic. I was referring to camomile tea."

He had to admit defeat and fetched a club soda for her and a Pepsi for himself.

"Now," she said, flipping open a smart leather notebook, "Let's try and find out something about the mysterious Euan Mackay."

Euan winced. "Mysterious?"

"So my contacts tell me. Even Otto Gelb said you were something of an enigma."

Euan was forced to smile. "I don't find that very surprising. However, I do assure you there's nothing very interesting about me."

Gloria ignored this and looked round the room. "Have you always lived in Venice Beach?"

"Yes. I was told it was where the upwardly mobile writers hung out and who was I to argue?" His flippancy drew no reaction from Gloria. "Actually it was Otto Gelb who found me this apartment when I first arrived and I've been here ever since."

Her face relaxed into a faint smile. "You keep your room very sparse. I mean, I just love the uncluttered look but this is verging on monastic."

Euan shrugged. "I like to live with as few trappings as possible. The only furniture I really like is books and I left my book collection behind in England."

She crossed and uncrossed her long legs. "Ah, yes, England. How long ago did you leave your native shores?"

"1987. October 16th."

"Good heavens. You remember the actual day?"

"Yes." His tones were clipped. "I remember the actual day."

She noticed the sudden tension in his face and decided not to pursue this. Instead she started to make a journalistic assessment.

He wasn't conventionally handsome in the Hollywood sense of the word but there was definitely a certain something about him. Otto was right. The man was an enigma. Obviously he was a little past his sell-by date, but he had a kind of lean and hungry look that made him definitely attractive. Maybe she would call him attractively craggy.

He lit a cigarette. "Do you mind?" She told him no, but meant yes. He went on cheerfully, "I have all the vices. I don't think I will come up to your reader's standards at all."

She ignored this. The last thing she wanted was a list of his unpleasant habits. Instead she said, "I'm told you are something of a lady's man."

Oh really! He vowed to give Otto a piece of his mind for landing him with this. His head had begun to thud again and he was just about to withdraw and swallow a few aspirins when Gloria persisted, "Do you think that's true? Are you a lady's man?"

He shrugged. "It's one of those meaningless titles. I expect it refers to the fact that I'm not seen out with any one particular woman."

"So you are footloose and fancy free?" He nodded. "You're uncluttered, like your room?" He nodded again and stubbed out his cigarette. Her probing continued. "So have you ever had a meaningful relationship?" She looked at him straight in the eye, as if to challenge him to give an honest answer. He groaned inwardly. A meaningful relationship? What the hell did that mean? Celia? Natasha? Were they meaningful? He hadn't a clue, but her stare was relentless. He was going to have to say something, so he finally said yes.

She came back sharply. "But it didn't last?"

"No, it didn't last."

"Was it in England?"

"Yes it was in England."

"Is that why you escaped to LA?"

Euan started to sweat. What was this, the Hollywood equivalent of the Spanish Inquisition? He decided to fight back. In dry tones he told her that he had been coming to LA anyway because he'd been made an offer which he couldn't refuse.

Gloria examined her notes and quoted the name of a Mini Series. "You had an immediate success. In fact you've been extremely prolific in the last..."

"Six years" he said helpfully. "Seven in October."

Gloria put down her notebook and gave him a look that sent a shudder down his spine. This woman was dangerous and far shrewder than her outward appearance had led him to believe. Her voice tone changed to one of conspiratorial intimacy.

"Do you mind if I ask you an impertinent question Euan?"

"Please feel free Gloria," he said drily.

"I have been checking up on you" she said and paused, wanting the fact that she had done her homework to sink in. "I know that your work, prior to coming here, was of a high literary calibre." She looked at her notes again. "Two distinguished adaptations for TV, a documentary drama that won international awards, an award winning screenplay that many felt should have had an Oscar nomination, and so forth. So I am intrigued. Don't you find what you are doing now rather, well, dare I say it, trivial? For such a good writer I mean?"

Euan shrugged. "It suits me to live here, the work is plentiful and the money is good...

She gave a scornful laugh. "Don't take me for a fool Euan. I don't believe that the money means that much to you."

"I am a Scot Gloria," he said trying to make light of it, "and we Scots are a very acquisitive race." She didn't look remotely convinced by this so he went on, "It actually takes a good writer to write, dare I say it, 'good trivia'. And there's nothing wrong with that. In fact in our modern stressful life, good trivia is a necessity. After all, we are in the entertainment business are we not?"

She looked at him, trying to decide whether he was taking her interview quite seriously. His voice, with its gentle Scottish lilt was a little difficult to fathom. She decided to change tack, but before she could do so, the telephone rang.

Euan frowned. He'd forgotten to turn on the machine. He got up.

"I'm sorry. I'll have to answer that. Will you excuse me for a moment?"

He went into the study and picked up. "Hello? Euan Mackay here."

"Hello Euan. It's Wal. Wal Simmons"

Euan stood rigid with shock. "Wal? Where are you? Are you here in LA?"

"No, I'm at home. I'm calling from London."

Euan felt a strange sinking feeling in the pit of his stomach. Wal? Ringing from London? That had to be bad news. Nobody had called him from England since his mother had died and that was at least five years ago. His mouth went so dry he could hardly speak. Finally he stammered out, "Is it Natasha? What's happened? Has something happened to Natasha?

Wal's voice was calming. "No, no, it's not urgent. I just need to talk to you at some point. Is this a bad time?"

"It's a little difficult. I have someone with me. Give me ten minutes. I'll ring you back."

"Of course. I'm at home. It's the same number."

Euan put down the receiver and walked back into the room.

Gloria noticed that he had gone rather pale. "Not bad news I hope?"

He shook his head. "Just a rather unexpected call from England. I said I'd ring back. I'd be grateful if we could wrap this up fairly soon. I do apologise."

This didn't please Gloria at all. She was beginning to be rather intrigued by Euan Mackay and thought that a prolonged probing might produce some fascinating copy. But for this she needed his full co-operation so she decided that a further interview would be the best course of action. She gave him a dazzling smile to disguise her annoyance and put her notebook away.

"Not to worry. I'll come back and see you at a more convenient time."

In a few minutes she was gone.

Euan made himself a pot of coffee and headed back towards the telephone. Although Wal was his friend and his lawyer, he was also related to Natasha and had made a promise to get in touch if anything was wrong. It was therefore difficult to believe that this was merely a social call, not after so many years. With slow deliberation he dialled the number. Almost immediately Wal answered. He must have been waiting for him to call back. Euan's heart beat faster and without waiting for any social preliminaries he burst out,

"All right, tell me. What's wrong?"

Wal's tones were soothing. "There's no immediate problem Euan. Yes, it is about Natasha but I could be bothering you quite unnecessarily. There's nothing actually wrong, well not really wrong..."

"Don't waffle. It's unlike you to waffle." Euan said irritably. "You're a lawyer. Just give me the facts,"

"All right, keep calm and I will. The facts are these. About eighteen months ago Natasha's paternal grandfather died, old Sir Malcolm Roxby Smith..."

Euan interrupted again. "She wasn't particularly close to him was she?"

"Not particularly, although I believe she liked the old boy and saw him on her frequent visits to her Norfolk cousins. It seems he took a special liking to her because in his Will, from the estate, he left her the Dower house and lodge, a fairly sizeable property."

There was a pause until Euan said impatiently, "Yes? And?"

Wal continued. "Natasha's original plan had been to sell it for what would have been quite a substantial sum. Then suddenly, about a year ago, she changed her mind..."

Another pause. In his frustration Euan almost shouted, "Wal for God's sake get on with it. The suspense is killing me."

"It's a trifle difficult Euan. I know how impulsive you are and I don't want you leaping to the wrong conclusion." Another pause and then he continued more quickly, "However I think you ought to know that she is now using the property for herself."

There was a sharp intake of breath as Euan said, "You mean she's left Gerry. Is that what you are trying to tell me? That she's left Gerry?"

Wal took his time and when he spoke it was with great precision. "I think that is an accurate assessment of the situation. They had moved to London because Gerry took up the appointment of a minor canonry at Southwark Cathedral. Then, nearly a year ago, Natasha came to see me and told me she was leaving Gerry to live in the house in Norfolk. I drew up the separation papers and that appeared to be that. Gerry has now left Southwark and gone to work in the South African townships."

There was silence as Euan took this in. Finally he said, "If this happened months ago why ring me now? Has something happened to Natasha since?"

Wal sounded hesitant, almost embarrassed. "That's just it. Nobody knows. She's become a total recluse. She communicates with no-one, not even her cousin Livvy. It's Livvy who's really worried. I thought Natasha might have written to you."

"No. I've heard nothing. We haven't communicated since I left England." He added bitterly, "That was the instruction wasn't it?"

Wal ignored this but before he had time to say anything else Euan burst out, "I'll come over. I'll catch a flight to England this weekend."

Wal was instantly alarmed. "There's no need for that Euan. Really, I'm sure she's fine, after all we'd have heard if..."

The line started to crackle. Euan yelled, "It's a bad line Wal, probably the start of another earthquake. I'll let you know you know what day I'm arriving. I'll need to stay with you to start with. Can you clear it with Miriam? Speak to you soon. Bye."

Euan replaced the receiver and sat back, feeling shaken. Natasha had left Gerry Masterson. In fact she had left him nearly a year ago. Then why in God's name hadn't she been in touch? She'd promised she would get in touch if things went wrong, yet she hadn't. The only thing now was to return to England and find out for himself. He felt a surge of excitement. This was just the excuse he needed to get away from L.A. There was nothing to keep him here. With a sudden burst of energy he made a list of things to be done. The apartment would have to be sold and his car. He started to make calls.

First thing the next morning he burst, unannounced, into Otto's office. Otto looked aggrieved. "Euan my boy, can't you make an appointment like everybody else?"

"No I can't. Not this morning. I have something important to say."

Otto looked at him. "Is it world shattering?"

"It is world shattering."

Otto lit a cigar and waved his client towards a chair. "In that case, shoot."

Euan put a script down on the desk. "First, I've finished the final draft. And final is the operative word here Otto. I won't change another word. If they want further work, or changes, they can get someone else in to do it. Understood?"

Otto waved his cigar by way of agreement. He was shrewd enough to know this wasn't the reason for Euan's febrile state, so he waited.

Euan took a deep breath. "Second and I know this may sound sudden but I am leaving LA. Going back to England."

There was silence in the room. Otto's face changed expression. One look at the man made him realise that Euan was serious. This was an unexpected blow. It would mean he was losing one of his best and most lucrative writers.

He said slowly, "That is a real shame Euan. I have some great projects lined up for you but I can't land them if you're not here, on the spot, in L.A. Is your mind made up?"

"Yes."

"I can't take you out to Harry's Bar and persuade you different?"

"No."

Otto shrugged. "How drastic a move is this? Is it for ever?"

"I just don't know. I need to deal with some urgent personal business. It could take a week," he paused, "or it could be a good deal longer." He decided not to tell Otto what he himself already knew, that he was making a final break with L.A. He'd already rung the accountant and his lawyer. They had been instructed to wind up his affairs as quickly as possible. He looked down at Otto and realised the little man could read his mind. They both knew what was at stake.

Otto put down his cigar, got up and walked across to Euan and gave him a hug. "Keep me informed of your movements and send me your goddam contact numbers. I don't want to have to send out search parties." He gave Euan a friendly slap on the back. "I'll be here for you when you decide to come back." When they reached the door of his office he added, "You're gonna find it very slow on the other side of the pond. You're a man who needs to keep moving otherwise you'll slow to a stop."

Euan smiled. "I've been moving so fast for the past six years I think I could do with slowing down." He suddenly felt quite emotional. He gripped Otto's hand. "So long Otto. Take care of yourself."

As he moved across reception he heard the telephones start ringing. He looked back. The little man was already at his desk, a telephone in each hand.

Three days later Euan was on the plane, heading for England.

CHAPTER ONE
SEPTEMBER 1994

As Wal Simmons replaced the receiver, a wave of panic swept over him and he groaned out loud, "Oh God Natasha, what have I done?"

Sinking back in his chair he realised he was shaking. The decision to call Euan might have been a grave mistake and if that proved to be the case the consequences would be disastrous. In those few minutes of telephone conversation he had managed to open a can of worms that any sane man would have kept firmly shut. Euan was now going to return from the States, descend on their house and then inevitably make his way up to Norfolk to see Natasha.

He stood up and on sudden impulse and completely out of character, he poured himself a glass of brandy and sank back again in his chair. Taking a gulp he tried to comfort himself with the fact that he had been put under great pressure. His mother had been nagging him for weeks to take some action. How was he to know that Euan would react like an impulsive madman?

He drained the glass and put it down. Another thought struck him and this brought him out in a cold sweat. He was going to have to break the news of Euan's imminent arrival to Miriam and in her present state this would do her no good at all.

He looked at his watch. It was nearly eleven so she would now be in bed. Just lately she had taken to retiring early in the evening. There was no point in waking her. With a bit of luck, if he went to work before she got up, he could leave her a note of explanation. He frowned and gave a long sigh. It wasn't that he wanted to be devious it was just so difficult to know what to do for the best.

Staring at the empty glass he decided another might help to calm him down. He sipped it slowly this time and thought about his wife. Poor Miriam, she was not having a happy middle-age. He had prepared himself carefully for the onslaught of the menopause. After all, he had been a successful divorce lawyer for nearly twenty years and was fully conversant with all the human frailties, both mental and physical. But nothing had prepared him for Miriam's sudden deterioration. He'd tried to be patient, God knows he had tried, but sometimes he felt he almost didn't know her. They called it change of life? More like a change of personality. It was incredible really. When he'd first met her she'd been a bright young lawyer with a potentially brilliant future. Then they'd married and because she was some years older than he, they'd started a family straight away. This had worried him at the time but she'd insisted it was what she wanted and then proceeded to throw herself into domestic and social life with gusto. The house and the children were run with great efficiency. She had been on endless committees, even finding time to run two charities and he'd marvelled at her endless energy, her enthusiasms and her quick mind. Now it was all he could do to have any conversation with her at all. Her violent mood swings took him completely unawares. Home life had become a minefield and the children had responded by leaving the nest as soon as they could.

Wal regarded his empty glass again and decided he might as well have another. It was doing him good, even if he was beginning to feel a touch befuddled.

Collecting his wandering thoughts he started to consider his offspring. Belinda, his eldest, had thankfully at last found herself a husband, a solid, pleasant young man and the two of them seemed to live a solid, pleasant sort of life but definitely on the dull side. Although he wouldn't have admitted it to anyone else, he'd always found his daughter a rather lumpy girl and in spite of Miriam's best endeavours she had never been destined for a brilliant career or for a brilliant match. So it had been quite a relief when boring old Nigel turned up. At least he seemed a dependable sort of chap. No, at least Belinda bless her, had caused them no trouble, unlike their eldest son Alexander. Alex was a continual puzzle to him. He was undoubtedly clever but from the start had been the cause of endless worries. It started at school with the usual problems of drugs, drink, even girls. Then a bad crash on his motor bike had set him back a year. At Oxford the boy appeared to calm down and to their great delight finished with a first, but this parental pride was to be short-lived. A few months after coming down from University he had joined an acting troupe which had taken him off to the Edinburgh Festival Fringe. What followed was a personal resounding success for Alex, making all the National papers and this led to him turning professional and at the moment he showed no sign of giving up his thespian ambitions.

Wal gave a shudder and drained his glass. What a waste. What a terrible waste. If it had been his younger son it would have been no surprise if he had landed in the theatre. Ben was good looking, charming and had an annoying way of always landing on his feet, but in spite of good schools and several cramming establishments, his academic qualifications had remained far from satisfactory. It was therefore something of a surprise that he not only went to work in the City, but was extremely successful and had proceeded to make a small fortune.

Wal stared into his empty glass and decided it would probably be unwise to have another. He really ought to go upstairs. Miriam would be well asleep by now. In any case, it was no good sitting here, wallowing in what might have been, or having regrets about his offspring. The brandy had obviously set him spiralling down the tunnel of self-pity and in all honesty, things weren't really that bad. He made a mental effort to pull himself together. After all, he was a successful lawyer and had survived the Recession. In fact divorces had become a good deal more plentiful in the last few stressful years and his work rate and income had consequently greatly increased. Unlike many of his friends he hadn't put his money into Lloyds and although his children weren't entirely satisfactory, they were to all intents and purposes making steady progress up the ladder of adulthood. He really couldn't complain about his wife either. Miriam might be going through a temporary bad patch but on the whole it had been a good marriage and in the early days she'd been a definite asset, being smart, clever, capable and ambitious for him. Without her he wouldn't have had nearly such a successful practice.

Feeling more cheerful he emptied the last of the brandy into his glass and dropped the bottle into the bin under his desk. He glanced at the family photographs on his desk and idly wondered what it would have been like if he'd remained a bachelor. He had very few bachelor acquaintances now and wasn't sure if he envied them, even with all the problems marriage could bring. There was his brother Luke, who'd been destined for a brilliant career, but instead had gone to India twenty-six years ago and never returned. An occasional postcard informed them that he was still alive. Two years ago his mother had received a photograph. Luke, thin and emaciated with shaved head, was sitting crossed-legged, in Buddhist robes, with a vacant expression on his face. If it hadn't been for the scrawled inscription on the back he wouldn't have recognised him. Was that a good existence?

The only other bachelor he knew well was of course Euan, but the fact he was single was more by mistake than by design. He recalled how at Cambridge Euan had bowled over the girls like nine-pins, causing much envy amongst his contemporaries, himself included. It was therefore something of a relief when Euan stopped his Byronic rampaging through the girls at Newnham and Girton and settled into a steady relationship with a rather serious medical student. After Cambridge he'd lost touch and when he next met Euan it was to learn with some alarm that he was having an affair with his beautiful, but married, cousin Celia. Although he'd never liked Celia's husband George, and pleased she should have found happiness with Euan, this was a potentially explosive situation. But before things came to a head there was that fatal car crash and Celia was killed. Euan had been devastated by her death and he and Miriam had done their best to help him through that time. The years went by and they had lost touch again. And then...

Wal drained the last of the brandy. The cold sweat returned as he remembered the evening, when, in this very house, Euan had re-met Natasha, Celia's daughter, no longer a gawky teenager but a beautiful young woman. From the moment they met it seemed almost inevitable that the two of them should fall in love. It was inevitable too, given their strong personalities, that it should have been such a passionate and tortured affair.

He ran his hands over his brow as he remembered the terrible months that led up to Natasha finally rejecting Euan and taking on what now turned out to be a disastrous marriage. At the time he had almost encouraged Natasha to marry Gerald Masterson. How was he to know it would be such a grave mistake? Gerry had seemed ideal. After all he was a clergyman, outwardly dependable, kind, with just a dash of excitement, being a celebrity vicar with frequent appearances on television. Was he wrong in thinking he'd be a steadying influence on Natasha? As he saw it, there was a desperate need to get her away from the clutches of Euan before they both ended up destroying each other. Since Celia's death he had felt very protective towards Natasha and although he would never have admitted it to Miriam, he felt rather more affection for her than he did for his own children. There was something incredibly special about her...

He stood up, a little unsteadily and stared at the telephone. What mayhem had he now unleashed? Euan had behaved admirably at the time of Natasha's marriage to Gerry and taken himself off to LA, out of Natasha's life. Now, because of that call, he was on his way back to England. Natasha, shut up in her Norfolk retreat, was completely unaware of his return and on top of everything else there were some very ugly rumours circulating about Gerry Masterson's private life.

It was a lethal mix and he still had to break the news to Miriam about their weekend guest. A task he was not looking forward to.

He closed the study door and stumbled up the stairs.

Miriam Simmons lay with an icepack on her head wondering where the hell Wal could have got to. He'd been on edge all evening and then, in the middle of the News he had disappeared to his study to make a telephone call and that was the last she had seen of him. She looked at her watch. It was half past eleven. What could the man be doing? Mind you, he couldn't be blamed for not rushing up the stairs for a night of sexual passion. There hadn't been many of those lately and if she continued feeling this way, not many to come either.

She adjusted her icepack. It was all so very unfair. None of her other women friends had suffered as she had. Every symptom mentioned in the menopause book had been thrown at her. She'd tried all the remedies. A year ago she'd had a hysterectomy but still felt each morning as if she'd been put through the mangle and the very idea of sex...

She sighed and thought grimly of how she'd tried talking to her doctor, but he'd been completely useless, suggesting she invest in a seductive black lace nightie, a solution she had quickly rejected. He also told her it would pass and her energies would start to return. Well she was now two years in and her symptoms showed no signs of abating. Wal, bless him, had done his best to cope. He'd even suggested moving to a smaller house but she couldn't face the upheaval. So here they were, still at Walbrook Grove, rattling around like two peas in a pod with the house deteriorating around them. The interior hadn't been touched for at least seven years. Once she'd enjoyed that side of things and been known for her excellent taste. Friends would ring her for advice. Not anymore. Some months back Wal suggested getting in a firm of interior decorators but she couldn't face all the endless decisions. So things stayed as they were, they didn't live exactly in squalor, but certainly in a dilapidated state. What did it matter? It wasn't as if they entertained any more. Now she panicked if Wal invited someone back for dinner. Belinda's wedding two years ago, was the last occasion where she had really made an effort.

She glanced around the room and the lines "Oh chintzy, chintzy cheeriness, half dead and half alive" came into her mind. Her clothes, some clean, some not so clean, lay strewn across the floor and her tights hung drunkenly over the stool of her dressing table. Maybe she should give the place a face-lift, even if it was only the bedroom. She climbed off the bed, picked up her clothes and stuffed them into the laundry basket. Tomorrow she told herself firmly, she would have a blitz.

Taking the icepack into the bathroom she opened the medicine cupboard.

It was full of bottles. There were remedies for the sweats, the shivers, hot flushes, palpitations, headaches, dry skin, nausea... Would the agonies never end? She applied a layer of Chanel skin cream to her face and wondered gloomily if she would have the energy to face the Resident's Committee the following day. Since the onslaught of menopause she'd given up nearly all her charity work, but as long as they stayed in Walbrook Grove she felt obliged to continue as Chair Person.

She heard footsteps on the stairs and returned to the bedroom. Wal swayed through the door and bumped into the dressing table sending her perfume bottles flying. His usually pale face was surprisingly flushed as he moved unsteadily towards the bed.

"Good God Wal. Have you been drinking?" This wasn't said with reproof but with total bewilderment. Wal never drank during the week and only indulged mildly at weekends.

Wal loosened his tie. "I've had a couple of brandies." He sat down heavily on the bed and his face wore a defeated look. Miriam felt suddenly worried and sat down beside him.

"Has something happened? Who was that you were ringing?"

He remained silent for a moment. At last he said, "I rang Euan. Euan Mackay."

She was startled. "Was that on a professional matter?"

Wal shook his head. Miriam frowned and then the light suddenly dawned. "Oh no Wal, tell me you didn't. Tell me you didn't call him about Natasha?"

Wal didn't answer but sat hunched staring at the floor. Miriam started to pace round the room in agitation. "How could you be so stupid? We've had seven years peace from that blasted man. Seven years in which to recover from the trail of devastation he left behind him. And now you've had the stupidity to contact him without even consulting Natasha?"

"I had to ring him," Wal said flatly, adding defiantly, "I made a promise to get in touch with him if anything went wrong. And how could I consult Natasha? She won't talk to us. My mother has been begging me to do something and I felt it was just possible Euan could throw some light on the situation."

"And could he?"

Wal shifted uneasily on the bed. "No he couldn't."

This drew a snort from his wife. "What a surprise."

He felt his temper rising. "There's no need to be sarcastic. I had to give it a try. It may not have occurred to you but something could have happened to her and I owe it to Celia to keep an eye on Natasha."

Miriam's temper also flared. "And do you think involving Euan is doing your best by Celia? My God, if I'd had a lover and then that lover had turned round and had a passionate affair with Belinda I'd be turning in my grave, swearing revenge."

This was an idea so comically ludicrous Wal had an urge to burst out laughing. Then he looked up at his wife's angry face, blotched with cream and the urge to laugh swiftly faded. He made an effort to calm things down. "I did it reluctantly but with the best of intentions. After all it is very worrying that nobody has been able to see or talk to Natasha for so long. She's refused to reply to letters, her telephone is permanently on the machine and when you do leave messages she doesn't answer them back. Her cousin Livvy even called at the house, only to be told by the housekeeper that Mrs Masterson was out and she didn't know when she'd be back..."

Miriam broke in impatiently. "If she has a housekeeper she must be all right, otherwise that housekeeper would have said something."

Wal shook his head. "Not necessarily. The housekeeper might not know the severity of Natasha's mental state."

Miriam sat down beside him and said more calmly, "Have you considered that Natasha might just want to be on her own for a while? If the rumours are true, her marriage broke up in a pretty unpleasant way. She may need to give herself time to recover without having friends and family descending on her like a flock of vultures."

Wal considered this. "That is possible, but I still say it's not natural. How old is Natasha now, twenty seven?"

"I think she's twenty nine."

"Well that's far too young to cut herself off from the world."

"Oh, there's an age limit is there?" Miriam gave a sarcastic laugh. "So tell me, at what age are you permitted to become a recluse? Did anyone inform Greta Garbo of this?"

"You're being ridiculous," Wal snapped. "I just meant it isn't natural for someone so young to shut herself away like this. She might be having a nervous breakdown. She might need help. If there was an outside chance that Euan knew something it was worth a try?"

"And then what? Shut her up in a funny farm?"

"I don't know." Wal yelled. "I just want to make sure she's all right." He wanted to add, "you stupid woman" but didn't. There was silence and he started to undress. He went to the bathroom, brushed his teeth and then returned. As he climbed into bed he realised he still hadn't told her about Euan coming to stay with them. He lay back and stared at the ceiling. Finally he blurted out, "Euan's coming back to England."

Miriam gave another snort. "Well that doesn't surprise me in the least. He was probably just waiting for an excuse…"

Wal said quickly, "He'll be staying here for the first few days."

She sat bolt upright. "He'll be WHAT?"

"Staying here" and he added lamely, "we do have plenty of room."

"That has nothing to do with it." Miriam blazed. "I'm not having him here. He can go to a hotel."

"No he can't," Wal said firmly. "He's one of my greatest friends. I haven't seen him for over six years so I am not having him stay in a hotel." He looked at his wife's furious expression. "For God's sake Miriam, I don't know why you've suddenly taken against him. I seem to remember that when Natasha married Gerry your sympathies were entirely with Euan." He turned away from her and put out the light. "Anyway, he's coming here on Sunday and that's that."

Miriam also put out the light and lay thinking. She had to admit there was some truth in what Wal said. If she were being totally honest it was only lately her resentment against Euan had built up, very likely brought on by fear. It was from the moment she'd heard about the break-up of Natasha's marriage and she knew there was a possibility the dramas with Euan would start up again. She just couldn't face that.

Not now, not at this moment in her life.

She gave a deep sigh. If only he hadn't turned up at that damned party all those years ago, the affair would never have happened and Natasha wouldn't have been driven into the arms of the ghastly Gerry Masterson.

And there was another thing that irked her. She couldn't help thinking that there was something almost indecent about having an affair with the daughter of your previous mistress. It was perverse. But then there was nothing straightforward when it came to Euan. He had this extraordinary effect on people. Belinda had been besotted with him for years and then just look at Wal. He wouldn't hear a word against the man and was now insisting he stayed in their house, even though he knew it was the last thing she wanted.

She turned restlessly in the bed, her mind in turmoil. It was no good. She was going to have to get up and make some herbal tea. Sleep was beyond her now.

Wal heard her leave but made no comment. They'd only have gone back to bickering and he'd had enough of that for one night. Apart from anything else there was another problem looming and that was his mother. She rang him daily about Natasha, urging him to do something. How would she react to this latest development with Euan? Not well. He was sure of that.

He closed his eyes. That was enough for tonight, it would all have to wait until morning.

Dolly Linklater sat at the breakfast table and looked irritably at her husband. She had been talking to him for at least three minutes and unless he'd had a sudden attack of deafness there was no excuse for him to ignore her any longer. It was too bad. There hadn't even been a grunt out of him. He was buried in his paper and she might just as well have been communicating with the wall.

"Tinker!" she finally exploded. "I wish you'd listen to me."

Her husband looked at her with a bewildered owl-like expression. "Sorry," he said, tapping his newspaper, "there's a particularly interesting bit about the new By-pass..."

"Oh really Tinker!" Dolly exploded in exasperation. "Blow the bloody By-pass!"

Seeing she was genuinely upset Tinker put down his paper. "Sorry old thing, tell me what's bothering you."

"It's Natasha," she held up her hand to stop him from saying anything, "now I know Wal isn't your real son and Natasha isn't your real great niece, but when you married me you took on all my problems as well..." How very true Tinker thought but said nothing as she continued. "...so if I'm worried, you ought to be worried with me."

There was certainly logic to this. "Why are you worried about Natasha?" he asked.

Dolly looked exasperated. "Haven't you been listening to anything I've been saying over the last few weeks?"

Tinker thought quite probably not, but out loud he said, "Remind me."

"She has nobody to turn to, not even her dreadful father because he now resides in Switzerland. I always knew he was a rotten egg. How Celia could have married him I really don't know. And if that wasn't enough he persuaded their daughter to make a disastrous marriage..."

Tinker cut in. "But I understood Natasha had now left Gerry."

"Well of course she's left Gerry," Dolly said irritably, "but now the poor darling has taken herself off to the wilds of Norfolk, where she has shut herself away, totally isolated." Tinker smiled. He was used to Dolly's dramatics but it still amused him. She caught the smile and sounded cross. "I don't know what you find so amusing Tinker. This is serious."

He was immediately apologetic. "I know my dear, but you did make Norfolk sound like Siberia." He paused. "We could always go and visit her..."

"But that's just it. We can't. Nobody can. We're not even sure if she's in the house. For months now she hasn't replied to telephone calls or letters and she has this fierce housekeeper who turns everyone away."

Tinker had visions of Mrs Danvers but merely said, "I'm sure we'd have heard if something were wrong. Isn't the child with her?"

Dolly nodded. "Yes, but I don't know how Laura is either. I haven't seen the child since she was two. She must be five by now. I can't understand it. I know Natasha was always independent but this behaviour is totally irrational."

Privately Tinker thought Natasha was behaving rather sensibly. She'd obviously gone through a traumatic time and needed some peace and quiet on her own, without her family.

"And then there's Wal," Dolly continued. "He's being no help at all. The trouble with my son is that he's so busy dealing with other people's nasty divorces he's become completely insensitive to the needs of his own family." Tinker had always found Wal a gentle and thoughtful man but again kept his council. He really didn't have an option as Dolly was now in full flight. "As for Miriam, I just don't know what to make of her of late. She used to be such a bright, energetic woman. Now she's just a lump. And it's no good you looking shocked Tinker. She is a lump. Every time we've been to see them I notice she's getting worse. When I think how beautifully she used to keep that house it's a tragedy. I mean, look at it now. It's getting shabbier by the minute. I've spoken to Wal about it but he takes no notice. And it's not as if they were short of money. They could well afford help but Miriam refuses. She has even given up on her appearance. Mind you, I was never very taken with her sort of look, too like Margaret Thatcher for me, but she always managed to appear elegant. Now she just looks a complete frump and I gather she's no longer on any of her committees…"

Tinker wondered how soon he would be able to return to his paper but realised some sort of contribution was expected of him. "What about Belinda? Can't she help?"

Dolly was dismissive. "Not if her cousin Livvy can't. Livvy was always closest to Natasha and she's as worried about her as I am. There's nothing for it Tinker. We must have a family council of war. I shall ring Miriam and suggest we go up for Sunday lunch. Do you agree?" Without waiting for a reply she swept out of the kitchen. Tinker sighed, picked up his paper and went back to his boiled egg and bread soldiers. Last time they'd had a family conference it was to try and stop Natasha's wedding to Gerry Masterson and a fat lot of good that had done.

Dolly dialled Wal's home number and was unsurprised to find Miriam in. "Now Miriam," she said in brisk tones, "I think it's time we all met and talked through the Natasha problem." She waited for Miriam to say something but as she didn't she continued. "It's probably best if we drive up to you. What about this Sunday? Then Wal will be home. Maybe Belinda and her husband, what's-his-name, can join us. We could come for Sunday lunch..."

At the mention of Sunday alarms bells began to ring in Miriam's head. Sunday! That was the day Euan was arriving. If Dolly saw him she'd hit the roof. "Actually Dolly," she said, trying not to sound as if she were hyperventilating, "this Sunday won't be possible. Wal has a client arriving, from America. He'll be tied up all day. I'm so sorry."

"How very tiresome of him," Dolly said crossly. "Oh well, not to worry, we'll have to arrange something for one evening next week. I'll look at Tinker's diary."

Miriam replaced the receiver with a mixture of exhaustion and relief. She felt she was walking on eggshells. A minute later she rang Wal and turned the whole problem over to him.

Wal waited nervously in the Heathrow Arrivals Hall for Euan to appear. When he finally did make his entrance he noticed with some satisfaction that Euan was looking a little older. At last he's catching up with the rest of us he thought.

"Good of you to meet me," Euan said as they shook hands. "I didn't expect it." They made their way to the lifts and Wal saw there was very little luggage in the trolley. Maybe Euan was only planning a short stay and his spirits lifted.

"How was the flight?" he asked.

"Long." Euan gave a smile, the craggy charm still definitely there. "I need a shower and a shave. Ten hours in a cramped space leaves a man feeling very uncivilised." As they climbed into the car he looked at

Wal. "I hope it was all right, inviting myself to stay? Just say the word if it isn't and I'll move into a hotel."

Wal assured him it was fine and inquired if he had any plans.

Euan seemed vague. "Entirely fluid, I'm playing it by ear until I've contacted Natasha."

The car gave a swerve. "It really wasn't necessary for you to come over," he said nervously gripping the steering wheel, "there's nothing dramatically wrong with Natasha."

Euan privately thought that the break-up of the marriage and her reclusive state were dramatic enough reasons, but decided to keep it light. "Well it was a good excuse to see England again. I'd begun to be a bit homesick."

They chatted idly for most of the journey, but as they drew near Walbrook Grove, Wal suddenly said, "I think I ought to warn you about Miriam." He hesitated, not quite sure how to continue. "She had an operation about a year ago and quite frankly she still isn't over it. You may find her rather stressed and on edge."

This greatly surprised Euan. Of all the people he had known in England Miriam was the last one he'd expected to change. She'd always been so confident, even formidable. He glanced at Wal. The poor man looked tired and stressed himself. She must be bad. "Look," he said, "you've obviously quite enough on your plate without my landing on you. I'll only stay a couple of days and then make other plans." Although Wal said nothing Euan could tell he was relieved at this. He continued, "Perhaps I could come and see you in your office tomorrow. Then we could talk things over in private."

Wal said at once, "Of course, good idea, come around midday and then we can go and have lunch."

As they drew up outside the house, Belinda, who had been looking out of the window on and off for the past half hour, gave a shriek of excitement and called out to her mother, "They're here. They've just driven up. Euan's arrived."

CHAPTER TWO

The following morning Euan woke early in the spare bedroom of Walbrook Grove and as he slowly focused on his new surroundings his thoughts returned to the events of the day before. What a change had come over these people in the six years he had been away. Could it really all be blamed on Miriam's menopausal problems? Could one person make so much difference? It was as if the proverbial pebble had been thrown into the middle of the pond and the shock waves were now spreading out in ever increasing circles. The whole family had been thrown off kilter. Even the usually placid Belinda had been in a somewhat volatile state, alternating between the gushing and the anxious. If she had enquired one more time about his jet lag he would cheerfully have strangled her. What concerned him most was the state of Wal, who now jumped nervously every time his wife made a move or joined in the conversation. Knowing Wal as he did, he was sure he would have tried everything he could to help her; patience, kindness, understanding. But Miriam seemed beyond that. One look at her had been enough. The woman was in urgent need of professional help. He took out a cigarette and lit up. A thought suddenly occurred to him. What about Dr Strutter? He had been wonderful with Celia, although that had been nearly fourteen years ago. The man must be in his sixties by now and quite probably retired. Still, it might be worth making enquiries.

He looked at his watch and saw that it was only 5.30. His internal clock was still on LA time. There was no point in making a move for at least an hour. He didn't want to risk waking up the whole household.

He lay back and thought again about the previous day. The dinner had been an ordeal of the worst kind, stodgy food and stodgy conversation. Oddest of all was that nobody mentioned Natasha once. The conversation, such as it was, had been kept deliberately general. They had questioned him about his life in LA and he had given a rather vague account, throwing in some lurid details about the race riots. In return he asked them about life in England during his six year absence. He regretted having missed all the fun of the Thatcher downfall and at least expected an account of the night of the long knives, but this was not forthcoming. It seemed that the whole episode had been wiped from their memories. They briefly mentioned the struggles of the Recession, the problems over Europe and he got the feeling that a general malaise had hit the country. It was all very depressing.

There was one minor diversion when Belinda's husband arrived to collect her. He'd been at some business conference and made it pretty plain that he was tired and anxious to get home. Not that Nigel looked capable of injecting a great deal of excitement into the proceedings but at that point he would have welcomed any diversion. The evening had broken up pretty quickly after that. He had suggested a last nightcap to Wal but this had been declined. It was as if he were too nervous of the consequences to accept.

An hour later Euan made his way quietly down the stairs. There was no sound from anyone. The supper dishes were still as they had left them on the dining room table. He'd offered to help with the clearing up but Miriam had replied that the cleaning woman would deal with it in the morning. Even so, she could at leave have removed the dirty plates to the kitchen. In the Walbrook Grove old days the food had been whisked away from under you before you'd even had time to finish.

He opened the French windows and walked out into the garden. The sun was just filtering through the low lying mist. There was a damp, mushroomy smell, so reminiscent of an English Autumn. It is what he had missed in California, damp leaves and gentle rain. Soon there would be frosts and bonfires. He felt better already.

Looking down the garden his eyes were drawn to the seat under the tree. With a rush of emotion he remembered how he had met Natasha on that first fateful evening. The image was so vivid it was almost as if she were standing there right now. It has been an October day like this when he'd come to this very spot to say goodbye. He shivered. Maybe it had been a mistake to return. Maybe it was all too late. That old life was over. What was the point in trying to rekindle a flame that was probably no longer there? The old proverb, 'Let sleeping dogs lie' sprang to mind. And yet, the dogs were no longer sleeping, the situation had changed. As long as Natasha's marriage to Gerry lasted he had vowed not to interfere. Now all that was over, she was on her own again and free. Or at least, free of Gerry. For nearly seven years he'd been trying to forget her, forget the skinny, waif-like creature with her chestnut hair and large brown eyes. He'd tried to forget the husky voice and gurgling laugh, but he hadn't been able to. For him it was an unresolved part of his life and he needed resolution, whatever the final outcome might be.

He sat down on the seat and made a plan. He'd write her a letter. If she didn't want to see him she could tell him so. He wouldn't force himself on her. Looking out over the garden he was certain of one thing. He wouldn't go back to America. It had nothing to offer him anymore. He would be staying in England, even without Natasha.

Wal appeared at the French windows and called out, "Would you like some coffee?" Euan joined him in the kitchen and found Wal standing in front of an enormous and gleaming coffee machine. It's my new toy," he explained proudly. "The children gave it to me for Christmas. It does everything, Espresso, Cappuccino..."

Euan smiled. "Just regular for me and make it black and strong." He stifled a yawn and added, "Belinda would be gratified to know that I am now definitely suffering from a touch of jet lag."

Wal carefully poured out the coffee and Euan found the pride he took in his toy rather endearing. It certainly made the rest of the old equipment in the kitchen look positively antique. The years in LA had made him realise the inadequacies of English electrical gadgetry. He glanced at the refrigerator. It was ridiculously small. You could have fitted three of that size into his American one. Seeing him staring at the fridge, Wal asked anxiously if he was hungry.

"No, no." Euan quickly reassured him. "Coffee is all I ever drink in the morning."

Wal put down his cup. "I ought to be going. The tube is so unreliable these days. If it's not strikes or breakdowns it's a bomb scare."

Euan thought privately that Wal probably couldn't wait to leave the house in the morning but all he said was, "I'll see you around midday. I presume you're still in the same office?"

"Yes," Wal sounded almost apologetic, "the same ones." As he reached the door he asked, "Are you on for lunch as well?" Euan nodded and Wal seemed pleased by that. Lunches out were his only chance of a decent meal. "Good, I'll make a reservation."

Euan arrived in Wal's reception area on time and was politely told to wait. Nothing much had changed here. There was still the background babble of shrill voices saying, "Simmons and Woolcock, can I help you?"

After a while a long-legged receptionist in a very short skirt stood in front of him and said, "Mr Simmons will see you now Sir." He decided he was too tired to feel excited by this nubile specimen who inquired politely if he knew the way to the office. Euan assured her he did.

Wal looked happier in his own surroundings and more like the Wal of old. He waved Euan to a seat. Euan obediently sat and lit a cigarette. "Do you mind?" Wal smiled. "No I don't. I get a lot of smoking in here. I take it as a sign of nerves." "Nonsense," Euan replied, "it's the sign of a bad habit. Lately I've been trying to cut down, but at the moment I need something to keep me awake." He blew out the smoke and looked at Wal. "Tell me everything you know about Natasha."

Wal shifted uncomfortably. "Obviously I can't tell you everything. Some things were told to me in confidence. But I will try to give you the general outline of events." He put his hands together, as if collecting his thoughts and when he did speak it was in his precise legal tones.

"If we go back to the early years of their marriage, I think it would be fair to say that as far as we knew Natasha was fairly content. Miriam and I visited them once or twice in their Cotswold Rectory." He paused. "I have to say it was the most beautiful house. Natasha always did have great style, just like Celia, and she had made the place absolutely charming..." He caught a look of impatience from Euan and continued quickly, "Anyway, as I said, we did go to see them. The last visit was just after their daughter Laura was born..."

Euan stiffened. "I didn't know there was a child. Nobody told me about any children. How many are there?"

"Just the one," Wal looked a little guilty. "I would have told you about her, but quite frankly, on reflection, I thought it best..."

"To let sleeping dogs lie." Euan said pointedly.

Wal sighed. "Well, yes, I suppose so. It did seem best." He laid his hands flat on the desk and frowned, as if trying to concentrate. "As I said, it all seemed fairly happy, on the surface. Although I do remember Miriam remarking that it was a rather odd relationship."

"Odd?" Euan spoke sharply, "In what way odd?"

Wal shifted uneasily in his seat. He liked to deal in facts, not all these untidy emotions. "Well, it seemed somehow detached, devoid of any real affection between them. There were no rows you understand. They were almost too polite to each other. It was as if they lived two completely separate lives. Gerry continued to do his television work where he was still something of a celebrity. Natasha spent most of the time in her painting studio. She seemed happy there and in fact all might have continued well if they hadn't moved back to London..."

"When was that?" Euan asked.

"It must have been nearly three years ago. It was a definite promotion for Gerry, a minor Canonry in Southwark Cathedral. But for Natasha it was a major blow. She had been settled in a place that suited her. Now she was uprooted and transported into a totally unsuitable property and this must have been dreadful for her. As I understand it there wasn't a house that went with Gerry's appointment as usually with Church appointments, so he had organised what can only be described as a bachelor pad, down in the Docklands area. I gather it was extremely well appointed with river views, architect designed, you know the sort of thing, but with no garden and of course hopeless for the child. Belinda went to visit a few times and became worried about Natasha. The poor girl knew nobody in that area and was completely isolated. It wasn't as if Gerry involved her in his work. Far from it, he was never in." Here Wal paused and began to fidget with the papers on his desk.

Euan spoke quietly. "So what happened? Was it just the isolation that made Natasha leave, or was it something else?"

Wal sighed. "Well, you may as well know. If you don't hear it from me you will hear it from someone else." He paused again.

Euan broke in impatiently. "For God's sake Wal, just get on with it."

"It's rather difficult to know how to tell you because it was all so vague." He shifted uneasily in his chair. "You see, about eighteen months ago some rather disturbing rumours about Gerry reached my desk, which led me to make my own investigation. It appears that Gerry Masterson was mixing in dubious male company and with one companion in particular, a young man who was already making a name for himself in the theatre called Peter Rich..."

Euan started. "Hang on, that must be the Peter Rich who used to live in Garrick Square. Gerry took a keen interest in him then, in fact I was convinced they were having an affair. He was up at Cambridge at that time."

Wal spoke grimly. "After he came down from Cambridge he almost immediately made a name for himself. From what I have gleaned from my son Alex, who knows about such things, Peter Rich is considered 'brilliant', Alex's word, not mine." Wal pursed his lips. "He also used some dreadful phrase like 'flavour of the month'. It's the usual story. This Rich fellow did a fringe production at Edinburgh which transferred to the West End and it caught the attention of the critics. You know how they like to make their discoveries. One critic in particular seemed quite besotted and wrote long pieces about him. Peter Rich is now all over the Sunday Magazines and is apparently hailed as one of the great young talents in British Theatre. I gather he's been snapped up by one of the major companies." Wal added drily, "You can call me a cynic but I suspect his sexual persuasion might have had something to do with his success in certain quarters and this really brings me to the crunch of the matter. The particular set to which I refer is well known for including prominent homosexuals. They are the voice of 'Gay Liberation' and all that sort of thing. Now I hasten to add I have nothing against Gays..." here Wal paused, "...but what with Gerry being a famous clergyman and Peter Rich always in the news, their association was inevitably noticed and gossip about them inevitably started to spread. Several of my journalist friends rang to warn me that a major story was about to break. I mean, it wasn't just that Gerry was always on our screens representing the clean and happy face of the Church of England, he was also a married man. I know the subject of AIDS is no longer uppermost in people's minds, but any death of a celebrity from the disease, and just lately there has been Nureyev and Freddie Mercury, makes the public nervous again. So a homosexual scandal involving Gerry would have been disastrous."

Euan groaned. "I can't say any of this surprises me. I always knew the man to be a closet homosexual. I tried to warn Natasha but she wouldn't believe me. She just thought I was being vindictive and jealous" He looked at Wal. "So how did Natasha react to all this?"

Wal put his hands together and looked thoughtful. "I honestly believe that for a long time Natasha didn't suspect a thing. In some ways, in spite of her air of sophistication, she remains an innocent. My only interest in all this was to protect her as far as I could. It was a delicate situation and while I was trying to decide on the best way to proceed, Natasha came to see me herself. That was just over a year ago. It was last August. I remember because I was about to go away for our annual holiday but the matter was so obviously urgent I had to postpone my departure for a few days."

This made Euan smile. Wal's annual holiday was sacrosanct and he was a creature of habit. For as long as he could remember Wal had always holidayed in Cyprus, for the same three weeks, every year.

"So," he said, "Natasha visited you."

Wal licked his lips as though they had gone dry. "Yes she did. I won't go into details, she will tell you those herself if she wants to. Suffice it to say she discovered that Gerry had been..." he hesitated and then, choosing his words carefully he said, "...that Gerry had been unfaithful."

Euan said angrily. "The bastard, you mean she caught him at it."

Wal ignored this and continued, "Natasha wanted an immediate separation. As I explained to you on the telephone, she had been left this house in Norfolk which she had been planning to sell. Now she decided to move herself and Laura up there to live. She asked me to deal with the details of their separation."

Euan leaned forward. "She didn't want a divorce?"

Wal shook his head. "No, at least, not at the moment, because it would have ruined Gerry's career, being a well-known man of the cloth."

"It would have served him bloody well right."

Wal looked at Euan and said severely, "Natasha may have been unhappy but she was never vindictive."

Euan couldn't stem his anger but all he said was, "What happened after that?"

Wal tidied the papers on his desk. "I had a most unpleasant session with Gerry. At first he went on the attack and told me that Natasha was neurotic and had over-reacted, that she had got things out of proportion, and quite a lot more of the same. I finally made him see that things with Natasha had gone too far to be repaired and in any case it was going to be extremely difficult to keep the whole scandal out of the papers. I think it was the latter that forced him to take action. He was a frightened man. He went to see his Bishop." Here Wal gave a ghost of a mile. "It's amazing what the Church of England can do when once put on the spot. For an organisation reeking of moth balls, they moved with both speed and efficiency. Gerry was immediately transferred to South Africa. A press release was issued to the effect that, Gerald Masterson, everyone's favourite TV vicar, had been hit by missionary zeal and had gone out to South Africa to work in the Townships during such momentous times. In the circumstances I found it rather nauseating."

Euan said grimly, "So our Gerry managed to escape and come up smelling of roses."

Wal shook his head. "Not quite because the rumours still persist. It's a story that just won't go away." He looked at Euan and said severely, "That is why we can't risk anything happening that might precipitate a scandal. This is for Natasha's sake. Do I make myself clear?"

Euan said huffily, "Perfectly clear, but it's no good getting at me. I was the good guy in all this if you remember. I behaved impeccably and removed myself from the scene."

Wal was fidgeting again with a stack of legal documents. "I only meant that the situation is still delicate. There should be a long period of separation before Natasha decides to do anything further."

Euan nodded. "I understand. No divorce and no publicity." He paused. "What about the child? Presumably Natasha has custody?"

"Yes, Laura remains with Natasha. Gerry does have some visiting rights but only by arrangement." He broke off and then said, "Actually that was the one thing that upset him. Much as I dislike the man he does seem to have a genuine affection for his daughter. He was very distressed about that aspect of things. Visiting rights aren't much good if you're in the depths of the South African Townships."

There was silence between them for a moment.

Euan suddenly asked, "What's Laura like?"

Wal threw his hands up in the air. "Good God Euan, I can't answer a question like that. I'm no good at describing my own children let alone anyone else's. Belinda will be able to tell you more about that."

Euan smiled. "Don't worry. I shall find out myself."

Wal said sharply, "So you're going to Norfolk then?"

"Of course, if Natasha will see me. I'm going to write to her first. Can you let me have her address?" Wal hesitated and Euan said, "You might as well let me have it Wal. I know it's the Dower House on the Roxby Estate. It won't take me long to find it."

Wal wrote it down on a piece of paper and handed it to Euan. "So, what are your plans?" he asked.

"I'll give her a week to reply and while I'm waiting I'll take the opportunity to call on my London agent. There are also some friends I'd like to see as well."

Wal looked at his watch. "We ought to go to lunch. I have a meeting at two."

Euan stood up. A wave of fatigue swept over him. "Actually Wal, would it be all right if we gave that lunch a miss? Exhaustion seems to have caught up with me. Can we postpone it to another time?"

Wal nodded and they made an arrangement for the end of the week.

As he reached the end of the street, Euan leant against a doorway and lit a cigarette. His hand was shaking. It wasn't so much tiredness, he realised he was far more shocked by Wal's revelations than he had expected. He walked slowly away from the office and found a quiet pub, where he ordered a pint and a sandwich and sat in a corner thinking things over.

On returning to Walbrook Grove he rather regretted not having mentioned Dr Strutter to Wal because he found Miriam lying on the sofa in the drawing room with all the curtains drawn and what looked like a wet towel draped over her head. He didn't disturb her but crept up the stairs to his room and packed. Leaving a note thanking them for their hospitality propped up against the coffee machine, he quietly let himself out of the house. He knew of a small hotel off Sloane Avenue which he now sought out and was soon happily installed in a room on the top floor looking out over the London rooftops.

The rest of the day was spent on the telephone, arranging meetings and social visits. The first of these was to be a lunch with Lady Fay Stanhope the following day. Fay was one of the few London friends he had missed when in California. They'd been thrown together while both were writing scripts for a television series. Large, affectionate and rather eccentric, it was Fay who had suggested, or rather insisted, that he bought the house in Garrick Square. She had organised the Square in those days, supervising who moved in, and then when someone moved out choosing the new resident with extreme care.

He hoped she would be someone he found unchanged.

It was with some feelings of nostalgia that Euan entered Garrick Square the following morning. His first glance went straight to the central garden which, as he remembered it, had been unkempt and untidy. He recalled a splendid old gardener who had struggled, without much success, to bring about some order amongst the chaos. Euan searched his memory for the name. Mr Alton! That was it. He'd be ancient by now and most probably dead, which might account for the fact that the garden had been completely transformed and in his opinion, not for the better. It was no longer an unruly mass of rambling roses and overgrown foliage. Now it was ordered with clear paths and violently coloured flower beds, more resembling a municipal park than the wild garden he had loved. Feeling a little shocked by this he glanced round the Square itself and noted the houses looked far smarter as well. What a transformation and all in less than seven years. The Square had certainly gone very upmarket. He idly wondered how much the houses would be worth now.

As there was still half an hour before he was due for lunch he started a slow walk round. Stopping outside Number 11 he thought grimly of the Square's great scandal. There had been a police raid and the resident, a Mr Pendlebury, had been dragged away in the early hours of the morning. He was later convicted of distributing child pornography and was presumably still behind bars.

Moving swiftly on he reached Numbers 15 and 16. These two houses had been knocked into one by the Rich family and rich they'd certainly been, a bit too much of the 'nouveau' variety for Fay. Arthur Rich's wealth had come from a very flourishing business which made bathroom fittings. Although not one of Fay's chosen ones, they had been well-liked and always generous with their hospitality and lavish parties. Euan suspected Doris and Arthur had found themselves rather out of their depth amongst Fay's chattering classes and he thought grimly they now faced a similar problem with their son Peter, the successful theatre director, who was very likely going to be named in a gay sex scandal. Doris in particular wouldn't cope well with that.

He walked on until he reached his old house, Number 23 and stood staring in disbelief. Had he really lived here? It looked extremely grand. The present occupant had obviously spent a great deal on renovations, the place positively gleamed. He glanced towards the basement and recalled how often he'd watched Natasha run up and down those steps. Euan shivered. The sun had gone in and there was a distinct chill in the air.

noved on to Number 29. This had been the home of his greatest Murdo Struthers, a retired publisher and a man of enormous cha... and erudition. Just before Euan left England Murdo had suffered a mild stroke. A year later he suffered another, this time fatal. He hadn't known about Murdo's death until he read his obituary in one of the English papers. The loss of this man filled him with great sadness. The obituary on the other hand filled him with great irritation. In the final paragraph they mentioned that Murdo had been divorced. What possible reason could there have been for mentioning that? Murdo's marriage had been a disastrous mistake and for the rest of his life Murdo had never hidden the fact that he was gay. He had lived with the same rather dim and unprepossessing man for over thirty years, so why hadn't the obituary said, 'survived by his life-long friend and companion, Desmond'?

There was no sunlight on the north side of the Square. As he reached Number 36 he shuddered. It had been the home of the Coopers and he had loathed them. Gavin Cooper had been the editor of one of the tabloids and his third or fourth wife an appalling specimen of womanhood, an aggressive Australian and an alcoholic to boot. Their forays into social life were punctuated by violent public rows usually ending with crockery being thrown. There was a child as well, known to all as 'Horrible Fat Henry', probably a Public School horror by now poor kid.

He walked briskly to the last but one house, Number 39, the house that had belonged to the Reverend Gerald Masterson, that is, until he had married Natasha in October 1987. It was the reason he had left for America and now, the reason he was back.

A distant clock struck twelve. It was time for Fay.

As he rang the doorbell of Number 8 he was greeted by the familiar sound of yapping. Fay obviously still had dogs. The door was flung open and there she stood in all her glory, a little older, but still an exotic vision in silk caftan, flowing chiffon scarf and long strings of coloured beads. She threw her arms around him with such strength he feared for his rib cage.

"Darling Euan! What a lovely, lovely surprise. I've been so excited since you rang. I hardly slept last night. Come in. Come in."

This was easier said than done as two yapping Pekes were leaping about in the way. "Quiet you naughty dogs. Quiet I say!" Fay sounded imperious but it had absolutely no effect. Eventually Euan managed to step over them and make his way into the living room. It was just as he remembered, a shabby, glorious mess, crammed full of antiques and heirlooms, most of which had seen better days.

"Sit down where I can see you," she commanded and handed him a large glass of sherry. "I hope you don't mind, I didn't ask anyone else. Selfish I know, but I wanted you all to myself."

Euan suddenly sneezed and then noticed a large and chipped Meisson bowl full of pot-pourri, on the table right beside him. It gave out a strong Oriental aroma, probably to counteract the ever-present smell of dog urine. He sneezed again and as soon as Fay turned round to pick up her sherry glass, he pushed the offending bowl as far away as possible.

"Now ducky," she said as she flopped into a large armchair opposite him, "first tell me how long are you here for?"

Euan smiled, he'd come fully prepared to be put through an intense interrogation so now said cautiously, "That rather depends..."

Fay clapped her plump hands together with delight. "I knew it. I knew it," she wheezed. "I told Boffy this morning. You are back to see Natasha."

At the mention of Boffy Euan looked surprise. Boffy had been Fay's second husband, a delightful, but rather gaga military gentleman. When there had been no mention of him on the telephone or any sign of him in the house, he'd presumed the worst. "Is Boffy here?" he asked.

Fay shook her head. "Alas no, the poor old darling now resides in a home quite near here. Alzheimer's I'm afraid. The last few years have been a dreadful ordeal and in the end I found I just couldn't cope any longer. The old love set fire to himself with his cigar and that was that. Once he'd recovered from his burns we moved him into the home. On most days he's docile enough." She gave a sniff and then all at once her mood changed. "Now Euan, I won't be fobbed off any longer. I want to know about you and Natasha."

Euan reminded himself that Fay was a writer of romantic fiction and liked to see life as a neat, rosy package. He therefore chose his words carefully. "I'm sorry to disappoint you Fay but I haven't seen or spoken to Natasha since I left England."

Fay looked momentarily crestfallen, then chuckled and said, "But that's all the better. It's like Jane Eyre and Mr Rochester."

"Oh really Fay," Euan spoke almost crossly, "it's nothing like that at all."

Fay pouted like a small child and Euan burst out laughing. "All right, you win. I did come over to see Natasha."

Fay clapped her hands with delight. "Then you heard about Gerry?"

Euan moved cautiously. "I heard he and Natasha had separated."

"But the rumours darling, the rumours, you've heard about them?" Fay rolled her eyes dramatically and spoke in conspiratorial tones, "I'm pretty certain the man is 'Uno de quello'." She picked up the sherry decanter and re-filled Euan's glass. "I always had my suspicions that Gerry was homosexual, ever since he arrived at one of my dinner parties in a dog-collar. I never mentioned it at the time, for fear of upsetting Boffy."

Euan well remembered Boffy sounding off about Nancy-Boys.

Fay added sadly, "That poor child. She was so young and innocent, what a terrible time she must have had. She was quite the most beautiful bride I have ever seen." She shook a reproving finger at Euan. "I've never really forgiven you for not whisking her away and saving her from a fate worse than death. Everyone knew she was madly in love with you and you with her. But I suppose I am a silly old-fashioned thing who can't get used to the fact that the days of chivalry are over."

"Actually I thought I *was* being chivalrous," Euan said, "by removing myself from the scene."

Fay said sadly, "Oh ducky you may have thought so, but you were terribly wrong," then added cheerfully, "never mind, the whirligig of time and all that."

Euan burst out laughing, he couldn't help it. Fay was quite

wonderfully ludicrous. "As I remember it Fay, the whirligig of time brought with it revenge and I am certainly not doing that."

She waved her arm in a gesture of irritation. "Don't quibble darling. Just tell me you are going to see her."

Euan put down his sherry glass. "I don't know. She may not want to see me. Apparently she is living like a recluse in Norfolk."

Fay clicked her tongue reprovingly. "What a place in which to be a recluse! Norfolk is a terrible county."

"I don't think she had much choice," Euan explained. "She was left a house on the Roxby Estate by her grandfather."

"That poor girl," Fay looked shocked. "I well remember the Roxby Estate from when I was a child. It took the full blast of the icy wind blowing relentlessly off the North Sea. No, there is nothing for it, you must go and rescue her as soon as possible."

"Like a knight in shining armour?"

Fay beamed. "Something like that." She hauled her large frame out of the chair. "And now, over lunch I want to hear all about your writing. I'm told you have been fearfully successful, as of course I always knew you would be, you clever boy"

They started to move towards the dining room and as they reached the door Fay turned to look at him. "You've aged a little darling. There's just a little more weight and your hair is a teeny bit grey. But you're still wildly attractive I'm glad to say."

Once seated at the table she added, "At least you are very much alive. It's so depressing these days, with all one's nearest and dearest getting increasingly decrepit. You never know who's going to fall off the perch next."

Over lunch Euan gleaned what he had already surmised about life in the Square. Not many of the residents he'd known still remained and Fay had lost interest in the Square's social life.

"It all floundered when darling old Murdo died," she told him sadly. "Desmond immediately sold up and left. You had already gone. The Coopers removed themselves, thank God, and so did Gerry's dreadful mother Joy. What a misnomer that was! Which only left the Riches and they went last year." Euan thought of Peter Rich and the potential scandal but decided he wouldn't broach that particular subject with Fay today. She went on, "In any case, poor old Boffy became ill soon after that and caring for him took up all my time. The one good thing is that the houses are now worth a fortune so I can always sell up. It will give me enough to see me through my remaining years in comfort."

She suddenly looked old and tired, almost fragile. Her eyes filled with tears. "Darling Euan, tell me, what *do* we do with our lives?"

He left soon after that, promising to keep her informed of events. As she enfolded him once more in her arms she said, almost pleadingly, "We did have fun all those years ago didn't we ducky, we did have fun?"

Euan felt he couldn't answer that, but gently kissed her on the cheek instead.

A week later, Euan hired a car and set out on his journey to Natasha and the Dower House, Lower Roxby, Norfolk.

CHAPTER THREE
NORFOLK

Natasha stared at the envelope, where her name and address were written in a distinctively neat hand. She knew immediately who it was from even though she hadn't seen the writing for nearly seven years. It shouldn't have been a shock. She had been half expecting it. After all, the news about her leaving Gerry was bound to have reached Euan sooner or later, so why this sense of panic?

She propped the envelope against the pot of marmalade and tried to decide on her best course of action. If Euan wanted to see her and she told him not to, she knew he wouldn't come. He would obey her wishes she was convinced of that. On the other hand, if she *did* allow him to come, what then? For nearly a year she had managed to keep her entire family at bay, Dolly, Wal, even Livvy. She was aware they would have found this hard to understand, but time and space were what she had badly needed, without being smothered with advice and affection, which they undoubtedly would have given her. But Euan? Euan was different. She had longed for him so often she was worn out with longing, especially over this past year. As long as he had stayed in America it seemed safe to indulge these longings. The ocean divided them and in the long hours of soul searching it had seemed unlikely to her that he would ever return.

Now he had.

She stood up and threw a log on the fire. It crackled, sending out a great shower of sparks. The open fires in every room were one of the things she most loved about the house and luckily there were several acres of woodland to supply her with all the logs she needed. It was just as well as there was no other form of adequate heating.

As she sat by the fire warming her hands, she recalled her first few weeks in the Dower House. It had been a time of quick decisions. The house was far too large for just her and Laura, so the first move had been to close off some rooms and make their living quarters smaller and more compact. The ground floor, apart from the kitchen area, had a large hallway, two big reception rooms, a dining room, and a small room she had kept as her bolt hole. She chose one of the larger rooms as their living room and this contained her piano and chaise longue. The other large room was as yet unfurnished but where she stored her painting things. Of the six bedrooms upstairs she had chosen the two with south facing windows for herself and Laura and there was one other bedroom she had furnished, just in case she should ever feel inclined to have a visitor.

She sighed. It was a large house and badly in need of restoration. The plumbing was Dickensian, all the rooms could do with re-decorating and at some point the re-wiring had to be faced and that would be a major expense. In spite of this she loved it. The high ceilings and long shuttered windows gave beautiful proportions to the rooms, filling them with light. Some might think her mad to take it on but the place suited her. It had rescued her when she'd been in the depths of despair and allowed her time to restore herself. One day she would go back to painting, but not yet, too many bad memories...

She pulled her thoughts back to the house. One of its great advantages was the kitchen area with the quarters above it. These were now the domain of Mr and Mrs Bondage, Tom and Gwen, or as she had quickly named them B and Mrs B. They had arrived as if by a miracle or more accurately via an advertisement in the local paper. It had been clear from the moment she arrived she was going to need help, but how could she afford it on top of all the other expenses? The obvious solution was to offer board and lodging to a housekeeper as part payment. The interviews had proved a depressing ordeal and she was about to give up when in walked Mrs Bondage, plump and cheerful, the very model of a model country housekeeper. She announced proudly that she had been in service all her life and in the early years had worked at Roxby Hall in the days of the late Sir Malcolm Roxby

Smith. Before she could stop herself Natasha told Mrs Bondage that she was the grand-daughter of Sir Malcolm and it was he who had left her the house. Immediately after she'd said this she regretted it. The class system, still so very much part of the estate life, embarrassed her. It was all the more embarrassing because she didn't come from an old family at all. Her grandfather had originally been plain Malcolm Smith, but having had great success with a soft drinks company, had sold out early making a fortune and with his vast wealth had purchased the Roxby Estate. He promptly changed his name to Roxby Smith, gave a great deal of money to charity and was subsequently knighted. Roxby Hall itself had been in a dilapidated state and her grandfather had decided to replace it with a new building, which although not hideous, had none of the Regency splendour of the old hall. Natasha was just relieved the Dower House had been left intact.

Sir Malcolm, on reaching fifty, abandoned his dreary wife and went off to live in the south of France with his second wife. The estate was made over to his eldest son Paul, and a lump sum settled on his younger son, her father George. Some years back Paul and his wife Maddie had also sold up and moved away. Roxby Hall was now an agricultural college and they also managed the estate and various farms attached to it. Only the Dower House remained untouched. Sir Malcolm had lived in it for a time with his fourth wife and it was for this reason she had been relieved her name was now Masterson because it has given her a sort of anonymity. However with this revelation she had blown her cover and worse still, Mrs Bondage seemed overjoyed by the discovery. Natasha quickly explained she was separated from her husband and he was now working abroad, so it was just herself and Laura. A look of pity crossed Mrs Bondage's face. There was a long pause until she finally came out with "What about Bondage?" For a moment Natasha had a vision of whips and black leather until Mrs B added that Bondage was her husband Tom, and he would have to come too. She'd added that he was a good handyman and did the odd bit of gardening. And that had been that. The Bondages had moved in and transformed her life. The kitchen was now run by Mrs B and the garden by B. They instinctively seemed to understand her need for privacy and became fiercely protective. The house and Laura occupied all her time and the months had quickly passed, allowing her 'to restore her batteries' as Dolly would have said.

She glanced over to the letter. Would all this be put in jeopardy now Euan had written to her? Suddenly she could bear it no longer. She moved to the table, snatched up the envelope and ripped it open. The card inside read, '*Natasha, I'm in the country and would like to see you. If you don't feel you can, or don't wish to see me, write and tell me at the above address. Or you can leave a message at Wal's office. If I don't hear from you I'll be with you sometime next week. Euan*'

A wave of anger swept through her. Damn the man, he'd thrown it back at her, left her to make the decision. Why hadn't he just turned up? Then at least he'd have been in the wrong and she could have sent him away without a guilty conscience. Now what was she to do? If she didn't reply, he'd definitely come. If she did reply saying no, she was certain she would always regret it. It was impossible.

Before she could deliberate further, the door burst open and Laura entered, with a very large and wet English sheepdog at her heels. Natasha regarded her daughter crossly. "Laura! Look at the state of you and Miffin too. How did you get so wet? You have to be ready for school in a minute. Go and get out of your wellies and ask Mrs B to fetch you some dry clothes."

Laura took a piece of toast and gave half to the dog. "I'm not wet," she said defiantly, "I'm more or less clean."

'More or less' was a phrase she had just learned and was now being used at every opportunity. Natasha was just about to take a firm line when Mrs B came through the door. "Come along young lady," she said firmly, "I told you to leave your boots by the back door." She looked at Natasha's flustered expression. "Don't you worry dear I'll clean her up and take her to school." She took the child's hand. "Come along Laura. We can't have you looking like that. Whatever would your teacher think?"

Laura didn't seem to mind what her teacher thought. "Can Miffin come with us to school?"

"Yes if we can find her lead. Now come along or we'll be late."

They departed and Natasha thankfully sank back into the chair. She didn't feel up to making decisions with Laura or anyone else. She picked up the card and read it again. After staring at it for a moment, she put it in her pocket her mind suddenly made up. Let him come. She might regret it, but she wouldn't stop him from seeing her.

As Euan approached the Great Yarmouth turning he experienced definite feelings of apprehension. There had been no word from Natasha, although he'd given her at least a week to reply. This silence had unnerved him. He'd felt sure she would have made some sort of contact if only to ask when he'd be arriving. Maybe it was true and she was having some sort of breakdown. Or maybe it was simpler than that. She just didn't want to have any further connection with the past.

He stopped the car and consulted the map. Lower Roxby appeared to be a few miles inland, about halfway between Great Yarmouth and Cromer. He also noted that this part of the county seemed to be littered with Roxby's. Apart from Lower Roxby and Upper Roxby, there was Roxby St Mary and Roxby itself. It was all very feudal and he idly wondered what it felt like to be a Roxby living in Roxby.

It was only just past two o'clock. He hadn't wanted to arrive until around tea-time so that gave him nearly two hours to kill. There was a choice. He could either go towards the Broads which he knew a little, having visited them once when he was at Cambridge, or he could drive towards the coast, which he didn't know at all. He decided on the latter and took the route that led him to Caister-on-Sea.

There was no sign of sun in the threatening grey sky and a high wind beat against the frail silver-green willow trees that lined the route. He was soon regretting not having gone to the Broads because a vision of horrors greeted him and one that combined all the worst aspects of what he had been told about English seaside resorts. There was nothing but an endless ribbon of Amusement Arcades, Fish and Chip shops, Bingo Halls and limp bunting.

He turned the car around and found a signpost directing him to California. Surely this must auger well?

It didn't. His hopes were quickly dashed. It was almost worse than the previous resort, with a large, drab caravan site thrown in for good measure. He couldn't even face a meal at the inaptly named Bermuda Beach Restaurant. Reluctantly he returned to the main road.

A little further and he arrived at Winterton-on-Sea. This looked slightly more promising. At least there was a church and a village green. He couldn't see a pub. In fact he hadn't seen a pub for miles. Didn't they drink in this part of Norfolk?

He took a bumpy road towards the beach and was greeted by a scene that looked straight out of World War Two. A bleak line of grass-covered mounds were split up by huge slabs of grey concrete. A high wooden look-out post, surrounded by barbed wire stood at the top of the beach. The only thing missing was a Nazi officer and a machine gun at the ready. A few yards away, perched crazily at the entrance to the beach, stood a white piece of board which announced that there had been a number of deaths from drowning in this area and the public should not swim between the two red marker posts.

He brought his car to a halt in the empty car park and a girl built like a Sherman tank, appeared from nowhere demanding payment. He asked her if there was anywhere he could find refreshments. She looked at him as if he were mad and after telling him it was out of season she pointed to a wooden hut next door to some dubious looking public lavatories and told him to try there. By this time he was so hungry he would have settled for anything, so he made his way to what he presumed was the beach café. A brassy girl, in black sweater and extremely tight jeans, was sitting painting her finger nails a lurid pink. She poured him a cup of stewed coffee and with an ill grace made him a cheese sandwich. It tasted of pear drops and he presumed he must be consuming a fair amount of nail varnish as well.

Having restored his blood sugar levels if not his taste buds, he walked down to the beach. It was deserted. The sand petered out as it approached the water line and the cold grey surf crashed loudly against the shingle, before drawing viciously back with the force of the strong undertow. No wonder you weren't allowed to swim.

In the distance a few tankers were dotted along the horizon. It was all dismally bleak. The wind was whipping the sand uncomfortably into his face so he turned round and walked back to the car.

Feeling profoundly depressed he drove slowly back to the main road. After about three miles the road suddenly curved inland and then ran straight and flat between farmlands as far as the eye could see. Once again the wispy grey-green willows with their pinkish red branches waved crazily in the wind. His spirits started to lift. This vast, empty landscape with its occasional wide expanses of rippling water, had a beauty all of its own. Windmills and churches loomed at him out of the Turneresque sky. He stopped and wound down the window, listening to the eerie humming sound which came from the wind whistling through the telegraph wires. Except for some cows and a great many birds, the vast landscape was totally deserted. On his left there was nothing but water and fields. On his right a high grassy bank hid his view to the sea. Otherwise all was flat. When the stretch of water finally ended the cabbage fields took over, row upon row of blues, greys and greens. Did we really consume that many cabbages?

At Happisburgh he stopped and again consulted the map. Lower Roxby was a few miles inland. He drove from the coast and now the countryside changed in appearance, no longer flat but gently undulating slopes of woodland. A signpost said, 'Lower Roxby 1 mile'. His heart was starting to thud uncomfortably. This could well turn out to be the worst decision he'd made in his life, but it was too late to turn back now.

The village began with a straggled line of small cottages. Some of them were covered in large pebbles that gave the pink brick a speckled effect. He reached the main street where there was the obligatory large church, a war memorial and at last, a pub, called the Three Horseshoes. This looked more promising.

He stopped at the village shop to take directions. It was the first time he'd heard a broad Norfolk accent but he understood enough. He was to make his way through the village, past the school, past the Roxby Arms and then at the curve of the road there was a stone wall and a lodge and that was the entrance to the Dower House. Euan followed these directions and was pleased to see that the Roxby Arms was not another pub but a small hotel. That could prove useful.

With his mouth getting drier by the minute he came to the small lodge and turned in at the gates.

Since the arrival of the card from Euan, Natasha had been in an extremely tense state. Mrs B remarked on this to her husband saying that evidently something had upset her but she didn't know what. However, at the weekend instructions had been given to air the guest room and make up the bed, as someone was arriving from America and would be staying for a while.

"'Tis some man no doubt," said Mrs B gloomily to Tom, as she shredded the peas with more vigour than usual. "Tis the root of the trouble, she's expecting a male visitor and it's upsetting her."

Tom tapped his pipe on the grate and remarked that it would be good for her to have some company, "'Taint natural for a young woman like her not to have company, male or female."

"She has Laura and us."

Tom refilled his pipe and said gruffly, "'Taint the same."

That had been five days ago. By the time there was the sound of Euan's car coming up the drive, the household was in a state of nervous anticipation. Natasha sat in the living room, unable to move, convinced she had made the wrong decision.

The car door slammed and Mrs B was at the door almost before Euan had taken his hand off the bell. He smiled charmingly at the plump woman facing him, in spite of her severe expression. She wasn't quite Mrs Danvers, but there was a definite air of disapproval.

"Is Mrs Masterson in? I think she's expecting me."

"Please step inside." The voice was far from welcoming. "Mrs Masterson is in the living room." Mrs B waved her hand towards a door across the hall and disappeared back into the kitchen.

Euan crossed the hallway and hesitated. Then the door opened and she was standing in front of him.

Neither of them moved or spoke but just looked at each other.

Euan eventually broke the silence. "Why didn't you write?"

This made her smile. "Isn't that what I said to you, when we met again all those years ago at Wal's?"

He nodded and closed the door. "Well, you didn't write, so here I am."

"So you are," she said shyly, and then, because she didn't know what to say or do next she moved towards him and put her head on his shoulder.

"I knew you'd come."

He made no movement. After a moment she broke away and sat one side of the fire. He sat down opposite and made a study of her.

"You haven't really changed," he said. It was true she hadn't, except for a look of wariness in her eyes.

She returned his scrutiny and laughed. "Well you've changed quite a bit."

"So everyone tells me, insisting I look older." He smiled. "For some reason they seem to be extremely relieved by this. I can't think why."

She laughed again. How he remembered that laugh and the husky voice. "I think it suits you," she said, "looking a bit older. You're not so much of a challenge."

His eyebrows went up. "I'm not quite sure how to take that. It's a little too enigmatic for me."

There was an awkward pause. Then Natasha spoke, the words coming out in a rush. "Oh God, how hopeless of me, I'm so unused to visitors. What time is it? I ought to offer you something. Food, drink, would you like some tea? Mrs B is bound to have some cake. Her cakes are delicious…"

Euan interrupted the flow. "Actually tea would be most welcome. I didn't really eat anything on my way here and I'm suddenly struck by pangs of hunger."

She leapt from the chair. "Right, tea it is. Mrs B will be delighted. I don't really eat much and she's been longing for a proper person to feed. Stay here and I'll go and tell her." She left the room.

Euan looked around. At one end of the room was a grand piano which he thought must have been Celia's. Next to it was a tall bookshelf and against the wall between the two shuttered windows was her famous chaise longue that he remembered so well from Garrick

Square. Apart from the two armchairs either side of the fire, there was no other furniture except for a round table by the door. On this were a great many framed photographs and he got up to have a closer look. The majority were of a solemn looking child he presumed to be Laura. There were also several of Celia and one in particular took his attention. It was of three people on a beach. The beach he knew at once to be Iona and there he was, looking very young indeed, with his arm round Celia. They were both looking down at the twelve year old Natasha. He remembered the occasion clearly and how they'd asked a fellow tourist to take it for them.

Natasha came back into the room and said, with an air of apology, "I'm afraid the house is in a rather unfinished state. I am organising it slowly but it seems to be taking a long time."

"It's all rather grand isn't it?" Euan's tones were faintly mocking "a large house and grounds, a lodge, even staff."

Natasha was immediately on the defensive. "I suppose it must seem so, but it isn't really grand at all. I'm doing up the rooms myself one by one and I hope in the end to make it comfortable rather than grand. Of course it's financially draining, any old house would be. A lot of restoration needs to be done. As for the staff, well, B and Mrs B work in return for their board and lodging. It's a good arrangement as I need the help. I couldn't do it all by myself and this was the only way I could afford."

Euan was about to apologise for his mild mockery when the door burst open and a filthy child and an equally filthy dog burst into the room.

"Mrs B says that tea is ready in the bolt hole."

"Oh Laura," Natasha wailed. "What have you been doing? You're absolutely covered in mud."

"I've been gardening, with B."

"Well you seem to have brought most of the garden in with you. Go and get cleaned up and then you can come back for tea. And take Miffin with you and leave her in the kitchen."

The child obediently turned and dragged the dog from the room. Natasha noticed Euan had a strange look on his face and said anxiously,

"You did know about Laura didn't you?"

"I heard about her last week from Wal" he said dryly, "before that you might just as well have been on another planet."

She looked rather guilty. "I'm sorry. I thought of telling you but then decided not to. It just seemed better not to involve you somehow and then it was difficult to go back on the decision when the circumstances changed." She paused and said with a smile, "Rather like you not writing to me after Mama died."

He let this go and followed her into the bolt hole. A lavish spread was laid out on a small table in front of another fire. Natasha poured out the tea. "Help yourself to food. As you see, there's plenty of it."

Euan looked at the scones, cakes and honey. "Very Rupert Brooke," he murmured.

Laura came back into the room, obviously having been polished by the redoubtable Mrs B.

"Come and meet Euan," Natasha said. "He's a friend of mine from America."

The child crossed over to him and eyed him warily. Then she held out her hand. He took it and formerly gave it a shake. "Hello Laura."

"Hello You-Wan" she struggled with the name and they both laughed

"You can take your tea to the table Laura. It's easier and we can still talk to you there." Laura tried to balance her mug on the plate. Natasha intervened. "One thing at a time, take the mug first." With a great deal of concentration the child obeyed. Once sat down she turned a rebellious face towards her mother.

"Mrs B says Miffin can't come in for tea."

"Mrs B is quite right. Miffin isn't as clean as you are now. Besides, she might knock over the tea things on the low table. You know how she wags her tail."

Laura considered this. "I could tell her to sit. She always sits when I tell her."

Natasha said patiently, "I know darling, but she's still too dirty to come in here. Finish your tea and you can go back into the garden."

"Why is she called Miffin?" Euan asked, by way of diversion

"Well, she is really Myfanwy. She was nearly a year old when we got her and her name was already established but Laura had difficulty pronouncing it, so we sort of compromised. Miffin was Laura's Christmas present last year." She sighed. "She's a lovely dog and very placid, but she does get filthy. I mean, she's like a walking rug anyway and her coat is permanently matted with mud, if not worse. Every now and then she gets into the neighbouring farmhouse and then we have to hose her down."

"She stinks of cow shit," Laura agreed.

"Very graphic" murmured Natasha.

"That's what B says. He says 'that dog stinks of cow shit'.

"Well we've got the idea, "Natasha said briskly. "When you've finished your tea Laura you can go back to the garden for a little while." She paused. "What are you so busy with out there?"

"My potatoes, I've finished them more or less." The rest of the tea was crammed into her mouth and she slid off the chair. "I'm going now," she managed to say.

Euan watched her departure and laughed. Natasha looked at him and said rather apologetically. "Not the best behaved child in the world."

He smiled, "but definitely a character. In some strange way she has a look of Celia, although the colouring is different."

"Do you think so?" Natasha seemed surprised. "I didn't think she looked like anybody in particular especially with that dark colouring. She's a bit of a changeling. I'm afraid I've let her run wild and she's fast becoming a gypsy, but it's good to see her happy after London."

Her face suddenly took on a strained, closed look. Euan had an urge to comfort her and somehow take away that pain, but it was too soon. He put down his cup and stood up.

Natasha looked up at him. "What are your plans?" she asked.

"The long or the short term plans?"

"Well, either."

"Short term I'd like to stay here for a few days if that would be all right?" He waited for her to say something but when she didn't he continued, "Long term is a little vague. I have a book I want to write…" he broke off.

"Is that in England or in LA?" she asked.

"England. I won't be going back to LA. I've grown tired of the place." He didn't want to say more at the juncture and she seemed to accept this.

She also stood up, "Let me show you round the place. I've had a bed made up for you in the spare room. You'll find it a bit sparse I'm afraid."

He smiled, "I'm sure it's fine."

There was a moment's silence. Then Natasha said hesitantly, "Euan, I'm really pleased to see you and I know there's a lot to catch up on, but can we take it slowly? I don't know how much you've been told but I'm in a slightly bruised state at the moment…" She stopped, evidently unsure how to go on.

Euan took her hands in his and held on to them. "I know," he said gently. "And I understand. Really I do."

CHAPTER FOUR

Euan sat in the garden reflecting on his first week spent with Natasha. For the past two days it had been an Indian summer and in spite of being October there was a mellow sun and a gentle stillness in the air. It was just such a day he had missed in LA and it ought to have made him feel good. But it didn't. In fact he was feeling distinctly unsettled. If he'd hoped it would be easy to re-establish their relationship, he quickly realised he was wrong. Natasha seemed to have constructed a protective barrier around herself which she allowed nobody to penetrate, not even him. On that first evening she had described herself as bruised. He instinctively knew the wounds went much deeper and although he hoped they weren't permanent, they were certainly going to take time to heal.

Picking up a pebble he threw it across the lawn into the flowerbed. The frustration of having found her again and yet having to tread so carefully was beginning to wear him down. It was a situation that would need all the patience and tact he could muster if he wasn't to frighten her off. At present it seemed she couldn't trust anyone and certainly wasn't ready to go back to the way they were.

Damn Gerry. Damn him to hell. That man was responsible for wasting nearly seven years of his life and the wait clearly wasn't over. There was no knowing how much damage Gerry had inflicted, or indeed, if she'd ever recover.

The sun went behind a cloud and there was a sudden chill in the air. He stood up and started to walk across the lawn towards the vegetable garden. Of one thing he was certain. His feelings towards Natasha hadn't changed. Not that he had really doubted they would. From the moment he saw her again he was filled with that strange mixture of protectiveness and desire, of longing and lust, feelings he'd not had with anyone else, not even Celia. So he had a dilemma. He wanted to pick up from where they left off but wasn't sure how Natasha would react if he made a move. Would she be capable of loving him again?

He stopped walking as another major obstacle struck him and that was Laura. He couldn't ignore the fact that she made a difference. Apart from anything else, she was a constant reminder of Gerry and his thoughts towards the man became even more murderous. The presence of this child was a definite intrusion. It wasn't hard to see that from now on Laura would always come first with Natasha, which meant he would have to take second place and that wouldn't be easy. Would he really be able to live with that?

Feeling restless and unsettled he looked across the lawn towards the house, yet another object of Natasha's affection. It was her house, nothing to do with him. He felt a stab of jealousy. How ridiculous was that, to be jealous of a house! But he could see the pleasure it gave her and he found it hard to bear. At times he almost felt like an intruder.

He reached the walled vegetable garden and sat down on a stone bench. Lighting a cigarette he tried to sort out his confused thoughts. It was difficult to know where he stood. Natasha kept telling him how content she was with her life and how the house had given her all she needed; independence, seclusion and freedom. Yet, he knew by the way she looked at him across the table, by her provocative remarks, by how she held his gaze, by how she suddenly blushed; that the old attraction was definitely still there.

Did this mean she wanted to take things further? He needed to know.

Old Tom Bondage was at the far end, pottering amongst the rows of peas and beans. In the middle of the vegetable garden there was a circle of herbs and Natasha had told him all their names, wonderful names like Balm, Comfrey, Tarragon and Savoury. She seemed as proud of the garden as she was of the house.

He looked back at Tom Bondage who saw him and waved. Euan waved back giving an inward sigh. The Bondages were yet another factor in his uncertainty about Natasha's new way of life. They were obviously devoted to her and ideal for the job but they made him feel uncomfortable, particularly Mrs B who still eyed him with suspicion and always seemed to be hovering, watching him.

He stood up, stretched and started to stroll back. Surely Natasha wouldn't want a life of such cosy complacency for ever? Where was the rebellious spirit he'd seen in her all those years ago?

On impulse he made his way down the drive to the ivy-clad lodge. The gate was broken and hanging from its hinges. Gently lifting it he put it on one side. The tiny gothic-style building was secluded by a box hedge which obviously hadn't been trimmed for years and was now wildly overgrown. Through the grime-covered windows, he could just make out the interior. It was small but had definite possibilities and the idea came to him that this would be a perfect spot for writing. He would ask Natasha for the keys and explore it further. He suddenly felt more positive. Now was definitely the time for decisions. Natasha had to be forced to open up and talk. He'd had enough social chatter to last him a life time. No progress could be made until she gave him the full account of what had occurred between her and Gerry. It was like a festering sore. Unless she lanced it there would continue to be a barrier between them. Instinctively he knew this wouldn't happen in the house so the only solution was to get her away, if only for a few hours. So he made a plan.

Over lunch he said casually, "How would you like it if I took you out tonight?"

She was immediately wary. "Take me out where?"

He laughed at her alarmed expression. "Take you to dinner somewhere."

Natasha looked doubtful. "I don't know. Mrs B has all the meals organised for the week. I don't want to upset her..."

Euan tried not to sound irritated. "Surely Mrs B will be cooking for B anyway? I'm sure if you tell her you're going out she will quite understand." Natasha remained silent, so he played his trump card, "Of course, if you don't want to go out with me..."

Natasha said quickly, "No, it's not that." She paused and looked down at her plate. "You're not going to believe this but I haven't been out to a meal since I arrived here. There's been no need, nor have I wanted to see anyone." She looked up. "I would like to have dinner with you. I'm just a bit nervous," and she added, "but we could try the Roxby Arms. I'm told the food's quite good there but if you wanted somewhere grander…"

Euan was brisk, fearing she might change her mind. "The Roxby Arms sounds fine," adding with a smile, "why not keep it in the family? You square it with Mrs B and I'll book a table."

At eight o'clock he and Natasha faced each other in an almost empty dining room. She was wearing a low-cut green dress which suited her but he decided not to increase her nervousness by telling her how beautiful she looked.

"This is like something out of Terence Rattigan," he whispered, as he glanced across the room at a military gentleman who was the only other occupant.

Natasha gave a weak smile. She had agreed to the evening against her better judgment knowing exactly what Euan's motives were for getting her out of the house. He eyed her a little anxiously. She looked very pale and there was pain in those expressive eyes. He hoped to God this was a good idea.

The waitress arrived with the soup which turned out to be surprisingly good. Euan asked for the wine list and ordered the best red on offer. By the time the second course arrived Natasha began to feel better. The dining room had filled up and they no longer felt they had to whisper. She was also on her second glass of wine, or was it her third? Euan noticed the faint flush in her cheeks and something of the old sparkle return. He re-filled her glass and ordered another bottle.

"Euan you shouldn't," she protested. "I'll fall over. I've hardly been drinking at all."

"It's good for you and you don't get drunk on good wine"

"Stuff!" she said laughing and then her expression changed, "I suppose you despise my way of life and find it boring."

He thought for a moment, choosing his words carefully. "No, not boring at all. It has an enviable calm." He regarded her with a penetrating gaze and went on, "I think it is probably exactly what you need at the moment."

She was grateful for this. "Yes, it did seem the only way I could survive."

The second bottle of wine arrived and some good Stilton. Natasha took a deep breath. The moment had arrived and she could shirk it no longer.

"How much do you know about me leaving Gerry?"

Euan shrugged. "Not much, just the few basic facts that Wal told me." He added gently, "You don't have to tell me Tash, but it might be good for you to talk about it to someone."

Her eyes filled with tears as he called her Tash. He was the only person that did and she hadn't heard him say it for a long time. She knew he was manipulating her but she didn't mind. It had been inevitable he would eventually break down her reserve and he was right, in some ways it was almost a relief.

So she began, deliberately keeping it factual and her emotions in check. She started with the wedding day itself. It had been a ridiculously grand affair and she'd found it a terrible ordeal. Even before they arrived at the reception came the realisation of the awful mistake she'd made in marrying Gerry. Stupidly she had grasped at his offer of security and protection and then was hit by the fact that she didn't love him at all, but by then it was too late and she was married.

"I was guilty you see," she explained, as if needing him to understand. "Guilty of having married him when I knew I didn't love him. I had acted selfishly and was determined to atone. I somehow had to make the marriage work and at the beginning I thought I could."

Euan leant forward, "I actually know the exact moment you realised you'd made a mistake. It was outside the church when the photographers asked you to kiss Gerry. You see, I saw it all."

Natasha looked puzzled. "How could you have seen it? You weren't even there."

Euan said grimly, "I saw it on the television screen. It was on the news, 'Famous TV vicar gets married' and all that rubbish. They went into close-up of the two of you kissing. It was then that I noticed your eyes and I just knew."

"I thought you had left for LA."

Euan shook his head. "I should have done. My plane was delayed. I was sitting in the airport lounge and there you were on every bloody screen. Jesus, you looked so beautiful it was torture."

"Oh God, what a mess I made of everything," she said sadly.

Euan decided not to let her off the hook just yet. He wanted her to feel some of his pain. "So how was the honeymoon?" he asked.

She looked down at her plate. "Terrible. Looking back I realise Gerry must have picked up one of the stewards on the plane. When we got to the hotel he said he had to go out to meet someone. I was too tired to even find this odd and went straight to bed. He didn't come in until very late. It was hardly a first night of passion."

"Very Byronic," murmured Euan and explained, "Byron awoke on the first night of his honeymoon and cried out, 'Good God I am surely in Hell!'".

This made her laugh and the atmosphere relaxed. Euan poured more wine and she continued. "Things were a little better once we were installed in the Rectory. I wasn't an ideal Rector's wife but I did enjoy meeting people and tried to join in with some of the activities. We entertained quite a bit and the house was lovely. The best thing about it was my painting studio..."

"Ah yes, the painting studio," Euan couldn't keep the bitterness out of his voice. "Wasn't that how Gerry finally bribed you into marrying him?"

Natasha sighed. "I suppose it must have seemed like that, but that studio made all the difference to my life. After Laura was born I spent most of my time in it. Gerry left the domestic side of things entirely to me, including looking after Laura." She added quickly, "It wasn't that he wasn't fond of her but he was squeamish about babies, well, all the physical side of things really..." She shifted awkwardly in her seat. "You must understand that in the beginning Gerry wasn't a bad husband, especially in public. He would lavish me with compliments and presents. To outsiders we must have looked like a happily married couple. He was popular and successful and I honestly didn't mind that we had no sex life. Everything might have been all right if we hadn't moved to London."

Her face suddenly had a sad, faraway look. Euan knew she could never have endured that sterile, unemotional life for long, so why did she pretend? He called the waiter over and asked if they could have coffee and brandies in the drawing room. Once installed by the fire, she took a deep breath. The full story had to come out now. It didn't need detail, just the facts.

Euan prompted her, "You moved to London. Was that when things started to go wrong?"

She nodded. "Yes. You see if Southwark had been a Cathedral with a proper Close or if there had been some sort of community life as there had been in Stockton it might have been all right, but from the moment we arrived in London, Gerry seemed to forget about me entirely. He didn't even involve me in his decision to take the job. I had always known he would get promoted at some point but it came far earlier than I expected. It was obvious Gerry had just used Stockton as a stepping stone doing his obligatory three years as a country parson so he could move on to the Cathedral life he wanted and of course, the new job being in London was an extra bonus."

Euan broke in. "Did Gerry give up his television work when you were in the country?"

Natasha shook her head. "Not entirely. Obviously he was no longer in charge of religious programmes but he still made a great many appearances and was invited on to chat shows and programmes like that. He became the BBC spokesman for anything to do with religious affairs. If anything his public profile was even greater than before." She gave a scornful laugh. "He never said anything anyone could disagree with, always sensible, cheerful and bland. I would ask him why he didn't try being controversial and then he would pat me on the head and say, 'Natasha's in one of her devilish little moods today.' God he was so patronising," she said angrily.

Euan decided to bring her back to the subject of London. "Who chose the flat?"

"Gerry did. He kept saying he'd take care of everything. I wasn't involved in any of the arrangements. The last few months in Stockton I hardly saw him. He was terribly secretive. A week before the actual move he took me up to London. I didn't know what to expect, although at that point I presumed he had found us a house. I knew there were some lovely houses within reach of the Cathedral; Kennington, Camberwell, Peckham, even Greenwich. I envisaged something rather like Garrick Square."

Euan interrupted, "Was his mother still living in Garrick Square?"

"No, that house had been sold. She moved down to Kent." Natasha hesitated, "Anyway I couldn't have gone back to Garrick Square, not with all the memories."

Euan pushed on, "Wal said you moved into a flat on the Isle of Dogs."

"Yes, we did. When Gerry first took me there I went into a state of shock. Apart from anything else, it was a really grim area, not developed as it is now and not a suitable place for Laura. There were no green parks, no good schools, nothing to recommend it at all."

"What on earth made Gerry choose such a place?"

Her voice was bitter. "Well, the flat itself was stunning, but only for a bachelor. I think by then that was more or less how Gerry saw himself." She shuddered. "I'll never forget the drive down. That terrible route out of the City, the endless drab buildings and derelict warehouses, the Limehouse Tunnel and out on to the West Ferry Road to Milwall. I remember Gerry saying that there'd be nothing for me to do. It had all been done and taken care of. He just didn't understand me or even try to. I had been looking forward to organising a new home. It was one of the few things in our married life I'd enjoyed. Anyway, he was right it had all been 'done'. It was all chrome, glass and brick, like a feature in one of those smart architectural magazines, a vast space on the top floor of a newly converted warehouse with glass windows going down to the floor and a frightening drop to the river below. It sounds ungrateful because the views were spectacular and the flat itself sparkling, contemporary and fitted with every gadget known to man. But from the moment I walked in, I hated it and felt immediately alone and isolated. There was nowhere I could put my things, let alone my painting stuff. Certainly none of my own personal furniture fitted in." Her voice was bitter. "Gerry sometimes took my breath away with his insensitivity. He just informed me that all the contents in Stocton were being sold and we were starting again with everything new. He didn't even consider I might not want to do that. I managed to save my most precious possessions, my chaise longue, desk and some pictures. I put them in store. Otherwise the furnishing was all Gerry's choice. The flat had one large living room, three bedrooms off one side, one of which became Gerry's study and a kitchen and dining room off the other. There was no garden, not even a balcony. Gerry became angry when I raised objections telling me it was the 'up and coming area' and the property was a 'great investment'."

Natasha drained her coffee cup. Euan could see she was beginning to tire but didn't want her to stop now. "Were your first impressions right? Was it an awful place to live?"

"Yes it was. Immediately after we arrived, Laura became restless and difficult. In the country she had been a healthy, almost placid child. Now she started on a seemingly endless series of illnesses. It wasn't surprising really. The flat and surrounding area were completely unsuitable for a small child. When she was three I started her at a little school in Greenwich but it was a struggle getting her there and she never really settled. I became increasingly worried. During our first summer I took her to stay with friends in Italy..." She broke off. "Do you remember my telling you about Edward? He died while I was living in Garrick Square."

Euan nodded. He well remembered the impact Edward's death had made on Natasha. The man had been like a father and grandfather rolled into one and she had been far fonder of Edward than she had been of her own father.

Natasha gave a wan smile. "Edward's wife, Francesca, was so horrified by my tales of the Isle of Dogs and my isolated life, she wanted me to leave Gerry there and then and stay on with her in Florence. I was tempted I must admit." She looked at Euan. "It was the second time Francesca had asked me to stay on. The first time was just before I married Gerry. She tried so hard to stop me from marrying him. Mind you, everyone did that. Perhaps if they hadn't tried so hard, I might..." Her voice trailed away. Euan smiled at her and said, "Are you trying to tell me you're perverse and obstinate Tash?" She smiled back. "I suppose I am, although in my defence I was being pulled both ways. My father thought Gerry quite wonderful. He loved his celebrity status and practically pushed me up the aisle."

Euan thought yet again that bloody George had a great deal to answer for but didn't want to discuss her father now and get away from the main subject so he said, "Did Gerry join you in Italy?"

"Good heavens no, I think he was delighted to be left on his own in his bachelor pad, relieved of my constant nagging for us to move. He never understood my hatred of that flat, just thought I was being ungrateful."

"So you returned?"

"Yes, we returned." A sudden shadow passed over her face and she shivered. "It was an awful time. Relations between us deteriorated fast. Gerry had changed somehow that summer. It was as if he couldn't stand me even being in the same room. We slept in separate beds. He became sarcastic and unpleasant and only occasionally took any notice of Laura. Every so often he'd turn up with some ghastly lavish present; huge dolls in pink taffeta, ornate jewellery boxes, frilly dresses, you can imagine the sort of thing. He'd call her his little princess. It was sick-making really. The poor child didn't know where she was. Most of the time he was never in then suddenly she'd be overwhelmed with affection and presents."

She paused. "Would it be possible to have some more coffee?"

Euan found a waiter and ordered coffee and another brandy for himself. Once she had taken a sip she started again. "There was a time when I thought it might help to have another child. After all I had conceived almost immediately, Laura was born ten months after we were married. Our sex life had dwindled completely after that, something I didn't mind at all." She hesitated before saying miserably.

"After my suggestion for another child, when he was drunk enough we went to bed. He was brutal and uncaring. It almost felt like rape and I vowed never to try it again." Euan felt his anger rising but was careful not to interrupt. Natasha's voice became flat and unemotional. "I suppose in a feeble way I just gave into it all. Looking back I'm sure I was suffering from depression. I certainly had all the classic symptoms. I wasn't eating properly, or sleeping. I became lethargic and listless with occasional bouts of weeping. I did nothing and felt basically worthless. I certainly didn't want to see anyone. This went on for nearly two years and it might have dragged on for ever if I hadn't..."

She broke off.

Euan leant forward, "If you hadn't what?"

Her voice faltered almost to a whisper, "If I hadn't discovered the letters." She took a gulp of coffee. "It was all quite innocent. I had to go into Gerry's study to look for our TV Licence. Some men had called round to know if we had one. Gerry kept everything like that in a house file in his desk. He was very meticulous. Once a month we'd sort out the bills, so I knew exactly what I was looking for. Anyway, it was when I was putting the file back that I found them, at the bottom of the drawer, in a hand I didn't recognise. It was 'My dearest G' that caught my eye."

She looked at Euan. "I know it was wrong of me, but I felt compelled to read them. Curiosity I suppose. There were quite a few. They weren't dated and always signed in the same way, just 'P'."

Euan gave a start on hearing this initial. "They were love letters?"

"Yes. But not just love letters, graphic details and references to what must have been long sessions in bed together." She brushed her hand across her eyes and said almost fiercely, "I wasn't jealous but I was very angry. I felt betrayed. Dirty. Anyway, I replaced them all and toyed with the idea of facing Gerry with it. But on reflection there didn't seem much point. Our relationship couldn't have got any worse. So I just went back into a sort of limbo. And then Bill Martin paid me a visit..."

She stopped again and Euan looked at her questioningly.

"Bill Martin was one of the Canons at Southwark," she explained.

"I'd met him at Gerry's Induction and rather liked him. In fact, of all the other clergy I met he seemed by far the most friendly, a sort of round, jolly Friar Tuck. When we first arrived he'd tried to involve me in Cathedral activities but I always gave Laura as an excuse and in the end he gave up. Anyway, he came to see me out of the blue. We sat having tea and it was obvious he was on edge about something. Finally he asked me if everything was all right on the marriage front. He was rather agitated poor man. He explained carefully that he didn't usually pry into the private lives of his fellow clergy, but that recently there had been a bit of worry over Gerry's behaviour which had given rise to concerns. There had been indiscretions. His superiors wanted things stopped before they got out of hand. He spoke in vague terms but it was obvious they were nervous some scandal was about to break and he, poor man, had been given the job of sorting it out. I privately thought it would have been better if he had gone to Gerry direct. I explained that I rarely saw Gerry and that we led completely separate lives. I could see the look of pity on his face. It was humiliating and embarrassing. He then nervously suggested that I try and persuade Gerry to give up his television work so that he could spend more time with his family."

She broke off and looked at her watch. Euan was quick to reassure her. "It's all right, it's not late. Finish telling me."

She nodded and took a deep breath. "Poor Bill's suggestion was laughable. At that time Gerry was working on what I thought a terrible new series called 'Sundays by the Fireside'. He was obsessed with these programmes. It basically meant that he hunted down and cornered some poor old pensioner or sick disabled person and chatted to them about 'spiritual life' and 'the teachings of Jesus' and such like. They were then allowed to choose their favourite hymns. Awful, but it was his pride and joy. He called it a 'flagship of religious broadcasting'. I doubt the Archbishop of Canterbury would have been able to stop him from doing those programmes so I didn't stand a chance. Anyway Bill Martin begged me to talk to Gerry and then departed muttering something about marriage guidance and that his door was always open."

Natasha gave a hollow laugh. "I did try and talk to Gerry as Bill had asked but unfortunately didn't choose a good moment. It happened to coincide with the day one of the major papers printed an article absolutely slating Gerry's 'Sundays by the Fireside' programme. It was a devastating and personal attack and Gerry took it badly. I didn't know about this article when I broached the subject of Bill Martin's visit because I only read it later, so I wasn't prepared for his violent reaction. He immediately became very angry, demanding to know every detail of the conversation and kept saying 'What indiscretion is he accusing me of?' As I didn't know I couldn't answer this. In fact I suddenly became angry too and words began to fly. I asked him if there was any truth in Bill's accusation. Was there some indiscretion that I didn't know about? Well that did it. He ranted and raved for about ten minutes, then slammed his way out of the house. I had never seen him like that and for a moment I thought he was going to be physically violent. "

She took a gulp of coffee. "As it was near Laura's half-term I rang Belinda and asked if we could stay with her for a few days, hoping that it would give him time to calm down..."

Here she broke off and again looked at her watch. "Euan it's getting rather late. Don't you think we ought to be getting home?"

She's beginning to lose her nerve he thought. He took her hands in his and said firmly, "No. Don't stop now. Finish telling me. You went to stay with Belinda..."

She took her hands away and clasped them tightly together speaking in a whisper. "I've tried not to think about this for so long." Her eyes closed for a minute then she opened them again and her speech became fast and breathless. "I'd been at Belinda's for a couple of days when the weather suddenly turned bitterly cold. So I decided to go back to the flat to get some warmer clothes for us both. It was less than an hour's drive. It didn't occur to me to ring as Gerry was never usually at home." She paused. "But this time he was. They both were, naked, not in bed, but in the middle of the living room floor, on the rug."

Her hands twisted in her lap as she struggled with the words, until finally she burst out, "It wasn't like two human beings at all. More like rutting animals. They had no idea I was there. On and on they went, making weird, primitive noises. Suddenly I could bear it no longer. I just screamed. There was a moment when everybody froze. Then they both gathered up their clothes and went into the bedroom and I could hear raised voices. I sat on the sofa finding it difficult to breathe. I thought I was going to be sick. Then the man came back into the room." She looked at Euan. "I knew him. So did you Euan. He was the Rich's son Peter. We met him in Garrick Square."

Euan said nothing. This piece of news hadn't surprised him at all. He'd been expecting it as soon as he heard about the letters.

"That was it," she continued, "something clicked in my mind and it suddenly all made sense, Gerry's behaviour, his hatred of me, the letters signed 'P'. You had been right all along. Gerry was gay. I'd tried not to believe it. Now I had to."

She gave a grim smile. "Peter left without a word. Gerry came back into the room and we had a blazing row. At first he was angry with me for returning. Then he told me I was getting things out of proportion. I demanded to know if there were other men. He just shrugged and said a few. I then asked why the bloody hell had he married me if he was gay? He looked almost shocked at this and told me it was common for men to love both sexes. He then went on the attack and told me the failure of our sex life was entirely my fault. I think he set out to destroy what remaining self-esteem I had. He told me I was cold and frigid and on top of this I had behaved in a completely depraved manner by having an affair with the man who had been my mother's lover, and he pushed home the point by saying that even my father had been horrified by my behaviour when he had informed him of our affair."

Natasha looked at Euan, adding sadly, "For some time I'd had a suspicion it must have been Gerry who told my father about us. After all, there was no-one else who knew and it was a clever move on his part having just the desired effect. My God! How devious that man was."

Euan said under his breath, "A complete bastard," and he added, "I always presumed it was Gerry who told your father. As you say, nobody else knew."

She nodded and went on, "At that moment Gerry was like some

terrible, unrecognisable monster. I didn't even bother to ask him how he squared his behaviour with his religion let alone his conscience, because by that time I didn't care. I stood up and calmly told him I was leaving him. This stopped him in his tracks. I don't think he'd actually considered this as a possibility. He told me I couldn't leave him because the church didn't allow divorce and it would destroy his career. So I told him I couldn't care less about either him or his career and that I wouldn't be staying with him a minute longer."

Her voice now became brisk and matter of fact. "I went back to Belinda's and rang Wal. I told him I was leaving Gerry for good. The only redeeming feature in the whole ghastly business was this house. I had been going to sell it but suddenly it became a lifeline. I sent for our things, got all my furniture and possessions out of store and moved straight up here. I left Wal to sort out Gerry, which he did with great efficiency. Obviously Bill Martin had been right about the indiscretions. My departure clinched it. I also think Wal threatened to go to his Bishop. The next I heard was that Gerry had gone to South Africa and that a financial settlement had been organised for me. I've had no communication with him since, except for some Christmas presents he's sent to Laura. That is all."

There was silence in the room, except for the crackling fire and the ticking of the grandfather clock. Euan finally got to his feel and held out his hands. She let him pull her up and he held her to him for a moment. He could feel her shaking.

"Let's get you home," he said.

As they walked down the street Euan asked, "What did Gerry's mother make of all this?"

"She didn't know. Joy died about three years ago from cancer. It was all very quick. Just after we arrived in London I drove down to Kent with Laura to visit her. I could tell then she didn't have long. Gerry went to see her a few weeks after that and she died the day after. I tried to comfort him but he seemed totally unmoved by her death. His only comment was that it was good she had gone so quickly. I never saw any sign of grief." She added sadly, "I don't think Gerry ever loved anyone, except perhaps Peter Rich. But that was more like lust than love."

As they reached the top of the stairs she turned and said quickly, "Thank you for dinner Euan. Good night."

She closed the bedroom door and he thought he heard her sobbing. Shocked and angered by the evening's revelations he walked slowly back to his own room.

CHAPTER FIVE

Laura and Euan sat at the breakfast table the following morning and he watched her overloading her toast with marmalade. Carefully licking the remains off the knife she announced. "Mama's been sick. She's been sick all night, just like Miffin was when she ate the pheasant..." Mrs B came into the room. "Mrs B do you remember when Miffin sicked up the pheasant? All the feathers were still on it. B said Miffin had swallowed it whole, more or less."

Mrs B sounded cross. "That's quite enough of that young lady. Now look sharp and eat your breakfast. I'll be taking you to school this morning as your mother isn't well." Here she shot a look of disapproval Euan's way. "It's probably something she ate last night that's disagreed with her." She turned to go. "Finish your toast Laura and we'll be on our way."

As she slammed the door behind her Laura gave Euan a conspiratorial grin. "Mrs B's right batey this morning. That's what B says. Right batey." She stuffed the remains of the toast in her mouth and slipped from the chair. "Better go," she said making a face as she went out.

Euan burst out laughing. He couldn't help it. She really was a funny child. Then a yawn got the better of him and he poured himself a cup of coffee. It had been a bad night and he'd found sleep impossible, so he spent the time mulling over Natasha's revelations and trying to form some sort of future plan. By morning he had things pretty well worked out, although a great deal depended on her state of mind as to whether his plan was accepted. According to Laura she was in a bad way.

After a couple of hours and still no sign of her he made his way to her bedroom and knocked on the door. A frail voice told him to come in. She was lying with an expression of pain and her eyes were firmly shut. As he crossed the room she opened them.

"Oh God, I feel terrible. I haven't felt this bad for years, in fact, not since that time in Garrick Square."

Euan smiled. "If you remember I wasn't guilty on that occasion, it was totally self-inflicted. Would you like a cold flannel for your face?"

"That's what you offered me last time," she said a little crossly, "Don't you have any other remedies?"

"A few, but I think you'll find a cold compress will help." He fetched a wet cloth from the bathroom, handed it to her and she obediently put it on her forehead then hitched herself up in the bed. He sat at the other end watching her. Quite suddenly he burst out laughing.

"Oh really Euan, I don't know what there is to laugh about, unless you enjoy seeing people in pain."

"I'm sorry." He was immediately contrite. "I was thinking of Laura at breakfast. She told me you were sick, like Miffin was after swallowing a pheasant as she so graphically put it. She was very funny. I expect she's told the whole school by now."

Natasha made a face. "Horrible child, I had no sympathy from her either. In fact she seemed to take a morbid interest in my suffering. I couldn't face taking her to school and had to ask Mrs B to do it, so humiliating. Lord knows what she thinks of me."

Euan stood up. "I shouldn't worry. Mrs B holds me entirely responsible for your state. She practically accused me of poisoning you." He made his way to the door. "I prescribe a hot bath and then I'll make you a potion that will restore you to health. It's a special recipe, never known to fail."

"You sound as if you are an expert in hangovers," she said grumpily. "Well as long as your recipe isn't alcoholic I'll try it. I mean it Euan, nothing alcoholic."

"Trust me" he said.

An hour later she came into the living room still looking pale and went straight to sit by the fire.

"You have a choice," he told her. "You can have lime juice and soda, or my special mixture."

"I'll try your mixture." She took a glass from him containing a lurid coloured concoction and sipped it suspiciously. "How long does it take to work?"

"Not long. Any minute now you'll notice a distinct improvement."

Mrs B knocked and came into the room and asked in a voice laced with disapproval if they would both be having lunch. She was told yes and left. Euan made a face, "I think I'm in disgrace with Mrs B."

Natasha gave a laugh. "Don't worry. I'll tell her it was my fault for drinking too much."

Euan said gently, "You didn't drink that much Tash. You're suffering more from an emotional reaction than alcoholic."

She sounded huffy. "Well you were the one who wanted to hear the whole grisly saga."

They were both silent until Euan said briskly, "We ought to make a plan." Noting her wary expression he added, "More accurately I ought to tell you my plan." She still looked apprehensive but as she said nothing he continued, "I'm going to return to London, probably tomorrow. There are various things I have to do. I must return my hire car and I need to talk to my agents, both here and in LA." He paused. "I have decided to take a year off from television scripts to write a book..."

Natasha looked at him thoughtfully. How could Euan possibly afford to take a year off? She found it difficult to assess his financial situation. He never said much. She knew his Scottish roots had been respectable but certainly not wealthy, so it was not as if there was family money to live on. He must have made some money from his television work and there had been the sale of the Garrick Square house, but that had been seven years ago and if he was now thinking of taking a sabbatical...

As if reading her thoughts Euan said, "I'm actually comparatively well off at the moment so finance is not a problem. I saved a good deal of money in LA and I'd always intended to buy myself enough time to write this book..." He broke off, not wishing to go into the ideas for his magnum opus at this precise moment. He regarded her thoughtfully. "I have a proposal to make. You may, or may not like it, but please hear me out before you react." She nodded and he paused for a moment as if gathering his thoughts.

"Once I have finished sorting things out in London which could take up to a month, I should like to return." Her eyes widened but she didn't interrupt. "I think you and I need time together but we need to take it slowly and I don't want to cramp your space. So I had the idea of taking the lodge. This would mean we would be near enough to see each other, but far enough away to have our freedom and privacy. It's a sort of compromise." He looked at her. "We could try it out for a few months and see if it worked. What do you think?"

Natasha sat quietly turning the proposal over in her mind. It was unexpected but it could be a clever solution to a dilemma that had been causing her some concern. When Euan had said he was returning to London her immediate reaction had been one of panic at the thought of losing him again so soon. Similarly, when he'd said he was coming back to Norfolk she had panicked again. His presence had a disturbing effect on her. If he'd suggested being with her in the house she knew it would have produced problems and put them both under considerable pressure. Therefore the lodge did seem a very possible solution. She looked at him anxiously.

"The lodge will need a good deal of work. At first I was going to offer it to the B's but they preferred the quarters above the kitchen. Since then repairs to the lodge have been fairly low down on my agenda. It's also very small. Won't you feel cramped?"

Euan smiled. "You may find this hard to believe after Garrick Square, but I actually prefer small spaces. My needs are few. I can get my desk and books out of store and the rest I'll buy up here."

Natasha also smiled. "We're like a couple of nomads, trailing our possessions from place to place."

He stood up. "I don't want to rush you, but if you're feeling strong enough, we could go and look at the lodge now. Then if you're in agreement, I'll get Wal to put some legal agreement down on paper and I'll move back up here in a couple of weeks." He laughed. "It's a reversal of roles. First you rent a flat from me then I rent a place from you."

They walked down to the lodge together and Mrs B out by the dustbins watched them go. "I can't make out that Mr Mackay at all," she confided in Tom, "not at all."

Tom puffed at his pipe. "Well Laura likes him. And she knows a thing or two that one. I reckon she's a good judge of character."

This drew a snort from his wife. "Now I've heard everything." She attacked her pastry with extra vigour. "Fancy you taking into account what a six year old thinks. You're losing your marbles Tom Bondage and that's the truth."

Her husband said nothing but smiled good-naturedly. He was used to his wife's sharp tongue. It had no effect on him whatsoever.

Over lunch Natasha and Euan discussed the practicalities of the plan, suddenly energised and excited by their new project. She agreed the lodge didn't need much renovation. The plumbing and electrics would have to be overhauled, but it had the advantage of open fires in the living room and bedroom so no worries about keeping the place warm.

"Apart from the odd bit of furniture and kitchen stuff there isn't a great deal to find," Euan said. "I can probably buy all I need in Norwich but I will need someone to put up bookshelves once I get my books out of store..."

"B is the person to help you there," Natasha told him. "He knows everyone in the village so he can tell you who could do the work. They all meet up in the pub."

"It might be an idea to visit the pub myself," Euan said casually, "I might go tonight, sound out a few people and get things going while I'm away."

Natasha made a face. "You're welcome. Personally, I don't want to touch any alcohol for at least a week."

Euan smiled. "You already have. There was a hefty dollop of vodka in your medicine, along with tomato juice, lemon juice and a number of other secret ingredients."

She tried to look cross. "You were told no alcohol!"

"Are you feeling better or aren't you?"

It was gentle banter, the calm after the revelations of the night before. It had left them both shaken, but in different ways. Natasha's reaction had been purely physical. With Euan it was more in his head. He really needed time in London away from her in order to sort out his confused feelings. It was also vital if the anger against Gerry wasn't to build up and ruin everything.

They talked on through the afternoon. Only once did Euan make a reference to the past when he asked Natasha about her father. He'd never liked George and George had certainly never liked him and with good reason. First Euan had stolen George's wife and then threatened to steal his daughter as well. This had sent George into such a panic it was hardly surprising he had almost dragged Natasha up the aisle to marry Gerry. As for Natasha, she had never shown much affection towards her father even before her marriage. Now she sounded cold and detached.

"They moved to Switzerland just after Laura was born," she told him, "near Geneva. It suits the ghastly Inga, Switzerland being so clean and clinical." She added wearily, "I did make an effort to get on with Inga but never could. She was so totally different from my mother in every way. She was so..." she searched for a word and in the end settled for 'Germanic' which she spat out with venom. Euan smiled and Natasha went on, "I wrote and told them I was leaving Gerry. Father wrote back a pompous note saying he was sure I had done my best. Done my best! It was partly his fault I had married the man in the first place. He put me under huge pressure." She shrugged. "His letter didn't offer support of any kind. Not that I expected or wanted anything financial, but some sympathetic words at that time would have been very welcome. And he didn't even mention Laura. I think he was still smarting because Grandfather left me this house and nothing to him. They'd never really got on but I don't think it was a vindictive move. Grandfather was just being practical. The Estate had already been made over to my uncle, Father's elder brother Paul, and at that time a generous settlement of money was given to Father. There wasn't really anything else to leave. Father wouldn't have wanted this house. He and Inga already have plenty of money and property. But it still seemed to upset him."

She sighed. "Wills seem to do that," adding, "Aren't families the pits?"

Euan smiled. "My mother left her estate to my brother Cal, but in fact I'd told her to, so it wasn't a shock." He paused. "Unlike her death which was, because it was so sudden and I didn't have time to get back from LA."

Natasha looked at him, "I'm so sorry Euan. When did it happen?"

"Not long after I'd arrived in America. Murdo went a few days later. It was a bad week I can tell you." He looked at her. "Actually I think my mother knew she was dying when I last saw her. Her goodbye was somehow final. She wasn't emotional about it. She was never one to make a fuss and Lord knows she'd had a hard life."

Natasha observed his clenched jaw and said gently, "I remember your mother, from when we visited your house on our way to Iona for that holiday, all those years ago."

He relaxed and gave a smile. "She remembered you too, even when you were grown up. She'd always say, 'and how's the wee girl?'" He gave a laugh. "She was a canny lady. I think she guessed by my reaction on that last visit that there was something between us."

There was silence in the room and then Natasha said, "When will go you go London?"

"It depends on how much I can get organised in the Pub tonight."

She laughed. "Well don't overdo the drinking. We don't want your reputation ruined before you've even moved in."

It was well after closing time that Euan finally made his way back to the house. Natasha heard him come in and smiled to herself. He'd certainly given himself time to get acquainted with the locals.

Tom was saying as much as much to his wife, who wasn't best pleased by the way he'd staggered through the door and fallen into the armchair. She'd been ready for bed for at least an hour and was filling in time by making herself yet another cup of cocoa. "I knew that Mr Mackay was going to be a bad influence," she sniffed, "and my first instincts are never wrong. Just look at the state of you Tom Bondage."

Tom gave an inward chuckle. He'd had a very good night but

one look at his wife's hostile face told him he would somehow have to appease her.

"Our Clive came into the pub," he said, "and Mr Mackay's offered him a job, asked him to help him with his work."

It was a clever move. His wife was immediately interested even if still suspicious. "What sort of work?"

"I dunno really," Tom was vague, "sorting out books and papers, maybe fixing him up with a computer. It'll be good, summat for Clive to do."

Mrs B was silent for a moment mulling this over. She and Tom hadn't been able to have children of their own, so when her sister died they had taken on her only son Clive. His father was a drunk and had moved away from the area making no objections. Clive was a clever, highly strung boy. He'd done well at college and landed a good job in a computer firm. All went well until two years back the firm had closed down. Clive was then made redundant at only twenty four. After that he'd found it impossible to find similar work and had taken on a variety of different jobs but never settled. His health suffered and he became depressed. Last year, to their alarm he got into some very bad company. There was drinking and drugs. They'd tried to help but were out of their depth. This job with Mr Mackay could be a solution. Clive would be close enough for them to keep an eye on him.

"What is this work of Mr Mackay's?" she asked Tom.

Tom lit his pipe and announced, "He writes for the television. He's been all over, just got back from Hollywood and knows a lot of them film stars." He chuckled. "He told us some fair old stories."

His wife looked disapproving, "Who else was in the Horseshoes?"

"Oh, the usual crowd, Jocky, Old Matt, Zack..." Mrs B clicked her tongue disapprovingly. "Bunch of reprobates," she muttered. Tom added, "He's asked Jocky to repair the lodge..."

"Do you mean the Dower House Lodge?"

"Yes, Mr Mackay is moving into it."

"Does Mrs Masterson know?"

"Well of course she does. It was her idea. Seems Mr Mackay wants to write a book and he's going to do it in there." He looked at her and added, "He's an old friend of the family and knew Mrs Masterson's mother. I'll tell you summat else. The mother was killed in a car accident when Mrs Masterson was just a kiddie."

Something clicked in Mrs B's memory, a headline in the local newspaper about Mrs Roxby Smith being killed in a car crash. She remembered how upset old Sir Malcolm had been. "That poor lamb," she said to B as she filled her hot water bottle. "What a lot she has been through with no mother and a husband who's left her. Maybe it'll be good for her to have a friend around."

She began to see Mr Mackay in a new light.

The next morning Euan arrived down late for breakfast. Natasha regarded him over the top of her newspaper and enquired "Do I take it you'll be in need of one of your own hangover cures?"

Euan poured himself a cup of coffee and a glass of orange juice and drained them both down fast. "Not quite as bad as that, I'm a wee bit dehydrated that's all."

She smiled and put down her paper, "I gather you have charmed the locals. Mrs B was given a full account of your evening from B."

Euan winced. "Oh Jesus, that can't have pleased her. Don't worry I was careful to be discreet. I said you were an old family friend and that you were letting me rent the lodge. All very respectable I assure you. I also managed to organise the entire restoration, plus I asked a lad called Clive to help set me up with a computer. He's related to the B's."

Natasha looked at him admiringly. "That was fast work. Who is doing the actual repairs?"

"Someone by the name of Jocky," he told her. "It seems he can turn his hand to anything."

"Jocky!" Natasha exclaimed, "Euan he's the biggest rogue around. He certainly can do everything, from pilfering to poaching." Euan looked taken aback and she laughed. "Don't worry I'm sure it will be fine, he's a good workman and you will be there to keep a watch on him. And Laura will be pleased. Jocky gave her some baby chicks last year. Unfortunately the fox got them but it made no difference Laura still thinks he's wonderful." She went back to her paper. "I'm impressed. Once you get an idea, you certainly move fast."

"That's me," he said, "the 'Real Mackay'."

"Don't you mean the 'Real Mackoy'?"

He smiled and shook his head. "No I don't. Originally it was Mackay named after the Scotch whisky, but the Americans changed it to Mackoy on account of some famous boxer. Look it up in Brewer's if you don't believe me."

"Oh I believe you," she said.

CHAPTER SIX

After Euan's move back into the lodge, it didn't take long for the two of them to establish a routine. In fact it all fell into place so fast Natasha didn't really become aware of the way her life had changed until she stopped to consider it. Now six months on, with spring well under way, she had time to reflect on the difference Euan's arrival had made. It was a little like the curate's egg she decided, good in parts even if the parts were not quite as she had expected.

To her relief, Euan had plunged straight into his magnum opus and worked away at the lodge, writing in long bouts only occasionally interrupted by feverish pacing round the garden. On most nights he rounded off the day with a trip to the pub. In consequence she saw him little during the week, only sometimes when they had the occasional supper out. They always had Sunday lunch together to catch up on the week's news although on these occasions Laura tended to hold the floor.

Another source of relief was that he hadn't put pressure on her to renew their affair. It had been the one aspect of his return that she had dreaded. It wasn't that she didn't want him, half of her longed for them to start again, but Gerry had left her with too many bad memories and the physical act of love-making now filled her with fear and apprehension. It would happen one day of that she was certain but until she was ready Euan would have to continue to show patience. She was aware this must be causing him a certain amount of frustration, although he never directly made a reference to it. Sometimes he would make trips to London and Natasha idly wondered if these were for some form of female dalliance. She never inquired, feeling it was better to stay in ignorance.

There was no point in being driven into his bed from feelings of jealousy.

There was a certain irony she reflected, that in all the areas she had expected problems there had been none. She hadn't once felt threatened or pressurised, nor did she feel in any way a loss of her freedom or space. It was almost the opposite of how she had imagined it would be. However, there was one change in him that definitely had surprised her and that was his violent mood swings. She remembered the occasional moodiness from Garrick Square, but nothing on this scale. When he first arrived back from LA he'd seemed calm, dependable, kind and understanding, but this was short lived after his return from London. It didn't take her long to find out that Euan's moods went up and down with great rapidity. It was almost as if he were harbouring some great bitterness and all this pent up anger would suddenly surface and pour out of him for no apparent reason. Thankfully the most violent 'black dog' moods were infrequent but when they did hit he would become gloomy, morose and at times almost frightening. One minute he'd be at his most charming, the next, he would be foul-mouthed, bad-tempered and often cruel. After that there would be two or three days of awfulness that nothing seemed to shift. At first she had tried to show sympathy and understanding but her only reward was to receive a verbal lashing. It set her wondering if he had childhood skeletons buried deep waiting for some trigger to make them re-surface. It didn't seem possible that these moods were just caused by bitterness over the death of her mother and her marriage to Gerry, but without a course in Jung and Freud she couldn't get much further. The only remedy was to keep out of his way and wait for normality to resume. Just once, when he had come out of a particularly dark mood she questioned him about it. He seemed surprised she should have noticed and shrugged it off by telling her all creative people tended to have manic episodes. Natasha remained sceptical but didn't pursue the subject.

There was another worrying aspect of these moods and that was when he went out on a bender. He would then return in an abusive and drunken state. Once or twice he had turned up at the house like this and she had quickly sent him back to the lodge, for fear of his running into Laura. At first she also worried about what the locals at the Three Horseshoes made of it and said as much to Euan. He appeared amused that this should worry her but assured her that when he was into a real drinking session he went further afield. He mentioned several pubs; The Recruiting Sergeant, the Trowel and Hammer, the Whalebone and the Woodmen, none of which she knew. When she inquired why there was the necessity for these benders, he shrugged it off by saying, "Sometimes when I am having a mental block with my writing, it helps to find myself three sheets to the wind. For a few hours it blocks out the problems."

"But doesn't that leave you feeling awful?" she asked.

"Pretty awful, yes," he agreed, adding with a smile, "There's no point in trying to analyse why I do it. I just feel the need of a bender and then go on one. I'm not doing anyone any harm, only myself."

She was not so sure about this. It certainly wasn't pleasant to be in his vicinity when he was that drunk, but she knew if she said so he'd accuse her of being prim, or a Puritan, or worse.

There was also a more recent problem which worried her. Euan had lately been given to making scathing remarks about the state of marriage, especially with regard to children. It was obvious he had mixed feelings about Laura. There had been a dangerous moment at Christmas when a series of lavish presents had arrived from Gerry for his daughter. Euan's mood darkened with each one and this had almost threated the Festivities. Natasha had for once become angry and told him either to pull himself together or go away. To her surprise he had behaved quite well after that but usually she avoided the distress and hassle of trying to talk him round.

Between these moods there were long bouts of calm when he was once again his charming self. They would laugh and talk together and she would almost forget the difficult times. She also reminded herself of the strain he was under with this magnum opus which was obviously causing him stress. On several occasions he admitted that he was finding it difficult taking on such a serious and scholarly work after so many years of writing trivia.

One night, when they were out for supper, she questioned him about it. Euan was in a mellow mood and the evening had been relaxed, but as he talked about his writing he changed and became passionate and animated. When he was like this he became unlike anyone else she knew. She listened intently as he expounded his themes and theories. Although understanding little, she was reluctant to stop his flow by interrupting. He explained it was a complex subject, the changing vision of the Antichrist through the centuries and his research was forcing him to study the interpretations and personifications of evil. It seemed to him that somehow the human race had this need for evil and every decade threw up a new villain.

He had talked for a full fifteen minutes when he suddenly stopped. "I'm sorry Tash, you're the first person I've inflicted this on. It's difficult to let go when you're living with a subject."

She smiled. "Don't apologise, it's fascinating. I just wish I understood more. Have you been commissioned to write this book?"

He gave a hollow laugh. "Good God no, both my agents were horrified with the idea. They would far prefer me to stick to television scripts and subjects which are more wholesome and lucrative. However, I persuaded them it was an opus that I needed to get out of my system and they agreed I should take a year out."

"Who will publish it?"

"That's a good question. I hope eventually to find a publisher brave enough, but given the state of publishing in England and given that I am hardly writing a popular or commercial tome, I may well have a problem." He stabbed at his food with a fork. "It will upset the Establishment and it is the Establishment that runs everything in this bloody country." He looked at her worried expression and smiled. "Don't worry I have the Acadine approach towards my writing."

"What does that mean?"

"Acadine was a Sicilian fountain which was said to have magic properties. Writings were thrown into it to be tested. If they were good and genuine, they floated. If they were spurious and slight, they sank. Therefore if this book is the former, it will survive."

Natasha felt rather doubtful about this theory and instinctively anticipated stormy months ahead.

*

In the middle of all this pre-occupation with Euan there had been a pleasant development in her life. Out of the blue she had been visited by one of Laura's teachers who said she felt sure that Laura had musical talent and it might be good for her to have piano lessons. Laura had other ideas and said she wanted to learn the 'cello. There had been a 'cellist at a Christmas concert and it had obviously impressed her. She was so adamant about this that Natasha found her a teacher and also purchased a quarter sized 'cello. Since then her progress on the instrument had been remarkable. Most satisfying of all was that she really seemed to enjoy it and never had to be nagged into practising. She would spend long sessions on her own, happily playing and composing little tunes.

"I think she must have inherited her musical talent from my mother," Natasha said proudly. "It certainly isn't from me. I've always been tone deaf."

Euan was immediately at his most sarcastic. "I suppose you're going to tell me next that she's a child prodigy."

She looked at him. He'd been perfectly pleasant a few moments before, so why the sudden change? He really was the most baffling man. She tried to keep it light. "I wasn't going to say anything of the kind. I'm just pleased to see her enjoying the instrument so much. I certainly wouldn't force her into playing."

Euan snorted. "You're falling into that boring middle-class parent trap of that desperate necessity to push their children through the torture of scraping or blowing some defenceless instrument. Good God. What did music do to deserve the awfulness of pushy, ambitious mothers?"

"What absolute drivel," Natasha snapped. "If the child has some talent and enjoys playing it's only sensible to do what I can to nurture it."

"For whose benefit, hers or yours?"

She was genuinely hurt by this suggestion and retorted, "Hers of course."

He gave a mocking laugh. "Tell me that in a few years' time, when you are entering her for competitions, along with all the other prize-craving mothers."

This made her lose her temper. "Look, just because you were intellectually pressurised and made to cram for scholarships and top marks as a child don't lay your hang-ups at my daughter's door. Laura has some musical talent. I just want to make sure she has an opportunity to enjoy it."

"It'll be singing lessons and drama auditions next," he taunted her.

"Bloody bullshit Euan!"

He looked at her furious expression. "Good Natasha, very good, you're managing to sound almost convincing."

"Don't be so bloody patronising!" she yelled back at him, as she stormed from the room.

She hated him at moments like this. Why did he feel the need to sneer all the time? At the top of his sneer list was of course, the subject of family. Any mention of a relation, or the Roxby Estate, was likely to produce a torrent of sarcasm and derision. For this reason she postponed an invitation to see her cousin Livvy until he was safely away on one of his visits to London.

Livvy arrived before lunch on the most perfect of spring days. The Wordsworthian daffodils were waving in the breeze and there was a light green sheen on the lawn. As the cousins hugged, Livvy said, "Natasha this place is wonderful."

"You must have known the house," Natasha said as they walked indoors.

Livvy shook her head. "No, it was one of the few parts of the Estate I never visited. I think it was rented out to some foreigners when I was young, who used it as a summer residence. I remember Grandfather muttering on about the 'Bloody Huns in the Dower House'."

Natasha laughed and told her it had been empty for a few years before she took it over and explained that the whole house had needed care and attention so she was doing it up slowly, one room at a time. They went into the living room and Livvy caught sight of the photographs. She picked one up. "This has to be Laura. When do I meet her?"

"She comes back from school about three. I thought it would be good if we had time to catch up on things first. It's been so long…" She broke off then added, "I do feel guilty for not making contact. It was just that I desperately needed time to myself. I'm doing my best to catch up with everyone now. Dolly and Tinker are coming to stay at the end of the month."

Livvy smiled. "How is Dolly? I haven't seen her for years, in fact not since your wedding. Poor Dolly, she cried the whole way through the service and then all the way through the reception. Tinker spent the entire time mopping her up."

Natasha laughed. "Actually Dolly was right about the wedding. The whole thing was an unmitigated disaster." She looked affectionately at Livvy, remembering how inseparable they had been as children. When her mother died, Livvy was the one person she had trusted and confided in. They'd been more like sisters than cousins. It wasn't until she left school that they went their separate ways.

"My God!" she suddenly exclaimed. "Do you realise I'll be thirty soon?"

"Well I'm ancient," Livvy said, "I've turned thirty two. How did we both get so ancient?" And they both laughed.

Over lunch Natasha gave Livvy the bare outlines of her life with Gerry. She listened with a mixture of sympathy and horror. As she finished Natasha said, "You do understand, I had to leave him, I couldn't have stayed on, even for Laura's sake."

Livvy gave a nod of understanding. "Of course you couldn't but I just can't make out why Gerry married you in the first place."

Natasha shrugged, "I've considered all the possible reasons, none of them very flattering to me. He was a man who needed to be married, given his situation and his career. It was too difficult for him to admit he was gay. Mind you, he still doesn't. He admits to nothing except to say he is bi-sexual. I personally think that is self-indulgent nonsense. You have to be one or the other." She added scornfully, "Anyway unfaithfulness is unfaithfulness, whatever sex you're with. But I'll tell you something that men don't understand. As a woman it completely destroys your confidence, to find that your husband prefers men to you. I just couldn't live with that. In the end my self-esteem couldn't have got any lower."

Livvy looked sad. "I'm afraid our upbringing and schooling didn't quite prepare us for all the problems adult life would throw at us."

Natasha had a momentary feeling of panic. Livvy hadn't mentioned Edmund or her marriage once. She knew there were no children. Was she having problems as well? She stood up. "As it's such a lovely day shall we go and sit outside?"

They walked through the vegetable garden and out onto the lawn, where they sat under a tree. Livvy sighed. "It's so perfect here. I do envy you the garden. We only have a patio in Norwich. I've simply covered it in pots and Edmund complains there's no room to move, let alone sit down."

"Why don't you move to the country?" Natasha asked. "You could keep horses again."

Livvy shrugged. "Edmund has to be near his work at the hospital. He's a very busy consultant. Anyway, I'm used to town life now. Over the years my tastes have changed." Her voice sounded wistful and Natasha was alarmed to see there were tears in her eyes.

"Livvy," she ventured nervously, "are things all right between you and Edmund?"

The voice that answered was over-bright. "Oh yes, we have a very good life, extremely full..." she hesitated, "but we have no children."

"And would you like children?"

"Yes," Livvy angrily brushed away a tear, "more than anything in the world, but it is sod's law Natasha. Those that don't want children resort to abortions. Edmund and I, well, we've tried everything but it's no good. We just have to be resigned to the fact that we're one more dot on the statistics of childless couples."

"Surely there's something you can do? I mean, they've made great progress in this field haven't they?"

"For some, yes they have, but not for us. We have the 'double whammy' as the politicians would say. Edmund has such a low sperm count it's almost negligible and I have blocked fallopian tubes. One problem they might have been able to cope with, but not both. God knows we have tried. I had two operations where they poured blue dye through my system, or rather tried to. Edmund had endless hormone injections. But all to no avail." She paused. "The problem now is that Edmund is totally against having any child that isn't his, so that rules out all the other methods and also adoption. It's not really rational but he's adamant."

Natasha was silent and then looked at Livvy, "What about you?"

She said briskly, "Oh I wouldn't have minded what we did. I just wanted a child, but Edmund won't budge. We spent hours in discussion and argument. We both cried a lot. It nearly split us up, but in the end we didn't want to live without each other, it was as simple as that. Now the subject is closed. There are the occasional bad moments when people make insensitive remarks like, 'Isn't it time you started a family Livvy?' or they tell Edmund what a wonderful father he'd be. It's just something we've learned to live with."

Natasha sat feeling shocked. "I feel hopelessly selfish Livvy. I've been so obsessed with my own problems I never even considered yours."

Livvy returned to her practical self and said briskly, "When you think of all the suffering and sorrow in the world we all need to put things into perspective. Edmund and I have a good life and I am lucky to have found a man I can admire and love. He's a brilliant doctor and we have plenty of friends and of course our cats..." She laughed, "Boosey and Hawkes. They were named after Edmund's favourite music shop. Did you know he originally wanted to be a musician? He played the trombone and he's a very good pianist."

Natasha nodded. "I remember him playing at your wedding." She was about to mention Laura's musical talent but stopped herself feeling it wouldn't be tactful at this moment to talk about her child.

Livvy went on, "We both joined the Cathedral choral society. Sadly Edmund had to give up through lack of time, but I really enjoy it.

You must come over for our next concert."

Natasha was about to ask for the date when she caught sight of Laura stumping across the lawn and her heart sank. Would it be a terrible ordeal for Livvy to have to meet her? Laura, unaware of any tension, threw down her lunch box and books.

"Phew!" she said with the air of someone who had just negotiated the Normandy landings. "I'm bushed."

"Bushed?" Natasha asked faintly, "Where did you get that expression?"

"At school," Laura replied and flopped onto the grass.

Natasha noticed a large tear in her school blouse. "What on earth have you been doing? Your sleeve is almost ripped off."

"I had a fight with Freddie."

"Freddie Mullins, the butcher's son? But Laura he's much older than you, and bigger."

"Well I pushed him over," Laura said proudly. "So he tore my blouse."

"Why did you push him over?"

"He said that playing the 'cello was for cissies, so I pushed him."

Natasha looked across at Livvy and to her relief saw that she was smiling. "Laura, this is my cousin Livvy."

Livvy held out her hand, "Hello Laura."

Laura stood up and shook it. "What's a cousin?" she asked.

Natasha looked at Livvy. "She doesn't have any cousins. Neither Gerry or I have brothers or sisters." She turned back to Laura and explained, "A cousin is the child of your brother or sister. My father's brother is Livvy's father."

Laura didn't seem very interested in this. "Where's You-wan?" she asked.

Natasha looked flustered and said quickly, "He's gone to London and won't be back until tomorrow. Now go and get changed and ask Mrs B to give you your tea."

With some difficulty Laura gathered up her things and stumped her way back across the lawn.

Livvy burst out laughing. "What a little tomboy. It's funny, I expected you to have a more ethereal child." She turned back to Natasha. "Who is this 'You-Wan'?"

Natasha sighed. "It's a long story. Let's go back indoors and I'll tell you over tea.

They walked back inside and once settled by the fire she recounted the whole Euan saga, from the time he was with her mother, to their re-meeting again and their life in Garrick Square, ending in her marriage with Gerry.

As Natasha broke off Livvy said, "If you had this passionate affair with Euan what on earth made you marry Gerry?"

Natasha sighed. "You may well ask. It's difficult to explain even now, because I don't fully understand it myself. Somewhere during that time in Garrick Square Euan and I went badly wrong. Maybe there was almost too much passion and we just couldn't sustain it. He became possessive, controlling and finally incredibly jealous. I reacted badly to this and we started having rows." She shrugged. "Gerry was there, always in the right place at the right time. With great skill he managed to come between us. I saw quite a lot of him, mainly to show Euan I was an independent person." She added bitterly," Gerry was a good listener and a seductively sympathetic ear. The more I saw him, the worse it became with Euan. I began to feel like a battlefield. Euan behaved like Svengali with me. I ceased to be my own person when I was with him. Added to this I was haunted by Mama and I had constant feelings of guilt. And then..."

"And then?" echoed Livvy?

"Well then my father got to hear about my affair with Euan and how I was living in his house. I now know it was Gerry who told him. My God that man was devious. Anyway, the balloon went up. My father summoned me home and there was the most terrible showdown. I returned to London and had another terrible row with Euan. I suddenly couldn't stand it anymore. I moved out and went back to Wal and Miriam. Gerry came to seem me, all tea and sympathy. It was such a relief to have kindness and understanding after being bullied and shouted at. Now I can see he had calculated the whole strategy and it was brilliant. He softened me up and then proposed." Natasha shrugged. "I just saw a solution to all my problems and accepted."

There was silence in the room. Then Livvy burst out, "But what about Euan? Didn't he try and talk you out of it?"

"Yes he did," Natasha gave a twisted smile. "He chose that moment to tell me that Gerry was gay. I didn't believe him and it made me despise him all the more because I thought he was just doing it out of jealousy."

"What a mess" said Livvy.

"It was," Natasha gave a great sigh. "Everyone tried to dissuade me from marrying Gerry, except of course my father. He was delighted. Apart from the fact that Gerry was a sort of celebrity, for him it was the ultimate revenge on Euan."

Livvy sounded severe. "I have to tell you Natasha, I always found your father a complete rat." They both laughed at this and Livvy added, "None of us ever liked him. It was difficult to think of him and Papa as brothers."

Natasha threw a log on the fire. "Don't you find it maddening that the awful people always seem to triumph? In the end both Gerry and my father won. Euan backed off and went to America. Once he'd gone, I didn't really care what happened to me anymore."

There was silence in the room, as they were both lost in thought.

Then Livvy asked, "Why is Euan back now?"

"He heard about the separation and returned to visit me, to see if I was all right."

"And he's moved back in?"

"Not into the house, he's staying at the lodge. It's a sort of compromise. We need to start again without any of the pressures of actually living together."

Livvy looked at her. "And is it working out?"

Natasha considered this. "I think the jury is still out on that one. A lot of time has gone by and we've both changed. I still feel the old attraction, but he's such a complicated and difficult person." She gave a smile. "He tells me all creative people are."

Livvy let that one pass. "Sex?" she asked.

Natasha shook her head. "No, although I know Euan wants it. I do too really, but I still have too many bad memories of Gerry. I don't think I'm ready for another physical relationship yet."

There was another silence.

"Does anyone else know that Euan is here?" Livvy finally asked.

"Only Wal, and you know Wal, always the discreet lawyer. I presume Miriam must know as well, but in the circumstances..." She broke off. "Have you heard about Miriam?"

Livvy shook her head and Natasha told her about Miriam's mental state as described to her by Euan.

A little later Livvy left. As she climbed into the car she said, "When you see Dolly, you must tell her that her cousin is running one of the farms on the estate. Her name is Florence Maddington and she's a great character, over eighty and runs the whole place single-handed. You should meet her. She's pretty 'formidable' as the French would say."

Natasha smiled. "I'd like that. And I'll come over to Norwich soon."

She watched Livvy's car as it turned out of view past the lodge and then walked slowly back to the house thinking it had been a strange, cathartic sort of day.

The following afternoon was again clear and golden. Euan returned from London and crossing the lawn to where Natasha was sitting he flung himself down beside her.

"Peace," he said, "perfect peace."

A moment later there was a burst of frantic barking from Miffin and suddenly all the dogs in the neighbourhood started to bark in unison. Then the cows began a low mooing. Euan looked bewildered. "Was it something I said?" Natasha pointed to the sky. There were about ten hot air balloons, every colour of the rainbow, floating serenely across the horizon.

"They may look beautiful" she said crossly, "but they always set the animals off. The farmers hate them."

Euan lay back and closed his eyes. "Never mind," he said, "Nothing is going to take away from the beauty of this moment."

Natasha eyed him suspiciously. "Good heavens, what brought this on? Did you have a successful time in London?"

"Not very," he said, his eyes still closed. "I'm just pleased to be back."

She took advantage of his mellow mood to tell him about Livvy's visit."

Euan opened his eyes. "We should go and see them. Take them out to dinner."

"What us together, going to see my family?" she mocked, adding, "Do you mean as an item?"

He smiled. "Why not, we are aren't we?"

This was Euan at his most unpredictable. He suddenly jumped to his feet and pulled her up as well. "What are we going to do about your birthday?"

She looked astonished. "How do you know about my birthday?"

"Belinda told me. She said it was your thirtieth, the day after tomorrow."

Natasha looked uneasy. "I thought you didn't do birthdays. Anyway, I wasn't going to make a thing of it."

"Well you should. Thirty is a milestone. It means you are catching up with me," and he laughed as he kissed her.

Over the next two days she couldn't fault his behaviour. He was charming, attentive and anxious to please. He listened to one of Laura's compositions and even managed to say something complimentary. As for her birthday, he insisted on making all the arrangements, ending up with a candlelit supper. Natasha looked in amazement at the room, filled with flickering candles of every shape and size.

"It was Laura's idea," he explained. "She told me you liked candles. I've given Mrs B the night off and arranged a cold collation. After all, we are celebrating your birthday."

Natasha burst out laughing. "It is like the seduction scene out of "Phantom of the Opera".

Euan put on some Chopin and opened the champagne.

At the end of the meal she said quite genuinely, "Thank you Euan.

That is the best birthday I ever had."

"There's more to come. You haven't opened your present from me yet. Wait here and I'll go and get it."

He left the room and there was a great deal of banging of doors and bumping noises. Then she was summoned. As she walked into the hall she stopped dead in her tracks and gasped. In the middle of the room there stood a huge stone urn standing on a pedestal. She walked slowly round it touching the intricate carving with her hand.

"It's amazing," she said at last. "How old is it?"

"Oh I don't know things like that, but the man in the shop said it was definitely an antique. I thought it would look good in the middle of your herb garden."

"Of course, that would be perfect. Thank you Euan" and she flung her arms round his neck.

He extricated himself and said, "I'm going to make some Gaelic coffee. You must drink it at once, while it is still hot."

As they sat by the fire, sipping their coffees, Natasha felt waves of happiness sweep over her. It might not last she told herself, but for this moment she was content just to wallow in it.

Near midnight Euan stood up and looked at her in a way that made her shiver. "Will you let me take you to bed?" he asked.

And she found she didn't have the will to resist.

CHAPTER SEVEN

"How could you? How bloody could you?" Natasha screamed as she wrenched at the gears. "I never believed you could be so crassly awful. What in hell's name made you behave like that?"

She screeched to a halt as the traffic lights turned red and looked at him angrily. Euan was slouched in the passenger seat, a supercilious grin on his face, his eyes half closed. The thought that he hadn't been listening to her only served to fuel her fury even more. She was beyond tears.

"I don't know how you have the nerve to sit there grinning. Haven't you got anything to say?" she shouted at him.

"You seem to be talking for both of us," Euan said wearily, "and no, I don't have anything to say."

The lights turned green. "There has to be a reason for you to have behaved like that?" she persisted.

Euan was silent. What could he tell her? He didn't really know the reason himself. Yes he'd drunk far too much which hadn't helped, but the real cause was much more complicated and at this precise moment his brain was too befuddled to give her any articulate explanation.

It started to rain and Natasha switched on the windscreen wipers. They made a dull, thudding hypnotic sound which did nothing to improve Euan's condition. She leaned forward and brushed the steamed up windows with her hand.

"Where the hell are we?" We should have seen the turning by now."

Euan made an effort to be helpful "We're in the purlieus of Norwich," he said, his voice very slurred.

"Well I know that," Natasha found it difficult to keep the irritation out of her voice. "We're on the ring road but I need to know where the turning is. Can you get out the map?"

There was no movement from the passenger side. A quick glance told her that the slumped figure was now asleep. "Bloody marvellous," she muttered to herself. "There are times when I really hate you Euan."

She drove to a garage and took directions. It was a wild and stormy night and she felt full of anger and resentment. Why wasn't he driving? Why couldn't he have taken the responsibility for getting them home? Then he might not have got so drunk.

Armed with instructions she climbed back into the car. There was no sound from Euan except the occasional snore, so she was left to ruminate on the events of the night alone. She felt in shock, mainly because it had all been so unexpected.

The evening had started in a mood of happy anticipation. Life had definitely improved of late. Euan had been less difficult and moody and since their sex life had resumed he was mostly at his charming best. So when he'd suggested taking Livvy and Edmund out to a restaurant for dinner she'd agreed. Maybe if they had stuck to that plan it would have been all right. Instead of which Livvy has asked them to dinner at their house. This was a mistake. She should have stuck to neutral territory for Euan's first encounter with family. But she honestly couldn't possibly have foreseen such a disaster. It had gone wrong from the start. They'd had difficulty in finding the house and consequently were late with Euan already tetchy. As soon as Natasha entered the room, she had an ominous sinking feeling. There was no particular reason for this, just a gut reaction, but as things turned out her instincts were horribly right.

The first couple they were introduced to were innocuous enough, Choral Society friends called Nigel and Annabel. He worked in computers and she described herself as a 'happy housewife'. Natasha saw Euan wince at this, but in view of the next introduction this was a minor setback. Livvy announced with a certain amount of pride in her voice, "Meet Marcus and Hilary Waters, our local celebrities. Marcus runs the Lidford Literary Festival which is one of the most successful festivals in the country."

Marcus held out his hand and said in a voice full of self-importance,

"I think you could say we're numero uno these days Livvy, especially after last year's coup." Here he gave a little wink at his wife.

Natasha felt a momentary panic as she saw Euan's expression change and knew he was about to launch into one of his famous put-downs. However, before he could open his mouth Annabel let forth a nervous laugh which rather resembled the whinnying of a horse. She did this at various intervals through the evening, which at first was startling but by the end nobody noticed it.

Marcus, of the nasal drawl, was a plump, oily little man, dressed inappropriately in crushed velvet which made him resemble a rather large cushion. His wife in contrast was tall, broad-shouldered and had the air of one who spent a good deal of time in beauty salons; the black tresses didn't have a hair out of place and the manicured nails were painted a violent shade of magenta. The leotard top was stretched over her perfect frontage and Natasha noted with amusement that there was maximum cleavage on show. The tight skirt fitted tightly over the most exercised of trim hips and the little lace-up boots were the last word in trendiness. The whole effect was heightened by a large amount of chunky jewellery and studded belts.

Livvy said, "You probably know Hilary better as Hilary Reynolds, the writer and broadcaster."

Hilary completely ignored Natasha and held out a languid hand towards Euan. "I do so hate labels don't you? I always think the description of journalist covers everything I do. After all, *you* are the authentic writer and I am thrilled to meet you." Edmund gave Euan a drink and he knocked it back in one as Hilary continued, "I believe you used to work in television over here? I seem to remember a series which won a great many awards."

Her gushing memory-act didn't impress Natasha. She knew Livvy would have briefed them about Euan and Hilary would have added her own research. It was probably why they had agreed to come. They were celebrity hunters and everyone else in the room was superfluous. Euan also recognised this and his face adopted a shut, mutinous expression. He gave Hilary an icy smile. "I've been in LA for seven years. Do tell me, does television drama still exist in England? I heard they only did American programmes these days."

Hilary gave a brittle laugh. "That's a teeny bit harsh I think. But do tell me Euan, what did you write in Hollywood?"

"Drivel," replied Euan and Annabel gave another whinnying laugh.

At this point Hilary grabbed Euan by the arm and swept him off to the other side of the room. Natasha was introduced to another couple but found it hard to concentrate. She saw enough to know that Euan had now knocked back his third whisky and there was an ominous glint in his eye. Just before dinner she went into the kitchen and found Livvy.

"You'd better tell Edmund to go easy on the booze for Euan. When he's been writing like this he always knocks them back fast and not always with the best results."

Livvy was looking flustered, so she replied a little vaguely, "Don't worry. I'm sure he's fine."

But of course he wasn't.

The rain began to ease off and Natasha switched the wipers to intermittent. She looked at her watch. God she was tired. The evening had exhausted her and she felt both mentally and physically wrecked. Maybe if Marcus and Hilary hadn't been there the evening could have been all right. Euan would have found the company boring but at least he might have remained civil.

She swerved to avoid a fox. The hazards of night driving in the country were endless and she didn't much care for it. The other day a deer had run out in front of her and in spite of slamming on the brakes, her front bumper had been removed. She wound down the window and let the night air blow on her face. The blast of cold wind momentarily woke Euan, who stirred, muttered something unintelligible and then fell back into his stupor.

Suddenly she found herself smiling. There had been one amusing moment amidst all the horrors. The dreaded Marcus and Hilary had been going on effusively about a book which had just been made into a film. It was a recent release so nobody in the room would have had a chance to see it and it was their obvious intention to make everyone look provincial and dull. At the end of constant name-dropping and fashionable references, Hilary said, "It is the most brilliant film and so true to the book, which is acknowledged as one of the great pieces of recent writing. You really do have to see it Euan."

Euan who had been unusually quiet through all this suddenly said, "I have."

Marcus and Hilary were overjoyed to have found a soul mate in this cultural desert. They both talked at once, "You have? But that's wonderful. Didn't you just love it?"

Euan cut them off, "I read the book. I saw the film. And then I threw up."

There was a stunned silence. For the only time that evening Marcus and Hilary were silenced. Then everyone began to talk at once. Things deteriorated quickly after that. Anything Marcus or Hilary said would immediately make Euan take the diametrically opposite view. In the end he just took to saying, "Bollocks!" or "Rats!" or "Piffle". Natasha looked round the room and could see the other guests were becoming increasingly uncomfortable and embarrassed. Thankfully at last Edmund came to the rescue suggesting they all got round the piano and this just about saved the evening. The Choral Society people came into their own and as song followed song, Hilary and Marcus pleaded a heavy schedule and left. Natasha finally managed to extricate Euan, but not before he'd consumed several large brandies.

She wound up the window as she turned into the drive and stopped outside the lodge. Turning the engine off she shook Euan awake and yelled in his ear, "Can you make it inside?" He nodded. Then went back to sleep. She went round to the passenger seat and hauled him out, more or less throwing him in the direction of his front door. Her last glimpse of him was standing rocking backward and forwards, trying to get his front door keys out of his coat pocket. If he's locked himself out she thought to herself, I don't care. He can just sleep on the front door step. I've had enough.

*

She woke the next morning with the feeling that she hadn't slept at all. Laura was in an unusually whining mood at breakfast and it was a relief when she was removed and taken to school. The arrival of the post did nothing to improve her disposition either. There were several large estimates for work on the dry rot under the stairs, an invoice from Zack who she apparently owed for six months work in the garden, and a letter from her Bank Manager to say that the last two months maintenance hadn't been paid into her account. This was odd because Gerry had always been punctilious about his payments. This didn't exactly mean she was threatened with a financial crisis, but it was worrying all the same.

It therefore wasn't surprising that Euan received a definitely frosty reception when he put his head round the door half an hour later. He looked pale and unshaven and made straight for the coffee pot.

"I hope you are feeling as lousy as you look," she growled.

He flopped into a chair. "I forgot to turn on the immersion so I have no hot water. Can I ablute in your bathroom this morning?"

She looked at him with distinct hostility. "I don't know how you have the nerve to show up here after your behaviour last night."

Euan held up his hands. "Pax please, I'm too hungover to fight."

"Good," she said.

He drained his coffee and poured another. "All right, mea culpa. I'd had a lousy day and I was tired. I drank too much and then took against the company. I know I behaved badly but I can honestly say I didn't think such ghastly, mealy-mouthed specimens still existed. They're Babbitts."

"Babbits? What on earth are you talking about?" Natasha asked crossly.

"Babbits are people who think they own 'Culture' and feel themselves superior to the rest of mankind. They know everything and understand NOTHING!" As he yelled the last word his face contorted with a look of pain. In view of his obvious suffering she tried to sound reasonable.

"Well, I didn't particularly like them either, but you didn't have to ruin the evening for everyone else. You became as bad as them, a shouting bully, heckling and rude."

Euan threw up his hands. "What can I say? I'm a recidivist. But those people drove me to it."

Natasha sighed. "I just wish you could have made an effort for Livvy. She'd tried so hard. It may have been mistaken but she invited those people especially to meet us."

Euan retorted angrily, "Then she's an idiot. That's exactly what those people want, to have the Livvy's of this world put them on a pedestal then crawl around and lick their asses."

"For God's sake Euan, just shut up!" Natasha sounded sharp.

Euan shrugged. "It's true." He looked at her, "but I didn't mean to upset you or Livvy." And he added sulkily, "Maybe you think I shouldn't go out at all."

"You go out often enough to the Pub."

"That's different. I find that relaxing. I'm not an outsider there. I don't have to worry about not having a double-barrelled name or not being a member of the so-called intelligentsia. Mind you, that lot last night didn't have an ounce of intelligence between them."

He sat glaring gloomily into his coffee and Natasha looked at him with irritation. This was all so childish and once again she was aware of this big chip on his shoulder. It would be impossible for them to have any social life at all if Euan was going to react like this every time, but all she said was "Do you mind not climbing onto your hobby-horse this morning Euan? Last night wore me out and I have enough problems of my own, quite apart from this stack of bills that needs sorting out." She paused. "Actually, while you're here there is something I need to discuss with you. I have Dolly and Tinker coming to stay next weekend. After last night's fiasco and given your views on my relations, it might be better if you made yourself scarce. Livvy may be forgiving, Dolly won't be."

She looked so serious Euan burst out laughing. "Oh dear, is the bad boy in detention?"

Natasha tried to keep her temper under control. "It's not funny Euan. I hated last night. I may have understood your reasons but I find it hard to forgive. Livvy is very special to me and I don't like seeing her upset. As for Dolly, well, what with Mama and everything it could get horribly complicated."

There was silence for a moment. Then Euan said, "I tell you what. Just to show you how repentant I am I'll go to London for a few days while Tinker and Dolly are here." Natasha didn't respond so he added, "Furthermore I will ring Livvy and apologise. Or would flowers be better? I had a friend at Cambridge who automatically sent flowers to his hostess and the female guests after every dinner party in case he'd offended any of them."

In spite of herself Natasha smiled. "Don't worry, I'll ring Livvy. I'm going to suggest she and Edmund come over to dinner here and when they do I trust you will be on your best behaviour."

"Yes Ma'am." Euan saluted and stood up, "permission to go and ablute now Ma'am."

As he stood in the shower his mood underwent a change. He'd done his best to diffuse the situation but the previous evening still rankled with him. Of course his behaviour had been out of order but Natasha's polite acceptance of such awful people infuriated him. It was the tip of the iceberg and if allowed to continue it would see him drawn into a social life that was both stifling and soul-destroying. When she had lived with him in Garrick Square she had been feisty and passionate. His memory was of someone who had spoken out strongly against the hypocrisy, cant and false values that had emerged in the eighties. He had seen in her a kindred spirit. But now?

He turned off the shower, wrapped himself in a towel and sat on the bathroom stool mulling things over. Of course it hadn't been easy for her, of that he was well aware, but having escaped from marriage and the clutches of Gerry, you'd have thought she'd want to enjoy her freedom and throw off the shackles of her background. Instead of which she seemed only too happy to start returning to her family and friends and again adopting their set way of life. Livvy was the start, Dolly was next, and soon the whole bloody lot would follow. They were like some dreadful octopus spreading their tentacles and sucking her back into their narrow social world. It had to stop. He certainly didn't want to be saddled with all that clobber. At some point soon she would have to decide between them, and him.

He stood up and started to shave his mind still racing. It was a fact and perhaps a strange one, but what had attracted him to both Celia and Natasha in the first place was that like him, they seemed to be outsiders. Both, through their circumstances, had become isolated just as he had done. He had been alienated from his friends by being the Minister's son. The abuse he had received from his father alienated him still further. Then at Cambridge he felt lost amongst the bright Public School set and further feelings of inferiority had crept over him when teaching at Civolds, a smart private school. He had certainly never fitted in at the BBC or any other television company. Even in LA he'd been recognised as a misfit and a maverick. This no longer bothered him but he hadn't come this far to be told to conform and settle down.

He put down his razor and smiled. A sudden vision of the home life of Marcus and Hilary Waters floated before him. That woman was a man-eater, sex mad and driven. He patted on some aftershave and came to decision. He loved Natasha and wanted her with him, but sacrifices could only go so far. For the moment he would continue to be patient and try and remain on his best behaviour but the strain was nearly killing him and the present situation couldn't go on for ever. Sooner or later she would have to leave the old life behind.

"I hope you're studying the map Tinker." Dolly spoke sharply, as she peered myopically through the windscreen. The journey from Oxford had already taken several hours and fulfilled all Tinker's worst forebodings. When planning the route he had been careful to avoid the motorways, partly because of Dolly's erratic driving and partly because he wasn't sure the 1947 Riley was quite up to it. So instead he made for Cambridge using minor roads. It was after Cambridge that the trouble had really started. They seemed to remain on the ring road for far too long and Dolly refused to stop. At last they found the signs for Newmarket and he now hoped they were moving in the right direction.

"What a boring county Norfolk is," Dolly said. "Of course it is known for being flat but quite frankly it is just this flatness that makes it so boring, it's flat, flat, flat!" She turned to him. "I think you can now leave the map Tinker darling and go on to Natasha's directions."

Tinker read them out. "We have to get on the A 11, after that it's quite simple."

"We're on the A 11" she shouted triumphantly, "I told you it wouldn't be complicated."

Tinker smiled but made no replay. Maybe he could now risk taking a nap? He was beginning to feel in the need of a snooze...

That was a mistake. Half an hour later he awoke in the middle of a farmyard.

"Oh Tinker," wailed Dolly. "I must have taken the wrong turning. You were asleep and I didn't want to wake you."

Tinker blinked himself out of oblivion. "Turn the car round Dolly," he said patiently, "and try not to run over any chickens. We'll go back up the track and take directions once we're on the main road."

Not for the first time he wondered why they hadn't taken the train.

Natasha looked at her watch. It was almost five and Tinker had said they would arrive early afternoon. She wished they hadn't opted to travel by car but Dolly had been adamant. She was a formidable lady even if she was nearly eighty. Nobody liked to contradict her. So it was with some relief she heard their car coming up the drive half an hour later.

A surprisingly sprightly Dolly alighted from the ancient vehicle. "Come along Professor," she shouted. "We've made it." She kissed Natasha on both cheeks. "Such adventures darling, we've done the entire tour of Norfolk! Poor old Tinker is a bit tired but he'll soon perk up after a cup of tea."

They went inside and Natasha put them either side of the fire. Mrs B brought in a tray of tea and introductions were made. Natasha regarded Tinker anxiously as he looked rather pale, although he insisted he was cold rather than tired. He explained that the heaters in the Riley were no longer working.

Natasha said, "It's a bit grey and gloomy today but I hope it will be better weather when I show you round. It's amazing what a difference it makes to the look of the place when it's in sunlight. We have terrific sunsets in Norfolk. I think it's on account of it being so flat."

Dolly shot Tinker a meaningful glance then turned back to her great niece. "You look far too thin darling. Can't the redoubtable Mrs B feed you up on cakes and puddings?"

Natasha laughed. "You have been telling me I was too thin since I was a child. I don't think I'll ever change, but I'm perfectly well I assure you."

The door opened and Laura, who'd been specially polished for the occasion, came into the room. "This dress itches," she said, tugging at the collar. "Can I change back into my gardening clothes?"

"After you've met Dolly and Tinker," Natasha told her severely. She'd given Laura a long talk about who they were and how important it was that she behaved well and that it might not be a good idea to mention Euan. Now she hoped the message had sunk in. Her daughter was horribly unpredictable.

"Come here child," Dolly said.

Laura looked genuinely puzzled. "I'm not child. I'm Laura."

Tinker nodded approvingly. "A perfectly logical remark to make," he murmured.

Dolly studied Laura. "It's quite incredible," she said after a minute or two, "the likeness to Celia. The colouring is different of course, but the likeness to your mother at that age is extraordinary. She has the same shaped face and set of the eyes."

"That's what…" Natasha broke off just in time. She had been going to say that was what Euan had said. Instead she finished rather lamely, "That's what Livvy said." Dolly didn't seem to have noticed but Tinker regarded her thoughtfully. He didn't miss much in spite of his vacant, owl-like expression. Natasha went on quickly, "Actually Laura seems to have inherited my mother's talent for music as well." She turned to Laura. "Why don't you play something on your 'cello for Tinker and Dolly?" The moment she said this she thought how Euan would have mocked her for making such a request. Laura however was quite cheerful about it, in the knowledge that once she had performed she might be allowed back into the garden. She had left Jocky and B talking about a muck-spreader and it sounded too good to miss. She took her 'cello out of its case and tightened the bow. "What shall I play?" she asked.

"Anything you like," Natasha said.

"I could play a tune I made up, but it doesn't have a name."

It was a strange, melancholic piece, but somehow so mature and moving that Natasha felt a rush of pride. Again she knew Euan would have mocked her but she didn't care. She looked across at Dolly who was dabbing her eyes with a handkerchief. Tinker too, seemed totally concentrated on the performance. The tune finished abruptly on a sort of question mark. Laura took away her bow with a great flourish and looked at her mother. "Can I go now?" she asked in a fierce whisper. Natasha smiled and nodded.

As Laura left the room Dolly said, "Remarkable, quite remarkable" She dabbed her eyes again and put away her handkerchief. "That is one very remarkable child. Don't you agree Tinker?" For once Tinker could agree wholeheartedly. Dolly turned back to Natasha. "Can you find her a good enough teacher around here? With that talent, wouldn't it be better to take her to London?"

Natasha smiled. "She's only six. I'll see how things develop. For the moment I am quite happy with her teacher. He's young and keen and Laura really likes him. I think it's a good thing at this juncture for her teacher not to be too rigid. He lets her compose and make her own way in her own time. It's why she enjoys it so much." She sighed. "She is so much happier here than she was in London."

By lunch time the next day Natasha was beginning to feel exhausted. Dolly was indefatigable and if Tinker was tired he never mentioned it. So she suggested a short rest after lunch before taking them on a surprise visit. This was to meet Florence Maddington who had been married to Dolly's cousin William. As they drove over to the farm Dolly became excited and her words came out in a steady stream. "My goodness, I haven't seen Florence for years, not since Bernard's funeral and that must be eight or nine years ago." She turned to Tinker.

"William was an only child and simply doted on by his parents. He had a distinguished career in the Navy and came out of the war a Rear Admiral. Sadly he died quite suddenly soon after that. I'm afraid I lost touch with Florence. Bernard and I were both living in Oxford and it's a sad fact that William and Bernard never got on. I don't know why but my brother Bernard always was a tricky character. He was really a hopeless father to Celia and an even worse grandfather to Natasha. I always liked Florence on the few occasions we met. I didn't realise she had a farm on the Roxby Estate. Isn't life full of strange coincidences?"

As they sat in the farmhouse kitchen, Natasha compared the three old people sitting at the tea table and was struck by their differences. Florence with her soft, curling white hair and china blue eyes was small and frail looking. Tinker was a rotund figure in his ill-fitting tweeds and baggy cardigan, his round face made more owl-like by his baldness except for the few odd tufts of hair. Dolly, although shrunken of late, was still a large woman with strong features and rather resembled one of the Bloomsbury set, her iron grey hair pulled back into a bun except for a few wisps that had managed to escape. Her high colouring was set off by loose-flowing linen robes, today a brilliant blue with a bright yellow scarf.

They certainly made an odd trio.

Florence may have looked tiny and birdlike but it soon emerged she was a strong character with an iron constitution and ran the farm on her own with the help of only one hand.

"After William died," she explained, "I carried on farming. We had decided it was what we wanted to do when he retired from the Navy. I just didn't expect the old bugger to pull up stumps so soon. The farm in Suffolk eventually became too much. I looked around for a smaller tenancy and didn't know about the Roxby connection until later. I met Livvy at some estate 'do' and she mentioned that her favourite cousin had a grandfather with the surname of Maddington." She turned to Natasha. "Did you know your grandfather well?"

Natasha shifted awkwardly in her seat. "Not really," she said. "After Mama died in the car crash it all became a little difficult. I did make an effort to see him, but I don't think he really liked children. If my grandmother had still been alive it might have been different."

"Poor old Audrey," Florence sighed, "she had so much talent just lacked the old moral fibre. She never stood up to Bernard and that was her big mistake. Mind you, he was a difficult man, a bully really and he behaved quite despicably leaving all his money to that dreadful woman. What was her name?"

"Gemma Woods," Natasha told her.

Florence chuckled. "I've never been present at a more dramatic reading of a Will. The place was in uproar, everyone shouting, even Wal. The only person who remained calm was you Natasha. I found that most impressive."

Natasha shrugged. "To be honest Gemma Woods bore the brunt of looking after him, not an easy task I imagine, so she probably deserved his money. The only thing I really minded about was my Grandmother's pictures, but I've managed to buy quite a few of those back."

Florence tut-tutted, "Disgraceful!"

Dolly who had been strangely quiet through all this said, "You know, Bernard was never quite the same after Audrey died…"

"Guilt," Florence exploded. "I know he was your brother Dolly and only my cousin by marriage, but he had every reason to feel guilty. He was awful to her."

"That's a little unfair Florence. I think he really grieved for Audrey and of course his drinking was a lot to blame."

"I'm quite sure it was, but that is really no excuse for the way he treated Audrey, or Celia." Florence gave a little smile. "It almost makes me thankful William and I didn't have children. Now I can leave what's left of my money to a Donkey Sanctuary without a guilty conscience."

They all laughed and the tension eased. The rest of the visit passed happily.

The following day Natasha had watched with some relief the old Riley make its way down the drive and felt that on the whole their visit had been something of a success. Meeting up with Florence Maddington had been a particular bonus and she smiled at the thought that even Euan might approve of her.

In the hours since their departure she had achieved a good deal. Jocky had agreed to sort out the dry rot for far less than the other estimates and on the spur of the moment she had arranged to take Laura to Italy for two weeks, a perfect way to spend her school holidays. In addition this would give time for Euan to simmer down from the dinner party debacle.

At the end of what had been a good day she walked across the garden to give B a message from Mrs B about the vegetables she required for their evening meal. As she returned to the house, she caught sight of a figure hovering by the lodge door and wandered down the drive to see who it was. It turned out to be Clive, Mrs B's nephew, so she asked him what he was doing.

"I'm looking for Mr Mackay," he said. The man had a surly, sulky manner that she found slightly offensive.

"He's in London and won't be back before tomorrow," she told him.

"I'll call back then," he said as he sloped off.

She watched him go. There was something about him she didn't trust and she certainly didn't want him hanging round the place. She would tell Euan this on his return.

Three weeks later Natasha was in high spirits. The Italian visit had proved a great success, Laura had loved it and the break was just what she'd needed. Jocky finished his work and declared the house free of dry rot. Best of all Euan seemed quite restored and was at his most charming. Life was back on an even keel, summer was on the way and she decided nothing was ever going to depress her again.

It was then that she opened the letter.

CHAPTER EIGHT

April 28th 1995

My dear Natasha,

I know this letter will come as something of a shock. However it is vital you should be made aware of my situation and take action yourself, as soon as possible.

I cannot stress this enough.

For some time I have been in poor health and last week I went up to Jo'burg for a series of hospital tests. The result is that I have tested positive for HIV, which as I am sure you know, eventually leads to AIDS.

It is difficult to tell how long I have been infected with the virus. I'm afraid the doctors could give me no idea. Although I pray you and Laura are not infected, you must both be tested immediately. Please send me the results as soon as you can. I will await the news anxiously.
I shall be over in England around May 17th and have suggested to Wal Simmons that we have a meeting in his office. The reason is that I have to sort out various financial settlements for you and Laura.
My financial advisor has lately made a series of unwise decisions and this means I will need to make some adjustments to my financial situation. In view of this I have momentarily had to

cut off your monthly allowance, but I do assure you this is only a temporary measure.

I do not want you to worry. My personal needs are few, my expectation of life is short and I am hopeful of being able to leave the two of you well provided for.

I will be staying in London with a friend of mine, the Reverend Thaddeus Smith. You will find his address and telephone number in the London Directory should you wish to get in touch with me before our meeting.

Incidentally, I have told no-one in England that I have the HIV virus. All that is known is that I am returning for hospital treatment.

Please God you are both in the clear. I can stand anything but the thought that I might have infected either of you with this terrible disease.

You are always in my thoughts,

Gerry.

Natasha put the letter down on the table and sat very still. Her heart was making a terrible thumping noise and the palms of her hands felt clammy with sweat. HIV? AIDS? The possibility of being involved in such a terrible illness had never crossed her mind. It was a remote disease, the sort of thing you read about in the papers, pitying the celebrity victim and then passing on to the next item.

Was it possible that she and Laura could be infected with HIV?

She read the letter again. Maybe Gerry had got it wrong. After all, Laura was conceived seven years ago and she had only slept with him a few times after that. She went to the bookcase and reached for her Family Medical Adviser. Looking up AIDS she stared at the small print and read, 'AIDS has a lengthy period of incubation. At the moment it is thought to be anything up to a ten year period but it could well be more.' She sat down again feeling a growing panic. Gerry could have been infected before they were even married. She knew nothing of his sex life before she met him. Come to think of it, she knew very little about his sexual habits altogether. Had he been promiscuous? Or did he just have one partner, that Peter Rich boy? Maybe he'd had hundreds, in which case he wouldn't know who he'd caught it from. The whole thing was a nightmare.

She put her head in her hands as she came to the realisation that at this very moment she and Laura could be infected with a killer disease. There were other implications as well. What about Euan? If she were infected with the virus, then he could be too.

The telephone rang and she jumped at the sound. Almost in a daze she picked it up. It was a teacher from Laura's school asking for her help with the school play. Natasha's brain felt numb. She could take nothing in. The teacher droned on and she finally stammered out that this was not a good time. Could she ring back? She almost dropped the receiver, her hands were shaking so much. After a little while she dialled Livvy's number.

The moment she heard her cousin's voice she poured out the entire contents of Gerry's letter. Livvy listened until she had finished and then spoke in calming tones. She would ring Edmund at once and ask him to arrange tests for them both at the hospital that afternoon. Natasha was to collect Laura from the school and bring her straight over to Norwich. This practical reaction had a calming effect on Natasha. She rang the school and told them she had to collect Laura for a hospital appointment. This done, she was just preparing to leave when the telephone rang again. It was Euan.

"Tash, how about supper tonight?"

She could only stammer out "I can't." Realising that must have sounded odd she added, "Sorry Euan, I'm just rushing out. I have to be at a school function tonight. Can we make it later in the week?"

He seemed content with this and said cheerfully, "All right. I'll leave you to your domestics. Let me know when you're free."

He rang off and Natasha found she was shaking.

The waiting that followed the tests was a terrible ordeal. If only the results could have been immediate. Instead she had a week where she was left in a state of terrified anticipation. She could settle to nothing. She snapped at Laura, yelled at Jocky and jumped every time the telephone rang. As Mrs B removed yet another plate with half the food untouched she gave Natasha a severe look.

"I'm sorry," she mumbled apologetically, "it's nothing to do with your food Mrs B. I think I must have a bug that's all."

After what seemed an eternity Livvy finally rang. "I've just heard from Edmund. It's all right Natasha. You're both in the clear. You are not infected with HIV."

"Thank God," Natasha managed to whisper. "Please thank Edmund. I'll talk to you later."

She went upstairs to her room and sitting on the edge of the bed she burst into tears. When she could cry no more she lay back on the bed exhausted and fell into a deep sleep.

A few hours later she woke to find Euan looking down at her, his face full of concern. He sat on the bed and took her hand.

"Tash what is it? What has happened?"

She sat up looking dazed "Oh Euan, it's you." For a moment she couldn't speak then pulled herself together. "Could you go downstairs and wait for me? I'll be with you in a minute."

Euan paced up and down the room, full of foreboding, his mind racing. Something had obviously occurred. Was it Laura? Was she suffering from some incurable illness? Or was it Natasha? Dear God, was he going to lose her as well as Celia? Life couldn't be that cruel. If that were the case, what would happen to Laura? The child would be virtually orphaned. She certainly couldn't go and live with Gerry.

Natasha came into the room pale but composed. She went straight to her desk and took out a letter which she handed to Euan. "You had better read this," she said. He took the letter from her. As he read the colour drained from his face. At last he put it down and looked at her. "Are you?" he asked.

"No," she said in a voice unemotional and flat. "I heard today. Both Laura and I are in the clear."

They were silent for a moment. Euan sat down and read the letter again. Suddenly he shouted, "Are there no end to the horrors that man is to inflict? Does he have no idea of the hell he has just put you through?"

"I think he must do," she said wearily and added sadly, "He must be having a pretty terrible time himself." She put her head in her hands. "Oh God Euan, the relief, I was really panicked. Not so much for myself but for Laura and for you."

Euan looked startled. "I hadn't even thought of that." He paced about. "That's the trouble with people like Gerry. They're so obsessed with their own lives, they don't ever think of the implications of their actions. I have nothing against gays or anybody else who deviates from the sexual norm, as long as they don't put other people's lives at risk."

Natasha was mildly reproachful. "I'm sure you weren't exactly a paragon of virtue yourself while you were in LA."

Euan gave a mirthless laugh. "My dear girl, everyone in LA is so terrified of AIDS they'd even take precautions with a carrot! Boxes of condoms would automatically be taken to parties. I can assure you the days of promiscuity and easy lays are a thing of the past. Check-ups and blood tests would be booked in on a monthly basis."

"What about you?" Natasha persisted.

He took her hands in his. "I promise you, I only ever had safe sex and yes, I had the check-ups and blood tests along with everyone else. The nearest I have ever been to getting AIDS is from Gerry bloody Masterson." He let go her hands and they were silent again.

Natasha finally said, "I don't think he has full blown AIDS yet, he's still HIV. Not that I know much about the disease."

Euan picked up the letter again. "What about this meeting? Are you going to it?"

She looked surprised. "Of course, why do you ask?"

He threw the letter down. "I don't think you should. If the problem is financial I have enough money for both of us. Why don't you take the opportunity to tell Gerry to get out of your life once and for all?"

Natasha looked at him. "You must know I can't do that Euan. I can't add to Gerry's suffering by cutting him off from his daughter."

Euan wanted to say that Gerry deserved every bit of suffering that came his way but one glance at Natasha's expression told him it would be inadvisable to do this. He stood up and went over to the table of drinks. "I'm going to pour us both a brandy. I think we need it." She smiled wanly as she took the glass. "You really should have told me about the letter before this," he said. "It wasn't right for you to go through the waiting alone."

Natasha sighed. "I wanted to make sure I was in the clear first."

Euan picked up the letter and looked at it again. "The meeting is only a week away. Do you want me to come up to London with you? I could do with a break from the writing."

She shook her head. "It would probably be better if I did this on my own. I won't stay long. The B's are taking their annual holiday soon and I must be back for that."

Euan smiled. "Clive told me about their famous holiday. They go to Blackpool every year."

At the mention of Clive something clicked in Natasha's mind. "Is Clive still working for you?" she asked him. "He was looking for you when you were away last week. I forgot to mention it." She paused. "There's something about him I don't quite like. He's shifty. I don't really want him hanging about the house."

Euan looked a bit huffy. "I was just trying to do your precious B's a favour by keeping their troublesome nephew occupied. But if you don't want him hanging around, so be it. I didn't have a great deal for him to do anyway and to be honest he was getting just a wee bit tiresome."

She smiled as she always did when his Scottishness crept in. He kissed her and said, "Let's have supper before you go to London. Meanwhile take it easy. You look washed out."

After Euan left Natasha sat down and wrote to Gerry with the results of the tests. It was only fair he should have the news at once. He was probably as worried as she had been.

*

A week later there was a call from Wal. "Natasha, Gerry is in England and wants to have a meeting with you."

"I know. He wrote and told me. When does he want it?"

"Next Wednesday at 12 noon, in my office," Wal sounded worried. "Are you sure that is all right with you?"

"Yes," she assured him. "I'll be there."

The first thing that struck her, as she walked into Wal's office, was that Gerry had aged alarmingly and had the appearance of an old man. It was somehow very shocking. He had always been so well preserved before, now he was desperately thin, with the skin literally hanging off his cheek bones, his complexion down to his scraggy neck was a yellowish grey tinge. His clothes, although still elegant, hung loosely about his skinny frame. She had expected him to look ill, but not like this.

He stood up as she came in and he kissed her on the cheek. She tried not to feel repelled but she was. It was if the man was decaying before her very eyes. He somehow already smelled of death but when he spoke she was struck by how much gentler his manner was. Gone was that air of cold arrogance that she had grown to hate.

"You look well Natasha. The country air must suit you." There was a moment of awkwardness and then they both sat down as he added, "Thank you for your letter. I was very relieved and happy to get the news."

If Wal was puzzled by this exchanged he made no comment. A secretary arrived with a tray of coffee. As she left Wal put his hands together and said, "I gather this meeting is to discuss your financial arrangements Gerry."

Gerry nodded. "That is correct. That and other matters…" He paused and looked at Wal. "I think you should know, as Natasha already does, that I am suffering from AIDS, therefore I do not have a long life expectation. Obviously this has a bearing on my financial situation and I need to make some adjustments."

Wal looked shocked. He had realised from the moment he saw Gerry that the man was very ill but had presumed it was cancer. He

Full Circle

stammered out, "My dear man, that's dreadful news. I am so sorry."

Natasha looked at Gerry. "I thought you said you were only HIV."

Gerry spoke in calm tones, "Indeed when I wrote to you I was. However, just before I left South Africa I went into hospital with a bout of pneumonia. AIDS was diagnosed." Here he gave a wry smile. "In some ways it's almost a relief. Once you are infected with the HIV virus it is only a matter of time before you develop AIDS. At the moment there are no drugs to cure the disease, although they are working on it. So my diagnosis has just cut down the waiting time that's all." He held up his hands, "Please, I don't want to discuss my illness. This meeting is to talk about provision for you and Laura." He started to cough and they waited for him to recover and settle back in his chair. His voice was tired and frail but he gave a weak smile as he said, "I feel a little like Job at the moment as my troubles come upon me thick and fast. Apart from my illness, my financial affairs have been badly mismanaged over the last few years and a large portion of my capital swallowed up." He looked at them. "Please do not worry I am by no means wiped out. Certain financial arrangements have already been put into a trust for Laura, including the proceeds from the sale of my mother's house, but this of course cannot be touched until she is eighteen." Another fit of coughing brought things to a halt and they again waited for him to recover. "The immediate problem is the monthly maintenance payment, which at the moment has to be adjusted down. This will only be temporary and I have a life insurance, taken out when we were first married, which will give Natasha a very substantial sum on my death."

Natasha shifted uneasily. It seemed absurd to be discussing money in view of all his other problems. All her life through every disaster, she had been given money almost by way of compensation. This had happened when her mother was killed and then again when Edward died. Now it was to be the same story with Gerry's death. She almost resented it. The constant refrain rang in her ears, 'At least you'll be all right financially Natasha,' as if that made everything all right. Well it didn't. Of course having money helped, but she would willingly have given it up if it had meant having her mother and Edward back.

She now turned to Gerry. "Quite honestly Gerry, I can manage at the moment. You should keep the money for yourself and your immediate needs."

Gerry smiled but said firmly, "Thank you, I do appreciate that, but quite honestly my needs are few. I still have my Church stipend and I shall continue to work in South Africa for as long as I can. When I return to England I will be staying with a friend until it is time for me to go into hospital. So you see, I am able to make provision for you and I would like to do so."

His ability to provide for her and Laura was obviously important to him so she decided to say no more. Gerry looked at Wal. "What I propose is to draw up a new settlement for maintenance if I may? My Will remains the same. My entire estate goes to Natasha, with separate trusts for Laura."

Wal nodded. "I understand. You seem to have organised everything with great efficiency."

Gerry said with mild irony, "I have the advantage of knowing my deadline." He took some papers from a file and laid them before Wal. "This is the present state of my finances. There is a proposal in there for Natasha's maintenance. I would be grateful if you would run your eye over it and then advise Natasha. If she agrees, the papers can be signed before I return to South Africa." He leaned back in his chair, suddenly looking very tired. "There is one further point I wish to cover before I leave you and it is one that is spoken in total confidence." He cleared his throat. "Obviously AIDS is a disease that brings out strong emotions in people and consequently of great interest to the media. I am well aware that if my name is connected with the illness, it may well make headlines in the more sensational areas of the Press. We have seen what they have done in the past with famous names from Rock Hudson onwards. Not that I have that degree of fame but I think I will attract some attention because of my television profile at the BBC for so many years." He paused. "I am a little fearful at what those headlines might be when the gutter press gets to know about the nature of my illness and..."

Natasha burst out, "Why should anyone get to know about it? We're not going to say anything."

Gerry glanced at Wal, who was looking worried, and said, "I think Wal would agree with me that these things have an uncanny way of getting out." Wal nodded and Gerry continued, "Someone will see a few pennies to be made of out of selling my story. Believe me my dear, I don't mind for myself. It is you and Laura I am anxious about. I would therefore ask you to consider changing your name back to Roxby Smith..." He broke off, "or there may be some other man in your life and you would like to take his name. Please believe me when I say I do not want to interfere. I am just trying to protect you both."

"Thank you," Natasha whispered. She sat feeling miserable. It seemed so horribly sordid that people would want to make money out of Gerry's illness, but she could see Wal thought it might be true. Would it be sensible to change her name? If she did how would Laura react? It would be difficult to explain it to her. She had only told Laura that Gerry was working abroad. Now she was going to have to explain about HIV and AIDS and one day about him being gay. The complications seemed endless. She became aware that both Gerry and Wal were waiting for her to say something. "I think I need to go away and think about this. I am not sure I can make an instant decision."

Gerry nodded. "Of course my dear, whatever you think is best. I am returning to South Africa next week and will let you know any developments." Natasha presumed that 'developments' was a euphemism for the worsening of his condition. Gerry stood up and looked at Wal. "You have my contact numbers in London. I hope you can get the papers through by the time I leave."

Wal nodded. "I'll take a look at them tonight and draw up something for Natasha to see tomorrow, before she goes back to Norfolk."

"I am most grateful." Gerry turned to Natasha. "If you'll excuse me I'll take my leave. I tend to get rather tired. They kindly said they would order me a taxi in reception."

She stood up too and then, looking in her bag, brought out a photograph and handed it to Gerry. "I thought you'd like to have this. It's the latest picture of Laura."

Gerry stared at it and his eyes filled with tears. "Thank you. I can assure you there's nothing that could have given me greater pleasure."

With that he abruptly left the room.

Natasha sat down.

There was a stunned silence. After a minute Wal looked at her across his desk, "Are you all right?" he asked. She nodded, unable to speak as he went on, "I must say, he's a changed man, very different from the last time I saw him and I don't just mean physically." He stared down at the papers. "From a brief glance I should say you are not going to have any financial problems in the long run. He's actually left you both well provided for. However, the immediate income has been reduced and is a good deal less. Will you be able to manage?"

Natasha nodded. "I think so, yes. I've almost finished paying for the major house repairs and I still have my mother's money and Edward's, both of which gives me a small income although I don't want to touch the capital. Also Euan is paying me rent for the lodge."

Wal looked over the top of his glasses. "Oh yes, Euan. How is that working out? Does he know about the Gerry situation?"

"Yes. I showed him Gerry's letter once I'd had the results of the tests and knew that Laura and I were in the clear."

Wal gasped. "Oh my God, now I understand. I hadn't realised... But you're definitely in the clear?"

"Yes we are." She sighed. "Euan's immediate reaction was for me to tell Gerry to go away, out of my life for ever. I can see things are going to be difficult because I feel I must see this through, although I've never had to cope with serious illness before. Anyway, Euan's not going to like this decision."

Wal looked concerned. "I don't think Gerry is expecting anything like that from you. Maybe if you just paid him the odd visit..."

Natasha shook her head. "No, I think there will be more to it than that. I'm just going to have to go away and think about how I can manage it."

On the day she returned to Norfolk, Euan took her out to supper.

"So," he asked, "how was it?"

Natasha was still feeling shocked by her London trip and didn't really want to talk about it. She stared down at her seafood salad and realised she had no appetite at all.

"What did he look like?" Euan persisted.

She thought of Gerry's gaunt and haggard features.

"Dreadful," she said, "Ill, thin and old."

"So he hasn't much longer to live?"

Natasha felt irritated. "You seem to be taking rather a ghoulish interest in all this aren't you?"

"I'm merely trying to be practical," he told her. "Gerry's condition is going to have an effect on both our lives and I want to know how long that might be."

Natasha shrugged. "I know very little about the disease, although he now has full blown AIDS, so I would say it will be months rather than years." She felt ill at ease even having to discuss it this way and told him so.

Euan ignored this and pressed on, "So what happens now?"

"He goes back to South Africa. I get on with life here. When he becomes too ill to work, he'll return to England."

"Presumably to die?"

"Yes Euan, to die." She pushed her food away. "I can't eat any more. I'm sorry. I know it's a waste."

"It doesn't matter," he said in slightly kinder tones.

He studied her face which had dark rings round the eyes. Damn Gerry, he thought. The bloody man is making her suffer all over again.

He decided to change the subject. "I know what I meant to tell you. Something happened while you were away. B only told me last night. Apparently Laura was watching the television when on came a repeat of one of Gerry's ghastly hymn-singing programmes. As soon as she saw Gerry Laura said, 'that's my father.' Obviously with her surname being Masterson, it didn't take long for Mrs B to put two and two together and she became extremely excited. Apparently she is a great Gerry fan. So it will be round the entire village by now, especially if she's told old Bessie in the Post Office."

"Damn, that's really bad news." Natasha was frowning. "The timing couldn't be worse." She told Euan of her conversation with Gerry and his request for her to change her name back to Roxby Smith.

"There seems little point in doing that now. Everyone knows who we are anyway."

Euan was silent for a moment. Then he burst out, "Why can't Gerry do the decent thing and stay in South Africa to die? That would avoid all the publicity and problems for you."

Natasha said sadly, "I don't think he can. Once he becomes too ill to work he will have to give up his job. He's already made the arrangements to return to London and will be staying with a friend in London." She paused. "There's really no point in trying to anticipate what's going to happen. We'll just have to face it when the time comes."

She knew Euan was angry with the way she was handling things. He had expected her to cut Gerry out of her life once and for all. But she couldn't do that in spite of all that had happened between them. This situation had to be seen through to the bitter end, for Laura's sake as much as anything else. It filled her with dread but for the moment she had to carry on as normal. There was certainly no need to say anything to Laura yet because it could be a good few months before anything happened and maybe Euan would have calmed down by then.

Their lives now slipped back into the routine they had established before Gerry's letter had arrived to disrupt things. Euan finished his book and started sending it out to publishers. The rejections then began to come in. The first was the worst. He had never experienced rejection of his work before and it came as a shock to his system. For days he mulled over the letter, veering between bewilderment and anger like a dog with a bone unable to let it go. Finally Natasha persuaded him to send the book to another publisher. This he did and went back into a positive frame of mind, until the next rejection came in. After that it became a monthly event. Each time the book came back he would rail against the stupidity of publishers and then spend the next few nights hitting the bottle.

Natasha ignored him on the bad days and made the most of the good ones. Otherwise time passed pleasantly enough and Gerry was never mentioned. As money was tight she set about decorating the house herself and spent long hours amongst the paint pots, wall papers and curtain materials. By the end of November she had reached the last room, Laura had reached her seventh birthday and Euan had been sent his sixth rejection.

It was just a normal day when the news came that Gerry was back in London. It took the form of a letter from St Andrew's Vicarage Holland Park and it was written in a neat round hand.

Dear Mrs Masterson,

Gerry wanted me to let you know he has now returned to England. He will be staying with me, although for the last week he has been in hospital. He is very ill now, but I hasten to add he is in no immediate danger and would like to see you.

I hope it will be possible for you to make the trip to London. Please let me know if I can be of any assistance.

Sincere good wishes,

Thaddeus Smith

She put the letter down and sat thinking. It was the moment she had dreaded but had quite prepared herself for. She also knew the reaction she would have from Euan but nothing he could say would persuade from the course of action she knew she had to take. She and Laura would move to London to be near Gerry while he was dying. The decision to take Laura with her had been fairly recent. It was mainly because she had been unable to erase from her memory the look on Gerry's face as he had looked down at the photograph of his child. How could she now deprive him of the opportunity of seeing Laura in the last moments of his life? It was entirely her decision. He had made no such demands and she admired him for this.

She rang Wal to tell him of her decision and although he sounded worried he was immediately practical and offered her the top floor of the Walbrook Grove house, which Miriam and he no longer used. This she accepted gratefully, not knowing how long they would have to stay in London. He added that he would ask Miriam to check out nearby schools for Laura. Again this seemed a sensible move as it was very possible they might have to stay on into the spring term.

After talking to Wal she rang Thaddeus Smith. He had a high, affected voice and she had a vision of a rotund, Dickensian character, the archetypal clergyman as portrayed in so many television dramas. He seemed relieved to hear she was coming to London. Gerry was still in hospital and there seemed little prospect of him being allowed to leave in the near future.

Laura was the next problem. The Christmas term had another three weeks to run. It seemed a pity to take her out of school, so she decided to go on ahead and collect Laura when the term ended. The child listened solemnly as Natasha explained that her father was very ill. At first she wanted to leave at once, but Natasha reminded her of the carol concert and Nativity play and that Miffin would need her and she soon became reconciled to staying.

The B's immediately showed sympathy and understanding. She didn't tell them the nature of Gerry's illness, only that it was terminal. "Don't you worry about a thing my dear," Mrs B had said. "We'll look after everything here. You just go away and do whatever it is you have to do."

It was an apt phrase and one that she used when facing Euan. "It's just something I know I have to do, so please don't try and persuade me otherwise."

"You want to be a martyr?"

"No, being a martyr has nothing to do with it."

"You told me you hated illness and hospitals."

"I do," she said crossly, "If you want to know I am absolutely dreading it. But whatever I feel, Gerry is going to have a terrible time and Laura and I are all he has. If I just walked away from the problem as you now suggest, I would never forgive myself."

He tried a different tack. "What about Laura? How can you load all this onto a seven year old child?"

She tried to curb her irritation. "I am not loading it onto her. She's already part of it. You may not like it Euan but Laura is Gerry's daughter. Life can sometimes be cruel and horrible. I wish I could protect her from all that is going to happen, but I can't. It would be far worse if some day she found out that I hadn't let her visit her dying father."

Euan was unconvinced. He tried every argument he could think of to persuade her from going. He pleaded with her, reasoned with her and finally became angry. It made no difference, she remained adamant. By the time she left for London Natasha sadly accepted a rift had developed between them that might never be healed. It was also likely that during her absence Euan would build up a further stock of anger and resentment. She knew she was taking a great risk with their relationship, but in spite of all this remained convinced she had to see it through to the end. It left her fearful and unhappy. There was no doubt about it. Gerry's dying was going to change everything.

CHAPTER NINE

The call from Natasha informing him of her imminent arrival in London left Wal feeling distinctly uneasy. It was an unhealthy situation and he could foresee nothing but complications ahead. Watching a man die from a slow and painful disease was going to be a traumatic experience. How much easier it would have been if Natasha had done the sensible thing and just paid Gerry a couple of visits. Quite honestly after his treatment of her the man deserved no more, but Wal had long ago accepted it was pointless to argue with Natasha, or to give her advice for that matter. She listened politely, then rejected whatever he said and went her own way. It was a damnable business and very frustrating. If he'd been able to understand her motives it might have been easier. For the hundredth time he asked himself what on earth was making Natasha put herself through such an unnecessary ordeal. It simply didn't make sense.

Once again she had left him with a dilemma. He desperately wanted to help, but didn't know how. Since Celia's death he'd felt a great responsibility towards her. There was really nobody else. Her father certainly took no interest any more. In any case Natasha had never had a good relationship with George and since he'd left the country they didn't see each other at all. No, it was now up to him to help her see this through.

He sat at his desk idly flipping through various papers, quite unable to concentrate on anything, his mind so taken up with Natasha's impending visit. He had wanted to tell her not to bring Laura, convinced it was a mistake to inflict on a young and impressionable child the vision of her father dying from such a distressing disease. How on earth would Natasha be able to inform Laura of the stigma attached to AIDS? It seemed to him an impossible task, but once again Natasha's mind was made up and he saw little point in arguing about it.

The very thought of AIDS made him shudder. He knew very well that it wasn't only homosexuals who contacted the disease, there were drug users and people given contaminated blood who were suffering from it as well, but it was the connection between gay men and AIDS that he found offensive however broadminded he tried to be. He told himself he was not homophobic, but accounts of the bath houses, sex orgies and the sheer promiscuity of the seventies and eighties had left him shocked. He couldn't stop himself feeling in a rather Puritan way that the illness was a punishment of some kind, even if this was an unfashionable view.

Another thought filled him with unease. What would happen if the scandal over Gerry broke as well? He started to sweat. It didn't bear thinking about. He remembered his headmaster saying in doomish tones, 'Remember boys, all pleasure must be paid for one way or another.' It was a dire warning that had never left him. The damnable thing was that Gerry wasn't the only person paying for his pleasure. It would have an effect on Natasha and Laura, even indirectly on him. And what was worse, he felt partly responsible for encouraging Natasha to marry Gerry in the first place. At the time he'd been convinced that after her stormy relationship with Euan she needed a time of quiet stability. How wrong he'd been. Now he was faced with the fact that he had failed her and because of this he'd also failed her mother. His eyes filled with tears as they always did when he thought of Celia, his beautiful cousin, taken from them so young in that tragic car crash. It was a sense of loss that was mixed with a certain amount of guilt. He and his brother Luke had persecuted Celia quite dreadfully when she was a child. It was a memory that haunted him because he'd never had a chance to make amends. The only way he could do so now was to look after Natasha and in this he seemed to be failing miserably.

He left his desk and walked to the window, staring into the garden. It had recently been landscaped, something that had been organised by his wife when the rest of the house was re-decorated. It had to be said that the one redeeming feature in this whole Gerry debacle was the effect the crisis was having on Miriam. Indeed it had been something of a miracle. Her reaction had been wholly positive. From the moment he had first told her about the situation, all her old energies had returned. Her organising skills, for so long dormant, went into overdrive. Interior decorators arrived and the house had certainly been transformed. It was now bright and cheerful, although lacking the chic décor of the old days. With the news of Natasha's arrival Miriam had busied herself making the rooms ready on the top floor. In addition she spent time researching suitable local schools for Laura.

Wal had been quite happy to pay for all the expenses involved in this, but found it puzzling as well. He'd become almost used to his wife's menopausal collapse. Now, quite suddenly, she had pulled herself out of it. Even their sex life had returned. For a long while he had been reconciled to a life of celibacy and adopted almost monkish habits with cold showers, disciplined thoughts, going to bed late and rising early. But his last birthday had changed all that. After a mellow evening, during which an unusual amount of wine had been consumed, Miriam had leapt on him with such vigour and determination he'd found it impossible to resist. Since then her demands had been undiminished and he'd been forced to arrive at the office quite late on several occasions.

At the thought of sex, Wal found himself wondering about Euan and Natasha. He'd only seen Euan once or twice on his brief visits to London, but in spite of delicate probing, Euan had not been forthcoming. Wal however, was convinced their affair must have resumed otherwise Euan would surely have gone back to LA. So how would he now react to Natasha's departure for London to take up a vigil at the bedside of a dying Gerry? Not very happily he imagined but he was thankful of one thing. Euan couldn't possibly come down to London to be with her. One look at Euan would be enough to kill Gerry instantly. Wal gave a chuckle at this thought and then quickly reproved himself.

He returned to his desk and his work. A few minutes later the sound of the study door opening made him jump. Miriam entered, wrapped up and ready for departure. "I'm sorry to interrupt Wal. Just to say I'm off now and I've left your supper in the oven."

"Off where?" Wal asked.

"My Yoga class darling, I go every Tuesday evening, remember?"

"Of course," he said quickly although he didn't. She had so many classes it was difficult to keep up.

"By the way," Miriam said, halfway to the door, "Natasha rang. She's arriving early tomorrow afternoon. Apparently she's arranged to go and see some friend of Gerry's, a Thaddeus Smith, but will be with us for dinner."

Wal snorted, "Typical of Gerry to have a friend with such an affected name."

"Thaddeus? I rather like it. I sometimes wish we'd been more adventurous with our children's names."

Wal was thankful they hadn't.

His wife departed and he wandered into the kitchen and pulled a shrivelled pie from the oven. Miriam's cooking was the one aspect of her recovery that had made no obvious progress. Perhaps instead of Yoga she should take a course of cookery classes. With some difficulty he stuck a fork into the rock-like potato topping and reflected that on second thoughts it might be better to give her a large cheque, with instructions to fill the freezer with food from Harrods Food Hall, at least for the duration of Natasha's stay.

Natasha pulled up outside St. Andrew's Vicarage and for a moment sat lost in thought. This was it then. There was no turning back now. She took the keys out of the ignition and at once realised how desperately tired she felt. The drive on wet and windy roads had been a long one and the nearer she was to reaching London the more apprehensive she became.

A blast of cold night air hit her as she stepped from the car. How dirty and ugly London seemed after the country. Leaves, empty beer cans and old newspapers were swirling about in the deserted, ill-lit street. Even the Christmas decorations looked tawdry. It was all very depressing.

The Rectory, a Victorian gothic building, looked far too large for one man. Perhaps there was a Mrs Smith? Surely Thaddeus would have mentioned this.

She rang the doorbell and it was quickly thrown open by a plump, florid man, dressed flamboyantly in a thick tweed suit, bright yellow waistcoat and spotted bow tie.

"Natasha," he cried, "come in, come in." He disappeared at great speed down a long dark corridor and she followed him into a room brightly lit by coloured tiffany lamps, with books untidily stacked on shelves covering every wall.

"Now, you sit in this chair by the fire," he said, pointing to a well-worn leather armchair, "and I shall sit opposite you. But first, let me fetch you a drink. I have just opened a passable bottle of claret but you can have anything you wish."

"A glass of wine would be perfect," she said as she settled into the armchair. There was a strong smell of lavender wax that mixed pleasantly with the wood smoke. "What a great fire. I do love log fires, although I didn't know you were allowed to burn wood in London. I thought there was some sort of smoke regulation."

Thaddeus looked a little shamefaced. "Oh my dear, you have found me out. I am an abject sinner. I ask pardon daily for the burning of logs and hope the good Lord forgives me, not to mention the constabulary and the local authorities. You see, I have a terrible problem heating this old vicarage as the antiquated system is quite unusable and I suffer dreadfully from the cold. A few years back a dear friend of mine took pity on my plight and sent me logs from his country estate, so how could I refuse? This kind gesture makes the difference between survival and disintegration during the long winter months. What a wonderful man. He saves my life every year and I send up daily prayers of thanks."

He bestowed a beaming smiling upon her, which had in it just a hint of mischief. Natasha decided there was a touch of Mr Toad about him.

"Do you live in this house alone?" she asked.

"Well, yes I do. That is to say I occupy half the house. The other half is used by students. I let them have it for a pittance as long as they say their prayers and keep the place clean and tidy. My formidable housekeeper, whom I have nicknamed Mrs Mussolini, goes in to see them once a week and reports back if she finds any naughtiness. Bless them, on the whole they are dear good souls and of course as poor as church mice." He sighed, "Students struggle so terribly these days. Were you ever a student?"

"I was at Art School in Florence," she replied and added, "but in all honestly, one of the lucky, un-struggling variety."

"What a relief," he raised his glass, "Is this wine all right for you?"

"It's delicious," she assured him, then asked, "Were you a student with Gerry at Oxford?"

"Oh dear me no," and he gave a chuckle. "Gerry is a good deal younger than I. We actually met at theological college. My decision for a career in the Church came rather late in life, when I was already established as a crusty old academic in Oxford. So I was a good deal older than the rest of the theology students."

Natasha made a study of him. He certainly looked more like a college don than a clergyman. There was that touch of eccentricity about him and his affected dottiness gave him the air of someone who was living in another century.

He suddenly said, "I remember you so clearly from your wedding. Oh my yes. You were very beautiful then but you are even more so now if I may say so. You have an ethereal quality about you which is very rare."

This compliment was so unexpected Natasha found herself blushing. "Thank you," she murmured.

Thaddeus didn't seem to notice her embarrassment as he went on, "I was engaged once too you know, to dear old Gwen. She looked like the back of a bus poor darling, but she was a good, kind soul. I'm ashamed to say it was her appearance that finally made me break off the engagement. It suddenly struck me that she bore an uncanny resemblance to Caroline, the unfortunate wife of George IV. I panicked she might be a reincarnation and called the whole thing off."

Natasha burst out laughing and Thaddeus pretended to look

ashamed. "It was a wicked, unchivalrous act but I'm happy to say it did not cause her prolonged distress. She married a good man after that and bore him six children. So it was a relief all round. You see it would have caused my mother great distress if I had married someone by the name of Gwen, even if it had been short for Gwendolen, which it wasn't."

Natasha was puzzled. "Is there something wrong with the name Gwen?"

"Oh yes, I'm afraid quite seriously wrong." He paused. "Are you familiar with the works of Sydney Smith at all?" She shook her head and Thaddeus leaned forward. "That is an oversight and one that must be remedied. I lament the fact he is so neglected these days. The Reverend Sydney Smith was a brilliant wit, visionary and humanitarian. But I digress. This great man gave his daughter the name of Saba because he was convinced that anyone with the surname Smith should have an interesting Christian name by way of compensation. My parents followed this sound advice and gave their three children distinctive names. My name Thaddeus means 'courageous heart' which is so very comforting, my sister is Penthesilea and my elder brother is Baruch from one of the books of the Apocrypha. So you see it would have been distressing if I had married someone by the name of Gwen."

"Couldn't you have found a wife with a more interesting name?" asked Natasha smiling.

Thaddeus shook his head. "Quite frankly my dear, I was born to be a bachelor. Believe me, I love the company of women but I prefer to remain single. It's from pure laziness you know. I selfishly lead a monastic life but without the deprivations which a true monastic discipline would inflict upon me." He chuckled. "I expect one day the good Lord will punish me for my indulgencies, but up to now he has been singularly kind."

He stood up and fetched the decanter. "Can I give you a drop more wine? It is doing you good. You have a little more colour in your cheeks."

She accepted and then asked, "Have you been here long?"

He thought about it. "It must be getting on for eleven years. I earnestly hope they won't prefer me to another living. I have absolutely no ambition to climb up the ladder of the Church of England and would be perfectly happy to spend my remaining years in this vicarage, draughty though it be. I minister to the sick and give strength and encouragement to the needy. I carry out my duties of Baptism, Marriage and Burial with conscientious zeal. I fight for the King James Bible and I use the old Prayer Book and I expect soon they will put me in the stocks for all this but until then I will continue to care for my Parish and am content to spend my time amongst good books and good company." He suddenly looked conspiratorial and said in an affected whisper, "I am meant to be researching a book on the life of St. Thomas poor doubting soul, but it progresses very slowly and I despair it will ever be finished. The publishers despair of me too. I say to myself thrice daily, 'Go to the ant thou sluggard,' but it does little good. There are too many other pleasant distractions." He gave a chuckle. "Last Christmas my parishioners gave me a present of a CD player in recognition of my having been their vicar for ten years. Well my dear, it has been a revelation. Before then I only had an antique gramophone that made all the music sound as if it was being scratched out on a dustbin lid. Now I settle back and listen to the most glorious sounds and am transported to another world." He chuckled again. "Aren't weaknesses fun?"

She laughingly agreed.

They were silent for a moment. Then she said hesitantly, "It really is good of you take Gerry in as you have."

For the first time that night Thaddeus became serious and his expression changed. "I'm only too glad to be able to do what I can, little though it be."

He put his wine glass down on the table and put his hands together. "We'd lost touch you know, Gerry and I. Certain rumours had reached me, in the way rumours do. I'd always suspected he was of homosexual persuasion, so when the news of your separation was made known to me I was saddened but not really surprised. It is always something of a torment to watch a friend go so far astray. By the time I saw him again Gerry had sadly plumbed the depths of degradation and become a lost soul. He has only recently begun to find the way back."

He stood up and threw another log on the fire.

"The tragedy of modern life is that the great Christian message of love, compassion and tolerance has become lost at the very moment it is needed the most, when the whole world is groaning with sin and sorrow. Gerry has been very alone, which is why I am so grateful to you my dear, for your act of genuine Christian compassion. He is facing this dreadful death with such fortitude and courage it will help him greatly to know he is not alone anymore."

Natasha was moved. She stared at the fire. After a moment she asked, "When did you know he was ill with AIDS?"

Thaddeus sighed. "It was last year when I met him again. I was on a visit to South Africa. We sat talking late into the night and he admitted to me then what he had admitted to no-one else. Mind you I'd had my immediate suspicions. I've sadly witnessed too many cases of AIDS not to recognise the symptoms. He was already painfully thin..." He looked at her, concern in his face. "When are you visiting him?"

"The hospital suggested tomorrow, late morning."

For a moment Thaddeus seemed lost in thought, as if uncertain how to proceed. Finally he said, "My dear, I do not want to alarm you unduly but I think you should prepare yourself for something of a shock. He is suffering from many different symptoms, some of them quite horrifying and if you are not prepared..." He raised his hands in a helpless gesture and then let them drop.

She said quietly, "I am not totally unprepared and have some idea about what this disease can inflict on people. But I suppose nothing can quite prepare you for the shock if it is someone you know. There is no longer that sense of detachment."

He looked directly at her. "I do admire your courage. I know many who would have run away from the challenge and I am not entirely sure I'd have had it in my heart to persuade them otherwise."

Natasha shrugged. "I just didn't see I could do anything else, although there are several people who tried to stop me. It has been very difficult." She paused, thinking of Euan and the strain of making decisions when her loyalties had been so torn, and then the additional worry that her decisions were indeed the right ones. "I have to admit I wasn't at all sure about bringing Laura down to see Gerry. I am hoping just one visit will be enough. I don't want her to be frightened. On the other hand I don't want her to regret not having seen her father before he dies."

Thaddeus gave a nod. "I think you are quite right. What we adults have to remember is that we no longer see with the eyes of a child. It is quite probable that her innocence will stop her from being too frightened. She will know none of the stigma attached to the situation and may be able to accept Gerry's illness far better than we think. I am constantly surprised in my visits to the hospital, how wise and practical children can be in the face of the most terrible suffering and death."

Natasha took great comfort from these words.

They talked on for a while and then she said with some reluctance that she had to leave. "I'm staying with my mother's cousin and his wife and I don't want to abuse their hospitality by being late for supper on my first night."

"Quite right my dear, off you go. But please remember my door is always open. You can come and see me at any time. I shall be anxious to hear how you are managing."

She left, promising to keep in touch.

The next morning Natasha found she had the Walbrook Grove house to herself. Wal left for work early and after a long breakfast Miriam finally departed for a work-out in her health club. Given Euan's dire descriptions of Miriam's physical and mental collapse Natasha had been greatly surprised to find her not only looking amazingly fit but full of energy as well. Miriam informed Natasha over the muesli and prune juice, that during the last few months she had taken courses with many different counsellors and tried several different therapies in order to re-establish her inner harmony of body and mind. Added to this she had undergone various treatments which included cosmetic surgery, lipo-suction and muscle toning. The list was rather bewildering but the results had certainly been successful. It struck Natasha, as she switched on the coffee machine, that Miriam was lucky to have a husband who could afford all the health gurus and endless treatments, but knowing Wal as she did she guessed he probably thought it was money well spent.

Pouring herself a cup of coffee she wandered into the living room. The house had also undergone a recent face-lift and was now bright and chintzy. It didn't have the elegance and chic she remembered of the old days but it was certainly a great improvement on the drab description Euan had given her. She sat down on the brightly coloured floral sofa and decided it was only Wal who remained a constant in this house, but even so he looked rather worn down by everything that had recently been thrown at him, her problems included. Natasha smiled to herself. He was a good, kind man and had always done his best to guide and protect her since her mother had died. Poor Wal, that couldn't have been the easiest of tasks. First there had been her affair with Euan, then marriage to Gerry, then separation from Gerry, then Euan again and now Gerry dying of AIDS. It had been a catalogue of disasters and through it all Wal had been a rock, always there to help when he was most needed, just as he did now by giving her a place to stay.

She drank her coffee and gave an inward sigh. She was also well aware how uncomfortable Wal was with the fact that Gerry was dying of AIDS. For him it was an untidy, unconventional disease and not one he would want to be associated with. Yet he would never say so for fear of distressing her. It was for this reason she had made the decision not to mention her hospital visits to Wal and Miriam the previous evening and had deliberately kept the conversation away from Gerry. Instead she had regaled them with a description of the eccentric Thaddeus Smith.

"I think I know him," Miriam had exclaimed suddenly, "I thought the name rang a bell when you mentioned St. Andrew's Vicarage and then I remembered. I used to do a charity evening for him to raise money for the homeless. You're right, he's a charming man. We must have him round to dinner. You'd like him Wal, I have a feeling his father was a High Court Judge."

"Please don't do any extra entertaining on my account," she had quickly protested, "I feel guilty enough as it is, landing on you like this."

"Nonsense darling, we absolutely love having you here," Miriam warmed to her subject, "and you are a wonderful excuse for us to have a few dinner parties. We've been far too lazy of late haven't we Wal?"

Wal had given a weak smile.

There was no doubt about it. Miriam's recovery was complete.

Natasha took her coffee cup into the kitchen. It was only ten o'clock, so taking advantage of a peaceful house she decided to make some calls. There were a few people who should know the reason she was in London although she wouldn't mention AIDS, just tell them Gerry was terminally ill.

Belinda in a rather heartless way seemed fairly unconcerned about Gerry, but delighted to hear Natasha was in town and promptly asked her to join them at the opera. This she accepted a little reluctantly. In her experience operas tended to be rather too long and on the heavy side, not really what she needed at this particular moment but at least it wouldn't give Belinda much opportunity to question her on the subject of Euan.

Before making her next call she took a deep breath knowing it could be tricky. Then she dialled Dolly's Oxford number. It was answered immediately.

"Hello, Dolly Linklater here..."

"Dolly, it's Natasha..."

Before she had time to say anything else Dolly burst out, "Darling what's happened? Are you all right? Is Laura all right? Where are you?"

Natasha adopted her most soothing tones. "We're both fine Dolly. I'm actually in London staying with Wal and Miriam. Gerry has had to come back to England. He's terminally ill in hospital so I might be here for a while."

There was a pause. She could hear Dolly relaying this information to Tinker before coming back on the line. "It has to be guilt darling. Guilt causes stress and stress causes cancer. We can only hope it doesn't take too long for both your sakes, although I presume you won't do more than a couple of visits. It's good of you to do even those." Natasha made no comment as Dolly went on, "More importantly, where is Laura? Is she with you?"

"No, she's still in Norfolk. The B's are looking after her. I'll go and collect her at the end of next week when term finishes."

"Splendid. It will be a good opportunity for us all to spend Christmas together. Belinda and her husband can join us. I can never remember the boring man's name. Tell Miriam I will ring her to make all the arrangements."

Natasha was alarmed. She hadn't even thought about Christmas and spoke as firmly as she dared, "Actually Dolly, I don't think it's a good idea to make Christmas arrangements just yet. I am taking things slowly and one day at a time as I've no idea how the situation with Gerry is going to develop…"

Thankfully Dolly seemed to understand this. "All right darling, but Tinker and I will be up to see you once you've fetched Laura. Now please take care of yourself and don't get worn out. Miriam knows all the remedies for stress. She's an expert now so take advice from her."

Natasha laughed. "All right I will. Give my love to Tinker."

She rang off feeling she had handled that one rather well.

The next person on her list was Fay Stanhope. She longed to catch up on all the Garrick Square gossip and who better for this than Fay.

Fay became almost speechless with excitement at the sound of Natasha's voice and bombarded her with questions, especially about Euan. Natasha made a mental note to be on her guard when she made her visit. The lady was not exactly the soul of discretion. They made a lunch date for the following week.

With her calls accomplished she washed up her coffee cup and decided on a stroll round the garden before leaving for the hospital. As she reached the kitchen door the telephone rang. Forgetting it wasn't her own house she dived back and answered it and was just about to put on her best secretarial voice when Euan's voice came down the line.

"How are you?"

Her heart missed a beat. She certainly hadn't expected him to ring. "I'm fine," she said. "Is everything all right with you?"

"Yes, but missing you. Have you seen Gerry yet?"

"Not till later."

"Let me know how it goes." He paused then gave a laugh. "I saw Laura just after you left yesterday. Apparently Miffin hurt her paw, not badly but according to Laura her friend Jocky mended it. She also explained Jocky had taught her how to 'set a hen'. I gather this means giving the hen eggs to hatch, so she'll probably be presented with a bunch of chicks next."

Natasha smiled. "Oh dear, I fear she's going to find London very boring in comparison."

Euan made no reply to this. He still thinks I'm wrong about that she thought.

There was a long silence and then he asked, "How's Miriam?"

"Surprisingly well and back to her old self," and she gave him a brief account of Miriam's miraculous recovery.

Euan grunted, "It sounds as if she's health obsessed. Don't let her get you involved in all that nonsense."

She laughed. "It's hardly likely."

There was another pause until he rang off telling her to take care of herself and to ring him whenever she needed to.

She replaced the receiver rather puzzled. That was a strange and unexpected call. Euan hated telephone conversations and yet he had been almost chatty. It was totally out of character. Did this mean he was feeling guilty at having given her such a hard time? Surely that wasn't possible. Euan didn't indulge in feelings of guilt. However she felt a sudden lightness of heart. Maybe he was coming round to her decision to be with Gerry after all.

He wasn't, far from it. Euan put down the receiver and the strain of his controlled cheerfulness gave way to feelings of anger. He went out into the garden and walked around, his mind racing. There was no getting away from the unpalatable fact that for the moment he had lost and Gerry had won. It was a bitter pill to swallow, especially when he had just been beginning to win back Natasha's trust.

He kicked a tree stump. How dare the man die of a terminal

illness? He couldn't possibly compete with that. At the sight of Gerry's suffering Natasha would probably forget every single thing that man had inflicted on her. Would his dying make him irresistible? She could well be filled with pity. She might even find a new kind of affection for the man, based on compassion.

He groaned out loud, "Natasha, how could you do this to me?"

Yet part of him reluctantly admired her. It was certainly brave, especially as she knew the risks she was taking with their relationship. Added to this was her decision to involve Laura and that could well prove a mistake. It was so typical of Natasha to stick to her beliefs. She was straight as an arrow with an inviolable integrity. It was impossible to change her mind once it was made up. All he could do was watch, wait and pick up the pieces when it was all over.

He gave a shiver and it was at this moment he noticed his kitchen window was wide open. That was strange. He certainly hadn't opened it. When he'd left earlier to go to the post office all the windows had been firmly shut and he had only been gone about half an hour. On his return he went straight to the living room to call Natasha. That meant someone else must have opened it.

He walked quickly back to the lodge and went into the kitchen. One pane of glass had been broken, enabling the catch to be opened. It quickly dawned on him that he had been burgled. In panic he started to look round the living room. The antique pen which Natasha had given him was missing from his desk along with a silver inkwell. His music centre has also gone and a silver cigarette box that Otto had sent him when he left LA. He ran up the stairs. A set of gold cuff-links, a travelling clock and a radio had gone from his bedroom. Otherwise the house looked untouched, although there wasn't much else of value to take except his books. It was actually the value of his books that had caused him to take out an insurance policy, thinking an old lodge might be vulnerable to fire or flood. Thankfully that would come in useful now.

He returned to the living room and sat for a while thinking. It occurred to him it must have been someone who knew the house well and also knew his movements. That made the chief suspects Zack,

Jocky or Clive. Reluctantly he decided the police had to be told. Most of the things he didn't mind about, but Natasha's antique pen? That he had to have restored to him.

He picked up the receiver and dialled 999.

CHAPTER TEN

It was irrational and she knew it, but Natasha had always had a fear and loathing of hospitals. There was no real reason for this. Her only hospital experience had been a brief stay as a child when her tonsils had been removed, but she only had to breathe in that disinfectant smell that pervades all hospital buildings and her antipathy returned. It did so now. The moment she entered the swing doors and saw the linoleum floor of the corridor stretching out in front of her she felt her heart sink but it was too late to turn back. With a determined step she made her way to the reception desk and asked a harassed looking girl for directions to the Mackenzie Ward. Without looking up the girl told her in flat tones she should take a lift to the third floor. Natasha wondered whether her voice was like that because she had asked for the AIDS unit, or maybe it was just indicative of the slightly depressed atmosphere that pervaded the whole place.

The lift, when it finally arrived was packed and stifling, so it was with some relief she pushed her way out on to the third floor. What struck her immediately was that here it looked far more cheerful. There was plenty of light from the long, low windows, the walls had been newly painted and opposite her was a sitting area with brightly coloured chairs, low coffee tables and large potted plants in every corner. A few men and one woman were sitting around talking and reading. Some were in wheel chairs, others were attached to drips. One man looked up and gave her a friendly wave. She waved back and made her way to the Sister's office, knocked on the door and went in.

"I'm sorry to bother you," she said to a woman who looked

frighteningly severe, "I'm looking for Gerald Masterson. Can you tell me where I can find him?"

The woman, she presumed was the Sister, indicated that Natasha should sit down. "Are you a relation?" she asked.

Natasha hesitated. "I used to be his wife, but we've been separated for some time now."

This news obviously surprised her and she took a moment to digest it before asking, "How long is it since you have seen Gerry?"

"About nine months," Natasha replied, adding, "But I do know how ill he is."

Standing up the Sister now spoke more kindly. "The doctor is with Gerry at the moment. I think it might be a good idea if he spoke to you before you see him. Please wait here."

She left the room. Natasha's heart began to thud uncomfortably and her mouth went dry. Why was it necessary for her to see the doctor? What could he possibly tell her that she didn't already know? He could only say that Gerry had AIDS and was going to die. Suddenly she longed to run away, to return to Norfolk and forget she ever knew Gerry. It had been wrong for her to come and Euan had been right. This was all a great mistake. She should leave now. She stood up. But it was too late. The door opened and the Sister returned accompanied by a tall man in a white coat. Natasha looked at the badge pinned on his lapel and read, Dr Michael Sternfeld. Her glance went upwards. He had a mass of untidy dark hair and large heavy features. It was difficult to guess his age, maybe late thirties.

He held out his hand. "I'm Gerry's doctor."

She shook it. "Natasha Masterson. I used to be married to Gerry."

"Won't you sit down?" He turned. "Is it all right if we use your office for a few moments Sister?"

The Sister smiled and suddenly looked less formidable, "Of course Doctor." She went out and the door closed behind her.

Dr Sternfeld sat down opposite Natasha and spread his hands on the table. She noticed they were large hands, but then he was a large man, almost ungainly. He asked a trifle wearily, "How much do you know about this disease?"

"Very little I'm afraid," she replied truthfully, "apart of course from the reports in the newspapers." She added, "Gerry is the first person I have known who actually has AIDS."

He took off his glasses putting them on the desk. He looked tired and his eyes were rimmed with dark circles, but she was struck by the colour of them. They were extraordinary, a deep blue-green, the colour of the sea. He was looking at her with an anxious expression. "It's an upsetting disease and visitors can sometimes be shocked by the appearance of the patient."

"I think I am prepared for the worst," she said quietly.

He had a pleasant, deep voice, but he spoke with an air of grave resignation. "Then you know we cannot cure him." She nodded and he continued, "It may seem that I am stating the obvious but so many friends, partners, relations come in here expecting miracles and there are none. Sadly, at this precise moment, all I can do is prescribe medication for each symptom as it materialises. I can do nothing for the disease as a whole. Sometimes the drugs we prescribe have unpleasant side effects. A lot of the time we are working in the dark. I hope in time things will improve and we will find a cure, but for now it's as well you should know the facts."

"I do understand."

"Do you live in London?" he asked.

She shook her head, "No, in Norfolk."

He hesitated. "How long do you plan to stay?"

Natasha held his gaze steadily. "I shall be here now, right through to the end." She could tell he felt awkward not wanting to involve himself with personal matters. He returned her gaze.

"I do not wish to pry into your relationship with Gerry but it is a great relief to hear that someone will be with him, so many here have to die alone. However I won't pretend it will be easy. Death from AIDS can be a traumatic and exhausting experience to watch. The will to survive is strong and some can delay death for a surprisingly long time, given their physical state. I have noticed that people with terminal diseases, and in particular AIDS, seem to choose the moment in which they want to die. You may find this with Gerry." He paused for a moment and she waited. "I'm afraid I also can't tell you how long he has. For now we have him stabilised but you can never tell when another symptom will manifest itself. He's had a few unpleasant treatments lately. One of them has left his throat damaged and you will notice his voice is weak." He suddenly smiled at her. "Your visit will be far better for him than anything I could prescribe. Don't stay too long. It will be best if you see him for short daily visits rather than spend long hours with him twice a week. He tires very easily."

His bleeper went off and he stood up and moved towards the door. "One last thing, I think I should warn you that Gerry is losing his sight. He can see a little at the moment but his vision is blurred." She followed him into the corridor. "If you want to see me at any time, please do. I'm nearly always to be found somewhere on the third floor." With that he was gone.

Natasha walked to Gerry's door then closed her eyes for a moment summoning up her courage. After a minute she gently pushed the door open and entered the room. Remembering what the doctor had said about Gerry's sight she walked right up to the bedside. His eyes were closed.

"Hello Gerry," she said.

His eyes opened and his face broke into the ghost of a smile. "Natasha," he said almost in a whisper, "I was so hoping you'd come. Thaddeus told me you might visit." She pulled up a chair and sat beside him. He made a face, "I'm afraid I'm not a pretty sight."

She smiled. "I have seen you looking better." To her relief he was not quite as bad as she had expected. Of course he looked desperately ill but there were none of the alarming symptoms she had been dreading, lesions or weeping sores. His head was close shaven, he no longer had a beard and there was a deathly paleness about his face. His eyes were so sunken they almost disappeared into their sockets and had a strange milky film across them. His cheeks and neck looked scraggy and rather bruised. There were various drips that he appeared to be rigged up to and an oxygen mask lay beside him on the pillow. She said encouragingly. "In fact you look better than I thought you would."

This drew a laugh from him, which quickly turned into a cough.

"Has it been very bad?" she asked.

"Not too bad," he wheezed. "At one time I thought I wouldn't make it back to England but as you see, I managed it. Thaddeus got me straight in here because he knew Michael Steinfeld."

"I've just met him," Natasha said. "He seems a good man."

Gerry gasped out, "He's regarded as something of a saint on this ward. He devotes his entire time and considerable medical skills to AIDS patients and it must be a pretty thankless task. You'll find him shy but fascinating once you get him to open up. Ask Thaddeus about him."

Natasha smiled. "I met Thaddeus last night. I really liked him."

Gerry nodded but said nothing. The effort of talking seemed to exhaust him. So Natasha told him she would now be staying in London and in two weeks would be returning to Norfolk to collect Laura.

Gerry spoke in a hoarse whisper. "Would it be possible to see Laura just once? Ask Michael, but I'm sure there wouldn't be any risk."

"Of course I will bring her to see you. That is why she is coming to London."

Gerry seemed overwhelmed by emotion. "I don't know what to say. I don't deserve it. I'm so grateful..." His voice trailed away.

Natasha decided to be brisk and business-like. "I gather your eyesight isn't too good. I could read to you if you like. I'm not sure I'll be very good at it, but I'm happy to give it a try. Is there any particular book you'd like?"

Gerry thought for a moment. "I think I would like John Bunyan's 'The Pilgrim's Progress.' Thaddeus will have a copy."

She could see he was starting to tire. "Is there anything else I can bring you?"

He shook his head. "Alas, I keep little food down so it would be wasted, just you and the book..." He closed his eyes.

She replaced the chair and when she turned back she saw that he had gone to sleep, so she tiptoed from the room.

When she reached the sitting area she noticed a lady with a tea urn was in the middle of the room. There was a good deal of laughter and conversation. The same man she had noticed on the way in turned to wave to her and she waved back. A sudden wave of relief, almost euphoria hit her. She had survived the first visit and it hadn't been as daunting as she had anticipated. Climbing into the lift she once again reflected that the third floor, with all its pain and suffering, was strangely the most cheerful area she had seen in the entire hospital.

She said as much to Thaddeus, when she called in on her way home. He immediately agreed. "Oh my dear, you are so right. I notice it every time I visit. The children's ward has the same kind of atmosphere, although sadly it is marred by the terrible anguish and desperation on the faces of the parents." He put a log on the fire. "Isn't life strange? Since visiting the AIDS ward I have noticed that the people involved with this awful disease seem to be the most selfless human beings it has been my privilege to meet. There are now many support groups, made up of men and women who work tirelessly to relieve the suffering of the patients. It's a paradox. On the one hand it is the worst of all possible diseases given its associations, and on the other it has brought out the best and most remarkable qualities in people, not least of course the bravery of those suffering from it." He sighed, "God works in a mysterious way."

He poured Natasha a cup of tea and once again they sat either side of the fire. "Tell me, how did you find Gerry?"

She gave him an account of her visit. "Did you know he was going blind?"

Thaddeus shook his head and looked shocked. "Oh my dear, that is a terrible blow. We had discussed the direction his illness might take and he did say his greatest fear was that it would attack his brain. I don't think it occurred to either of us that he might go blind."

"I'm going to read to him," she said. "Gerry suggested "The Pilgrim's Progress". Do you have a copy I could borrow?"

Thaddeus leapt to his feet. She had noticed on her previous visit that he was a man of sudden movements. Muttering to himself about re-organising his books in alphabetical order, he walked up and down his shelves until he suddenly darted towards one, pulled it out and blew away the dust.

Natasha took it. "I'm ashamed to say. I've never actually read the book myself, so I'm rather looking forward to it."

Thaddeus went over to his desk and began searching for something else, talking as he did so. "'The Pilgrim's Progress' is one of those books of which everyone has heard and very few have read. You'll need to edit it a bit. There are some rather long and tedious passages. You can mark what you want to leave out in pencil." He dived under some papers and emerged clutching a small volume. "This is for you," he said, handing it to Natasha, "your bedtime reading. It's the biography of Sydney Smith. I think you'll enjoy it. It's a present."

"That's very kind of you," Natasha was touched. "I feel I'm being given a belated education."

"In every way," Thaddeus murmured. "Can I give you some more tea?"

As he poured Natasha said, "Tell me about this doctor. Gerry said you knew him."

"Ah Michael," Thaddeus smiled. "Our fathers were great friends. I've known Michael since he was a small boy…"

"I presume he's Jewish?" Natasha asked. "I mean, with his name and his looks…"

"Well, of course you are right. He comes from a very distinguished Jewish family, who escaped the Nazis in the thirties. They originally settled in America. Michael's father, Jacob, married one of those formidable New York ladies, called Marnie. She in her turn came from another Jewish and again wealthy family. She now runs the family Art Gallery just off Bond Street. They arrived in London in the fifties, running away again, this time from McCarthyism. I have to tell you my dear their children are all brilliantly gifted. The eldest two have now gone back to live in the States. Michael, the youngest went to medical school in England. He was marked out for a great career, specialising in research, I think it was into immunology. Then he disappeared for a while. Jacob and Marnie were rather tight-lipped about it poor dears. It seems he was working in a hospital for AIDS babies and they thought he was wasting his research opportunities." He looked at Natasha, "Parents have to be so careful not to be ambitious for their children it can so often end in disappointment." Natasha smiled, remembering Euan's remarks about her pride in Laura's music abilities. Thaddeus continued, "When poor Jacob became ill with cancer Michael immediately returned to London and went back to his research. Jacob died nearly a year ago and almost at once Michael took up the job he's in now. He somehow manages to combine the care of his patients with continued research into a cure for AIDS. His poor mother worries he is killing himself with overwork, but he is a driven man. I thank the good Lord daily for his dedication."

"He does look exhausted," Natasha said standing up, "probably because he seems to be the only doctor on call." She looked at Thaddeus. "I ought to be going. Thank you so much for the books."

As Thaddeus showed her out he said, "You should talk to Michael about his work if you get the chance. He's fascinating on the subject and will give you a completely new insight into the disease."

She smiled. "I'm sure he's far too busy to talk to me and really if he has any spare time he should use it to get some rest." At the door she said, "I meant to tell you, I will be away for a couple of days at the end of next week. I'm going to fetch Laura."

Thaddeus nodded, "I remember you saying. Don't worry. I'll visit Gerry on those days. If you leave 'The Pilgrim's Progress' in his room I'll read to him while you're away."

The next day, Natasha sat by Gerry's bedside and solemnly read out, "As I walked through the wilderness of this world, I lighted on a certain place and laid me down to sleep. And as I slept, I Dreamed a Dream..." It was tremendous stuff so much so that having only intended to read for fifteen minutes she ran on for nearly half an hour, by which time Gerry had fallen asleep. After that she marked out the passages into short sections and this worked well.

Her days now began to fall into a routine. The mornings would be spent writing letters or visiting friends, then in the afternoon she'd arrive at the hospital and read to Gerry. Sometimes in the evening she she'd go out, one night she saw a film. Although "Toy Story" had just been released and could have been good first film for Laura, she decided in the end Laura might be a bit young and went to "Apollo 13" instead.

Occasionally she had supper with Wal and Miriam and once or twice she pleaded tiredness and escaped to the top floor to be on her own. She survived the opera evening with Belinda and Nigel, which to her great relief was "The Magic Flute" with no drawn out death scenes for her to endure. Even so she found she was exhausted by the end, made her excuses and took a taxi home, declining their invitation to join them for supper. They'd already met earlier for drinks and Natasha found them rather a tedious couple. Nigel was a good deal older than Belinda and tended to refer to her as the 'child bride'. They also had nauseous endearments for each other which included, 'my sweetness' and 'light of my life'. After the gruelling sessions at the hospital this cosy sugariness jarred on her nerves. But at least there hadn't been time for Belinda to question her about Euan.

The visit to Fay was far more amusing. She set out on a clear cold day with the sun shining and brilliant blue skies. This made her revise the critical thoughts she'd had about London previously. Today she thought that certainly no city could be fairer. Walking most of the way through parks and down terraced streets, it took her over an hour to make it to Garrick Square. Once there she took a nostalgic route right round the entire square and decided the houses looked a good deal smarter than they had seven years ago when she had lived in Euan's flat. The central garden was sadly no longer wild but organised and landscaped. That didn't seem right somehow.

Right on time she arrived at the Stanhope house. The door was flung open and there was Fay, resplendent in an orange and gold caftan. Natasha was at once enveloped in a stifling embrace. When at last released, she was led into the familiar drawing room and handed a very large glass of of sherry. She inquired about Boffy and Fay's two daughters, Marcia and Jules, prolonging as long as she could the inquisition that she knew would be forthcoming. Fay, spread like a beached whale amongst the velvet cushions on the sofa looked as excited to see her as a small child. There was still that whiff of wet Pekinese and pot pourri in the room, which reminded Natasha of all those wonderful Fay dinner parties that had played such an important part in her life when she had lived in Garrick Square.

"Now ducky, I want to hear everything," Fay said, re-filling Natasha's glass. "Are you and Euan together again?"

Her reply was cautious, "Sort of."

Fay clapped her hands together with delight, "Well of course you are. I just knew it. I told Boffy, although he doesn't take much in poor love with his dementia. You and Euan are such a romantic couple, just like Jane Eyre and Mr Rochester."

Natasha spluttered over her sherry. "Oh really Fay, we are nothing like that."

But Fay was unstoppable. "Of course you are. Will you continue to stay in horrid old Norfolk once Gerry has died?" This was so blatant it rather shocked her. It seemed a little callous to think of making plans for after Gerry's death in this way, but Fay had always been outspoken. As if to prove the point she said, "I suppose he does have AIDS?" Natasha hesitated and Fay sensing her uneasiness went on, "I'm sorry ducky, but it wasn't very difficult to arrive at that conclusion. The rumours about Gerry were rife for years especially after you left him. When you told me he was terminally ill and mentioned the name of the hospital, well it didn't take a great brain to guess the rest." She took out a handkerchief which had been tucked in her cleavage and dabbed her eyes. "The poor man," she sniffed, "I know he's brought it on himself but it's a terrible way to go by all accounts. How long has he got?"

Natasha hesitated again, "It's difficult to say. Actually Fay I don't think many people know about Gerry having AIDS so I would be grateful if you could keep it to yourself. This is not for me you understand, but for Gerry. If the press get to hear about it they will have a field day. You know, 'gay vicars' and all that…"

Fay put away her handkerchief and said in practical tones, "Quite right ducky, especially with the current obsession about 'sleaze in public life'. There's nothing those horrors who write for the Tabloids would like more than a juicy sex scandal in the Church of England. Thank goodness that terrible Gavin Cooper is no longer in the Square." She looked at Natasha. "I just hope you can manage to keep it quiet, although you may find you have a problem.

"Quite honestly, I don't see Gerry lasting much longer," Natasha told her. "He's very weak, painfully thin and has endless complications. He's going blind you know."

"Blind!" Fay looked shocked. "Oh my dear, that is truly dreadful." They were both silent for a moment and then she said in a dramatic voice laced with guilt, "You know I've always felt responsible about your having married Gerry. I mean, you did meet him in my house."

Natasha shook her head. "That is ridiculous Fay. The man was living in Garrick Square so I'd have met him anyway. Marrying him was entirely my decision, mistaken though it was."

The door was pushed open and the yapping Pekes burst into the room. Natasha was thankful for the diversion. When Fay finally managed to calm the dogs she asked, "What is Euan doing with himself while you're in London?"

Natasha explained about his 'magnum opus' and the difficulty he was having in getting it published. This produced a chuckle. "It will be good for Euan to struggle for a bit," she said. "He's always had it far too easy. However, I'm sure he will produce a great work one day. He's a major talent and I honestly believe a bit of a genius, although I know that word is over-used."

As she was leaving Fay once again enveloped her in a suffocating embrace. "I do so admire your courage ducky." She let her go. "Do you think I should go and see Gerry?"

Natasha thought about this for a moment. "No, I don't think so. He has almost no strength and it would be a strain for him. But you might write a letter. I think he'd really like that."

Gerry was indeed touched by the letter. He'd had a particularly bad night continually fighting for breath. By the morning he was exhausted and caring little about anything except the fact that in a few hours Natasha would be back to read to him. Somehow he had to summon up enough energy for that. A smile hovered about his lips as he remembered that yesterday they had reached the passage dealing with the 'Slough of Despond'. Natasha had looked anxiously at him, obviously worried this would depress him. How could he explain to her he was beyond all that now?

Two things remained on his mind. The first was to make his peace with Natasha. The second was to make his peace with God. And he didn't know how to do either. So he lay in bed wrestling with these dilemmas and desperately looking for answers. Long hours were spent examining his past and looking for reasons for his downfall. Often these thoughts would turn to bitterness and self-pity. If only he could have been sure of his sexual orientation, he wouldn't have thrown away his marriage in such a cavalier way. How ashamed he now felt. Why, oh why had he done this? Could all his problems be laid at the door of his difficult early life with the absent father and domineering mother? Most problems nowadays were blamed on parents and childhood, but in all honesty he didn't think blame could be apportioned there. Until his marriage broke up he had led a charmed life. Success had come to him easily and everything had fallen into place without any real struggle. No, it was purely out of weakness he had taken the path he had. He had become obsessed with sexual gratification and given in to every temptation. Sadly none of those brief encounters had brought him any lasting happiness. Instead he had been left empty and dissatisfied.

He turned restlessly in the bed and the effort to move made him gasp for air. A nurse looked in and put the oxygen mask back on his face. She told him again he should get some sleep. It seemed she had no other advice. 'Sleep? Perchance to dream.' It occurred to him he was as frightened of sleeping as he was of dying. Maybe there was no difference and dying was just one long sleep? If Shakespeare didn't know the answer why should he?

His thoughts went back to that fatal summer when Natasha and Laura had gone to Italy. For two months he had behaved like a madman, falling into a state of moral disintegration. There were orgies and parties every night. It had been heady stuff. Of course he'd been aware of the risks and thought he had been careful, but obviously not careful enough. The diagnosis of HIV had sent him into deep shock. His first instinct was for denial, but the fear he might have infected

Natasha and Laura made him face up to the disaster that had overtaken him. There followed many nights of anguish, nights of sweat and pain and the fear of when the next symptom would strike.

It did him no good to dwell on such things.

Instead he once again puzzled over Natasha's visits. There had to be a reason for them because he knew she didn't love him, never had. Nor had he loved her. Or had he? His marriage to her had been a calculated act at the time. Yet when he was in South Africa she had never been out of his thoughts. Visions of her beauty constantly floated before him and he would recall that strange combination she had, of childish innocence and inner strength. Natasha had been the only person he had wanted to see in England, but since her first visit to the hospital his terrible guilt had returned. He recalled the devious means he had used to force her into marrying him and afterwards his cruel and neglectful behaviour to her once they'd arrived in London. If only he could turn the clock back, if only he could have been a better husband, if only he had given her another child, if, if, if…

It was all too late now.

He pushed the oxygen mask away.

Two evenings ago he had been visited by Peter Rich and had told him not to come again. Peter Rich only served to remind him of what he once had been and of the life he had so stupidly thrown away. Why had he done that? He didn't even like the man. It had been lust, nothing more. Peter had been young then. Now he was no longer attractive, merely arrogant and full of his own self-importance.

He closed his eyes and when he opened them again a nurse was looking down at him. She put the oxygen mask on his face and shouted, "You've got a letter Gerry."

He winced. Why did she have to shout? He was going blind, not deaf.

"Do you want me to read it to you?"

"Later," he gasped, "later."

She put the oxygen mask back on his face and went out slamming the door. The stupid woman! Didn't she realise that every vibration stabbed at his body like a knife wound?

His mind wandered back to the enigma of Natasha. Again he asked himself the question, why was she visiting him? Undoubtedly it was a Christian act, but she had never struck him as a devout Christian. Indeed during her short time as a Rector's wife she had stoutly defended her belief in agnosticism. Could it be a sense of duty that made her come and see him? He doubted that too. He glanced at his bedside table and the photograph of Laura. Maybe that was the answer. Laura was the key. If so, it was a miserable thought. What would Laura ever make of him? His legacy to her was a history of failure. He had failed as father, failed as a husband and failed as a man of God. The tears started to trickle down his cheeks.

A door slammed and the large nurse bulldozed her way back into the room. She peered down at him, took off his oxygen mask and wiped his face. "Now, now Gerry, we can't have tears, this will never do." She put the mask back. "Shall I read you your letter? It will cheer you up." He nodded and she opened the envelope. "Oh my," she said, "it's very grand on headed notepaper and from a Lady Fay Stanhope."

She read it loudly and slowly,

Gerry dear, I was so sorry to hear from Natasha that you were so ill. I can imagine you will be suffering, but I also know you will bear all with courage, strength and fortitude. Poor darling Boffy has Alzheimer's and is suffering too. As we get older none of us are finding it very easy. Our thoughts and sympathies are with you and I am relieved that you should have that angel Natasha with you at this time and that you will soon be seeing your little daughter Laura. Take comfort from them, and the loving thoughts of your friends. Affectionately, Fay.

The nurse folded the letter. "Isn't that nice?" She put it in his hand. Now, you get some rest. Natasha will be here soon and we don't want you too tired for her do we?" She tucked him in.

Gerry closed his eyes and thought of Fay's letter. She was right. Natasha was an angel and he started to mutter 'angel, angel, angel,' over and over again as he gradually slipped into unconsciousness.

CHAPTER ELEVEN

Natasha once again sat in the Sister's office opposite Michael Sternfeld.

"Tell me what's wrong?" she almost shouted in her panic, "Gerry was all right when I left him yesterday. Or at least he was no worse."

The doctor looked at her anxious face and wished that just for once he could be the bearer of some good news. "Gerry had breathing problems which developed in the night," he explained. "The congestion in his lungs made his breathing shallow and consequently he was not getting enough oxygen and lost consciousness. We've now drained his lungs and he's sleeping. You could see him for a short while later on, maybe in an hour or so."

Natasha felt frightened. "Was it a near thing?"

He shrugged and spoke rather wearily. "There's only so much punishment the body can take. For the moment we have him stable, but you have to be prepared, these crises can happen at any time. Sadly one of them will be fatal."

Natasha nodded. "I do realise that. I'm sorry to get so panicked." She looked at her watch. "It's not really worth my while going home now. I'll stay in the hospital until he's able to see me."

Dr Sternfeld stood up. "There is a canteen downstairs, or you can go to what we call the 'Recreations Area' at the end of the corridor, opposite the lifts. If you need to see me later I'll be around."

She looked at him, "Don't you ever go home and get a break from all this?"

He smiled then, "Just occasionally."

She wandered down the corridor with the intention of finding a cup of tea. She walked past the patients who were sitting around but as she reached the lift area the man who always waved to her looked up and smiled. On impulse she went over to what she presumed was the 'Recreations Area' and sat down beside him.

"Hello," she said. "I'm Natasha."

He held out a thin hand that was covered in purple marks and gave her a shy smile. "I'm Kenny." She took his hand and held on to it for a moment. "Would you like a cup of tea?" he asked.

"I'd love one but isn't the tea for the patients?"

Kenny shook his head. "Of course not, it's for anyone sitting in this area. We have lots of visitors." He stood up and shuffled over to the tea urn. As he returned with her cup he asked, "So who is it you come here to see?"

"Gerry," she said careful not to give his surname. She had noticed that everyone on the ward seemed to be called by their Christian names.

His face took on a grave expression. "I think Gerry must have had a bad turn in the night. They took him to theatre. Poor Dr Michael had only just gone home and they had to call him back. He's a saint is that Dr Michael. He never gives up on us, although we're all hopeless cases. I say to him, 'Not much fun being a doctor in this ward, there's no success rate at all.' And he just laughs bless him."

Kenny had a camp way of talking and a face that was slightly comical. As with all the other AIDS patients he had a gaunt, ravaged look which made it difficult to guess his age.

"What did you do before you came in here?" she asked.

He gave a beaming smile. "I worked backstage in the theatre. I just love the theatre. It's my life. I've been working in it every day since I left school at fifteen and that'll be six years next month."

Natasha was shocked. He was only twenty-one, yet he looked much older. To be struck down so young, it was heart-breaking.

"I started in Panto," he told her, talking in short sentences in order to get his breath back. "I really enjoyed that. Last Christmas I worked at the Palladium. It was the best time I ever had. We were one big happy family. Everybody knew me. Even the stars used to say, 'Hello Kenny love, how are you today?' And we had some laughs. You wouldn't believe the fun we had." He looked at her and said proudly, "They've been everso kind to me since I came in here, visiting me, sending me cards and that."

"I worked backstage once," Natasha said, "I was painting scenery. I really enjoyed it."

"There I knew it!" Kenny sounded triumphant. "I knew you had to be something to do with Showbiz. I said so to Brian over there. Only we thought you might be to do with the ballet. You do look like a dancer" His expression changed. "We've had two dancers in here." He paused. "But they've both left us now."

Natasha presumed that was his way of saying they'd died.

Kenny suddenly gave an apologetic laugh. "We're ever such a nosy lot, those of us who sit around. Tell me, where was it you worked?"

Natasha put down her cup. "It was a fringe theatre, up in Mill Hill."

"Not the Open Door Theatre?"

She smiled. "That's the one."

Kenny became excited. "I know it. I had an actor friend who worked there. You are lucky. I'd love to have designed scenery. That was really what I wanted to be, a stage designer, but I didn't have the training. Did you go to Art School?"

"Yes I did."

He said wistfully, "I wish I could paint. I've always wanted to, ever since I was a kid."

On impulse Natasha said, "Why don't you start now?"

Kenny looked startled. "You must be joking! It's a little late for that. We're all lost causes in here love. All of us are on the way out."

"Well better late than never then," she said firmly. "I tell you what. Tomorrow I'll bring in some painting materials. Then you can make a start."

He was doubtful, "I dunno about that. Whatever would I paint?"

She thought about this. "It should be something simple to begin with, a plant or some fruit. I could help you."

Kenny clapped his hands in childlike excitement. "Would you really do that? Oh that's everso lovely of you. It really is." He called across the area. "Hey Brian, Natasha here is going to start me on painting lessons. Do you want to join in?"

Before she knew it, she had been introduced to the group and they were all enthusiastic. It left her a little overwhelmed, but she promised them drawing books, charcoal and paints.

Dr Sternfeld arrived in the middle of this and told her Gerry could now be visited. She followed him to outside Gerry's room.

"Just a few minutes today," he said firmly. "He's still very weak."

The next morning Natasha set out early to look for an Art shop. At last she found what she was looking for and purchased six sets of watercolour paints, some charcoal, a selection of pencils and a great deal of paper. By the time she went in to see Gerry the entire group were happily engrossed in trying to draw a geranium. She told them she would visit them before she left to view their results. Kenny called after her, "I hope you'll be pleased with our efforts!"

Over the next four days Natasha found she was arriving at the hospital earlier each morning and leaving a good deal later. The painting classes were unexpectedly great fun although she had no idea how long their interest would last. She enjoyed the dry humour of the patients, their rivalry, their enthusiasm and gentle ribbing of each other's efforts. There were six of them well enough to take part, the rest of the patients on the ward, like Gerry, were too ill to leave their rooms. Natasha soon learned about their backgrounds and their lives before they had come into the hospital. Several of them were drug users including Josie, the only girl amongst them. There was also one sad case, a boy of only seventeen called Mick, who was a haemophiliac. He had been given contaminated blood during a transfusion. They all talked openly about the disease and all of them discussed the possibility of a cure being found.

"They may never find one, or it may take years," said Kenny, "and certainly not in time for poor old Bill," nodding at a man in a wheelchair and he added, "or any of us here. We've all accepted that."

Natasha found it touching how they all included Bill. The disease had affected his brain but they showed him their pictures and he nodded and grinned. Occasionally he would let out low moans and then one of them would go over and hold his hand until he stopped.

She found their talents were as varied as their personalities. Josie seemed to have real flair for it. Natasha asked her if she could keep one of her drawings. It was of a geranium and the girl seemed genuinely delighted to let her have it and solemnly signed it. Other efforts were stuck up on the walls where they made a colourful display and caused much comment as visitors peered at them.

On the last day before her departure for Norfolk, Michael Sternfeld took her to one side.

"Starting those painting classes was really an inspired idea. At last we can now feel justified in calling it the 'Recreations Area'."

Natasha smiled, "It was really all Kenny's idea I just provided them with the materials. I've actually enjoyed getting to know them and it has helped to keep my mind off other things." She hoped he knew what she meant by that rather enigmatic statement. He gave her a long look and seemed about to say something, but then changed his mind. Instead he just smiled and said, "Thank you anyway," and started to move away.

Natasha called after him, "You do know I am going to be away for a few days? I did tell Sister." He turned and nodded. She went on, "While I am gone Thaddeus has promised to come in and see Gerry. He will let me know if there is any immediate worry and I have also given my number to Sister. I will be bringing back Laura to see her father."

"That will be a tonic for Gerry in itself." There was a pause and then he said quietly, "We are all going to miss you Natasha."

Later that afternoon she sat with Kenny, "I'm afraid I won't be seeing you for a few days," she told him. His face fell and she was quick to reassure him. "Don't worry, I am coming back. It's just that I have to go to Norfolk to collect Gerry's daughter to bring her down here to see her father." She didn't add 'before he dies' because she was fairly sure they both knew what she meant. It was easy to get used to these hospital understatements.

Kenny sighed, "Gerry is lucky to have a daughter. How old is she?"

"Laura is just seven."

His face took on a sad, wistful look. "That was the age of my kid sister last time I saw her. She must be ten by now. They don't let her come in to see me." He paused. "I really miss her." And he turned away.

These terrible, sad admissions really tore at her heart but she said as unemotionally as she could, "Well now you can meet Laura. I'll tell her all about you." He smiled at that, and she made her goodbyes. "You will keep up with your art while I'm gone won't you?"

Kenny beamed at her. "Don't you worry, we all will. I'll make sure of that love."

CHAPTER TWELVE

The three days spent in Norfolk were so full of difficulties and frustrations it left Natasha feeling thoroughly unsettled and on edge. It started from the moment she arrived back. Euan was waiting for her and almost before she was out of the car he told her the news of the burglary.

"Why didn't you tell me as soon as it happened," she said crossly.

He said laconically, "It didn't seem the moment to add your worries." She walked into the house and he followed. "However there's been a rather unpleasant development since and you need to be prepared for the worst."

With a sinking heart she put down her bags. "What do you mean 'unpleasant development'?"

"They've arrested Clive."

"Do you mean Clive as in the B's nephew Clive?"

Euan nodded. "That's the one. I didn't want you to see the B's without warning you first as they've not taken it well."

She said wearily, "All right, you'd better tell me everything." Peeling off her coat she threw it on the hall chair and went into the sitting room.

Euan looked at her. "Am I glad you're back," he said as he slumped into a chair. "Since Clive's arrest the atmosphere around here has been a wee bit tense to put it mildly, although B seems resigned to the fact that the boy is a bad lot."

Natasha felt thoroughly irritated. "He's hardly a boy. He must be in his mid-twenties."

Euan shrugged. "That may be so, but the B's still look on him as a boy since he was in their care and they feel responsible for his actions.

He may not be a criminal but he was obviously easily influenced and had apparently fallen in with the wrong people. They'd got him into drugs and he needed money to pay for his habit. I was easy pickings." He lit a cigarette. "Mrs B is the one who's taken it really badly. She's been very tight-lipped and constantly giving me hostile looks as if I were in some way to blame."

"She probably feels guilty," Natasha said, glancing through the post on her desk. "It must be a difficult situation for her to handle and she feels the shame and disgrace of it all. You know what it's like in a small village like this."

"I can't pretend I'm over-concerned with her feelings," Euan retorted huffily. "What about mine? I happen to be the victim in all this."

"Have you managed to get any of the stuff back?" Natasha asked.

He shrugged. "One or two things and luckily he hadn't managed to flog the antique pen you gave me so that's been returned. I think I'd have set about Clive myself if that had gone missing."

Natasha looked worried. "I don't suppose you were insured were you?"

He gave a rueful smile, "Well actually, rather unlike me, I was. Some of my books are quite valuable and it occurred to me that the lodge might be vulnerable to flooding or a fire!" He stubbed out his cigarette. "Anyway, it will give me a chance to update some of my equipment, so it isn't all bad. Clive must be incredibly stupid. It was obvious, even to the dullard they sent round from the local constabulary, that it was someone who knew the house and my habits."

She sat down already feeling exhausted. "What will happen to him?"

"Frankly my dear, I don't give a damn. I tried to do your precious B's a favour by giving him a job and this is how he repays me. They can put him in the stocks for all I care."

Natasha gave a sigh. "I always thought Clive had a shifty look. I told you he was hanging about at the lodge."

"He was probably casing the joint, working out how to get in." Euan stood up and moved towards the door. "If you think that is a problem, wait until you hear about your plumbing disasters."

Natasha felt numbed by her reception. She had at least thought there might be a sympathetic enquiry about how she was. With a major effort she pulled herself together and went off to investigate the problem that had overtaken her plumbing system.

This turned out to be both major and fairly catastrophic. A cracked sewage pipe very near the house had caused an unpleasant seepage into the garden which had proved both disagreeable and expensive. Jocky had been called in to replace the pipe but the work had left a large hole. Although he had promised to fill this in, he didn't know if he'd have time before the end of the year, so for the moment they had to live with it. Laura was apparently the only person who derived any pleasure from the situation. She had developed a morbid fascination with the demolished area and referred to it as the 'shit-hole', a phrase she had no doubt picked up from Jocky.

The following day, on her way to the school, Natasha reflected that her return home had not exactly been restorative and now felt stressed out and on edge. Laura had been particularly obstreperous, probably punishing her for being away, veering from wild excitement to temper tantrums. She really hoped this unusual behaviour would calm down before she took her in to see Gerry.

Adding to her discomfort was Euan's constant biting remarks. If she'd hoped he'd come round to her decision of being with Gerry she was wrong. He was as hostile as ever. In spite of every effort to keep things normal between them nothing worked and there were times when his blunt coldness really shocked her.

The day after her return she had asked, quite innocently, if he'd like to go with her to Laura's Christmas concert and he'd looked at her in genuine astonishment. "Why on earth would I want to do that?"

She stammered, "Well I thought you might enjoy it."

"Well I wouldn't. She's not my daughter so there's no earthly reason why I should put myself through the agony of listening to a lot of spoiled brats singing out of tune."

Something in her snapped. "You really are petty Euan. I am well aware she is not your daughter, but she is fond of you and would like you to be there."

"What, as a proxy father?" He gave a mocking laugh. "She's going to see the real one soon enough isn't she?"

She had left the room then. She couldn't deal with him when he was in these bitter moods and for the rest of the day tried to keep out of his way.

This was only the start of her problems. After tea on her first day back Laura came out of the kitchen looking unusually mutinous. "I hate the B's," she blurted out angrily.

"Why, what have they done?"

"B hit Miffin for going in the shit-hole."

Natasha tried not to laugh. "He was only trying to keep Miffin away. It's still pretty pongy."

"He shouldn't have hit her. I don't mind if she's pongy." She looked at Natasha and added gloomily, "Mrs B is making me a dress for Christmas."

"Well that's very kind of her. I don't know why you are looking so cross."

Laura seemed near to tears. "I'm looking cross because I am cross. I hate it."

"What's wrong with the dress?"

"It's horrid. It's a horrid colour and it scratches. It's too tight and I won't wear it."

Natasha sighed. "I'll have a word with Mrs B and see if she can let it out and make it more comfortable." She decided on a change of subject. "Why don't we take Miffin for a walk and tomorrow we will buy her a big marrow bone from the butcher's."

This seemed to cheer her up and she stumped off in search of the dog. Natasha felt her heart sink. It was not the best moment to criticise Mrs B's sewing as she still hadn't broached the subject of Clive and that was a moment she was dreading.

*

The following morning she went into the kitchen knowing both B's would be there. B was sitting staring gloomily into the fire. Mrs B was ironing.

Natasha cleared her throat and said nervously, "I was so sorry to hear about Clive. I know this must have been distressing for you both."

Mrs B put down her iron and said stiffly, "Bondage and I are extremely sorry for the inconvenience caused to Mr Mackay."

Natasha said quickly. "Please don't worry. He was insured and some of the things have been returned..." Her voice trailed away.

Mrs B didn't seem to be listening. "Clive is family," she said, "and we quite realise we must take some of the responsibility. But we can't help feeling he got in with the wrong people. They must have led him on, because he's a good lad at heart."

B suddenly spoke and sounded angry. "It all started when he lost his job. He were a good lad afore that. It was having no work wot's dunnit. And now the DSS is after him because Mr Mackay said the lad had done some work for him and Clive didn't fill this in on his claim form."

Natasha felt helpless. She could see how depressed and humiliated they were but there was nothing she could say or do to make things better, so she decided to tell them of her plans. "I'm afraid I have to return to London in two days' time and I will be taking Laura with me. We will be away for Christmas and probably into the New Year."

Mrs B's expression changed. "Of course dear, we understand. How is the Reverend?"

It was a long time since she'd heard Gerry referred to as the 'Reverend' and it gave her rather a shock. "I'm afraid he's sinking fast," she said, "but it's difficult to tell how much longer he will linger on."

Mrs B spat on the iron, "It's always a surprise is that. My Auntie Joan had no insides, no insides at all. But she went on for months after her last operation."

Natasha not wanting further details of Auntie Joan said quickly, "I'll keep you informed of course. I do hope you can manage here. I will have to leave Miffin..."

Mrs B said rather enigmatically, "I think we all know where our duty lies at times like these. We are not ones to shirk our duty." She noisily packed up the ironing board, "I hope I'll be able to finish the little dress I was making for Laura before you go."

Natasha caught sight of a heap of lurid pink and flowered material on the rocking chair in the corner. Stifling a look of horror she said, "That's very kind of you Mrs B but I do know what a lot you have to do, so don't worry if you don't manage to finish it. It will be something for Laura to look forward to when she gets back." She was pleased to note a look of relief on Mrs B's face at this. Natasha then turned to B, "I have asked Jocky to complete the plumbing and get the hole filled up. I can't tell you how sorry I am that you've had this added problem. Will you keep reminding him?"

B removed his pipe. "I'll tell him but I don't know it will do a lot of good. He's a law unto himself is Jocky." He tapped out the tobacco. "If I were him I'd have run a mile. Proper mucky job it were. He had a terrible time getting out that old pipe."

And for the third time Natasha had to endure a graphic description of the removal of the cracked sewage pipe.

As she fled to the safety of her bolt-hole she almost longed to be back in London. There was such an atmosphere of gloom since her return and the cold, damp December weather didn't help. She stared out of the window at the bleak garden and thought what a mess she was making of everything. She'd even been too feeble to tell Euan she didn't want to sleep with him. Except for the proverbial headache she just couldn't think of a plausible excuse for saying no, at least, not one he'd accept without an argument. As she lay beside him restless and unable to sleep she felt terrified at the gulf between them, a gulf that was getting wider all the time. He was so full of resentment and continually made snide comments, just at the time when she could have done with his sympathy and understanding.

At some point he'd said in a perfunctory manner, "So how is Gerry?"

"How do you think?" she'd replied. "He's dying."

"Well I know that, but how is he in himself? Is he restless, guilty, at peace, or what?"

She looked at him. "I'm surprised you are interested." Euan made no reply, so she went on, "He communicates very little and I really don't know about his state of mind. Physically he's thin, weak, and he's going blind."

There was a long silence. Then Euan asked, "How often do you visit him?"

"Once a day," and she turned away. "Do you mind if we drop this line of questioning? I don't want to talk about it."

Euan shrugged, but she could tell he was annoyed. He was like a vulture wanting to pick away at the subject. She tried a different tack. "What's happening to your book?"

His manner changed. "Well I do have some good news on that front. I've been in touch with a friend who has a small but elite publishing house and we have done a deal on a limited edition which will come out in the New Year."

She made an effort to show interest. "What sort of a deal?"

Euan was rather vague. "Well, he provides the printing, the distribution, all that sort of thing." He paused. "And I finance it." Seeing her look of alarm he laughed. "It's all right, I can afford it. I'm happy just to have the bloody thing in print for the select few who have the nous and the intellect to understand it."

Natasha felt that the 'select few' would probably not include her, but she said in what she hoped were encouraging tones, "I'm really pleased for you."

A silence fell between them and on impulse she told him, "I've started reading to Gerry, 'The Pilgrim's Progress'."

Euan gave a snort at this and said contemptuously, "My God, couldn't you have found the man something more cheerful than all that Puritan drivel?"

Natasha was indignant. "You may find it drivel, I certainly don't. I'm really enjoying it and the characters are terrific. I feel I know them, Mistrust, Ignorance, Giant Despair, Talkative..."

Euan said sarcastically, "So what character is your precious Gerry, Hypocrisy?"

She finally lost her temper. "Do you always have to be so bloody nasty and sneer at everything?"

Later he apologised, but she didn't feel forgiving.

The following day she dragged Laura out to deliver some Christmas cards. There had been no change in the weather and the lawn was beginning to look extremely sodden. Laura whined the whole way and complained of the cold. Even Miffin turned for home with obvious relief. There's not much Christmas cheer in this neck of the woods she thought as she opened her post. There was a card from Florence Maddington inviting her over for a drink. She decided it was something she'd like to do even if it did mean postponing her departure for London. She put a call in to Miriam and Wal and then rang Thaddeus. He told her there had been no change in Gerry but he would let him know about her delayed return. He added, "I'll tell Michael as well. You should know Natasha he thinks you are quite wonderful."

She was surprised. "Does he? I can't think why. We've only had two or three conversations."

"Well you've made quite an impression my dear," he paused, "on us all."

Natasha gave a wry smile. "I can't tell you how nice it is to be appreciated. I only wish I'd had the same effect on people up here. There's been nothing but moods and bad temper since I arrived back."

She put down the receiver and sat watching the sun sink down beyond the horizon. Her thoughts turned to Michael Sternfeld. She thought about his shy manner, his kindness and his dedication. And then she thought about his eyes, those extraordinary blue green eyes the colour of the sea...

The door slammed and Euan came into the room. He looked at her. "What's up? You're looking almost guilty."

"You made me jump that's all," she said quickly.

He sat down. "As it's your last night I thought I'd take you out to supper."

She explained about delaying her departure for a day in order to go and see Florence Maddington.

He shrugged, "Well that makes no difference. It's still my last chance to take you out, so what about it?"

Natasha stared at the fire for a few moments and then accepted, although she was still angry with him especially over his refusal to attend the Christmas Concert.

After he left she thought about Laura's performances and it made her smile. Laura had been a star and a disaster and all within ten minutes. Her 'cello solo had gone without a hitch but her performance as one of the shepherds was marred by dropping the lamb, which then rolled slowly down the platform steps with a slow thud, thud, causing the boy playing Joseph to forget his lines. Instead of being dismayed by this Laura had burst out laughing, setting off the rest of the shepherds, who all continued giggling through the rest of the scene. It also drew laughter from several members of the audience and it was only a severe frown from the headmistress that had restored order.

Euan arrived early and they had a drink in the house before setting out. He seemed positively cheerful as he told her his galley proofs had arrived and that correcting them would take up most of his time. Natasha was relieved to hear this and told him she had been feeling guilty about deserting him over Christmas.

"You and your guilt," he mocked her smilingly. "I don't know why you should worry. Christmas is not a Festival I indulge in except of course for the odd beverage."

However, over the meal he produced some startling news. "Since you mentioned Christmas, I've had the strangest invitation and you'll never guess who from." She couldn't, so she waited for him to enlighten her. "Marcus and Hilary Waters," he announced.

Her mind went blank. Then suddenly the penny dropped. That ghastly couple, that ghastly evening! "Them?" she said incredulously, "I trust you refused."

"No. I didn't actually. I accepted."

She stared at him in astonishment. "But you loathed them. I distinctly remember you said you'd never met such awful people in your life. So what are you going to do at Christmas, spend the entire day getting drunk and yelling insults at them?"

He smiled and said almost too casually, "I may have been a wee bit harsh but I was very drunk that evening. I've actually had dinner with Hilary since then. She's all right once you get to know her." She looked at him completely stunned and for some reason there was an odd sinking feeling in the pit of her stomach. Maybe she was wrong but she definitely had the impression Euan was being 'economical with the truth'. He continued to make light of it. "It's all quite innocent. Hilary wants to interview me about my book and Barry has agreed to read extracts from it for his next literary festival."

Natasha remarked drily, "So this Christmas Day visit is by way of a publicity exercise."

He gave a shrug. "That's one way of putting it," and added, "it's not as if you're going to be here."

She ignored this and said, "You could have taken this opportunity to visit your brother?"

Euan looked startled. "Why on earth would I want to do that?"

"Well you haven't seen him for a long time. You could have met his wife and children."

He threw up his hands in mock horror. "Spare me that," he said. "We don't all have these strong family ties you know. Believe me, it's a huge relief not to have to deal with all that clutter."

She felt snubbed and although she tried to ignore it at the end of the meal she pleaded tiredness and went to bed alone.

The next evening Natasha set off for drinks with Florence Maddington.

As they went into the drawing room Florence said, "It's good of you to spare the time in the midst of all your other problems." She regarded Natasha anxiously. "You seem tired my dear, but I suppose that's only to be expected. I know you and Gerry were separated but it's never easy to watch someone die in any circumstances."

Natasha thought about Gerry's gaunt face racked with pain, the struggle to breathe and his slow rasping voice. "No," she admitted, "it isn't," and on impulse she added, "He has AIDS you know."

A silence fell in the room. Natasha stared into the fire wondering whether it had been a mistake telling Florence, after all, the woman was in her late eighties. She looked up and found Florence watching her. "In that case my dear, you are even braver than I thought."

Natasha shrugged. "It's the people in that AIDS ward who are brave, the doctors and nurses as well." And she described her London experiences, from the meeting with Thaddeus, to descriptions of Kenny and organising the art classes. Florence listened attentively until Natasha finished. She collected Natasha's glass. "I think you could do with another drink."

The doorbell rang. "That must be Livvy," Florence said handing back her glass, "I do hope you don't mind, I told her you were coming and she was anxious to see you."

The cousins hugged and Natasha said, "I can't tell you how good it is to see you both. I had been feeling very down since returning to Norfolk. You wouldn't believe the doom and gloom in the Dower House."

She told them of the plumbing disaster, Clive's arrest, Laura's performance at the Christmas concert and the terrible dress Mrs B was making for her.

Livvy was sympathetic. "Poor Laura, I know just how she feels. I remember being crammed into a dress like that and hating it."

Natasha laughed. "As I remember it, you hated all dresses and were only happy in jodhpurs."

"Are you taking Laura to see her father?" Florence suddenly asked.

Natasha nodded, "Yes, for a short visit, I just hope it won't be too traumatic, for either of them."

"How is Gerry?" Livvy enquired.

"He's not good," and Natasha sighed, "I was just telling Florence about it. Sometimes I find the whole experience unbearably harrowing, at other times it is almost inspiring. The patients have a wonderful doctor. His name is Michael Sternfeld. When he's not on the ward he is doing research for a cure. I think he and Edmund would have a lot in common."

"They're a strange breed research doctors, workaholics all of them," Livvy mused. She looked at Natasha, "How's Euan taking it?"

Florence at once looked quizzical. "Who is Euan?"

Livvy said quickly, "I'm so sorry Natasha, I thought Florence knew..."

"It's all right," Natasha reassured her, "I couldn't say anything last time I was here because of Dolly. You know how she might have reacted." She turned to Florence.

"I don't know why I have made my life so complicated but it is and I find it difficult to explain my relationship with Euan even to myself, but I'll have a try."

She embarked on a brief summary of Euan's relationship with her mother, the meeting with him when she returned from Art School, the stormy affair that followed his return from America and now his residence at the lodge. "People keep asking me what is happening with us both and I never know what to say. Sometimes we're wonderful, sometimes we're dreadful." She paused. "At the moment, we're dreadful."

"Is that because of Gerry?" Livvy asked.

Natasha nodded. "He thinks I'm making a huge mistake going to London and also because I'm taking Laura."

Florence leaned forward. "Why does he think that?"

Natasha thought for a moment. "To be fair, I think he is genuinely worried things could go badly wrong if a scandal leaked out, but mainly he is angry and bitter about me and Gerry. He is convinced I should walk away from him once and for all. I just can't make him see my point of view. He can't make me see his. So it's deadlock."

"It sounds like another Svengali and Trilby situation to me," Florence said, "It seems obvious Euan wants to keep total control. I had a relationship like that once. In between the moments of passion we fought like tigers. He tried to dominate me and I fought not to be dominated. It wasn't a healthy situation but I just couldn't let go."

"So what ended it?" Natasha asked.

Florence looked at her. "I finally found one moment of strength and broke free. It was the most sensible thing I ever did, although terrible at the time. I then married the Admiral who was a good and kind man," her eyes twinkled, "although between you and me, a trifle dull. It didn't seem to matter. We had a wonderfully happy life together and the only wrong he ever did me was to die so young. I still miss the old duffer."

There was silence in the room except for the ticking of the clock above the fireplace. Natasha glanced at it and stood up. "I ought to be getting back. I leave for London early in the morning and I still have a mass of things to do."

Florence went out to fetch her coat and Natasha turned to Livvy, "I have some interesting news. Euan tells me he is spending Christmas day with Marcus and Hilary Waters."

Livvy looked amazed. "I don't believe it. Are you sure?"

Natasha nodded. "I found it hard to believe as well. Apparently Marcus is going to use extracts of Euan's book at his next Festival and Hilary is writing an article about him."

"So they're all sweetness and light?"

"Apparently they are."

"I wish I could be a fly on the wall."

Natasha gave a mirthless laugh. "I'm not sure I could stand it."

Just before leaving for London she walked down to the lodge to deliver Euan his Christmas present, a bottle of Tomatin his favourite malt whisky. The door was open and she could hear splashing sounds coming from the bathroom. She called up to him and he yelled back,

"I'm in the shower, be with you in a minute."

She went into the living room and put the bottle down on his desk. It was then she noticed a card, written in a large bold hand with a lot of exclamation marks.

Darling Euan,

That was the most wonderful evening. I so enjoyed your company, especially afterwards!!! Please let's meet very soon, before Christmas Day if possible. Love – and all the rest!!! Hilary.

Natasha started to sweat and felt suddenly sick. Slowly she read the card again. It could only mean one thing. Euan and Hilary were having an affair. Numb with shock she went to the bottom of the stairs and in as steady a voice as she could manage she called out, "I've left Laura waiting Euan, so I can't stop. I'll ring you from London." Without waiting to hear his protests she ran up the drive and almost dragged

Laura into the car and then drove off at speed. In an effort to calm herself she started telling Laura about London and all the people she was going to meet.

"When do I meet Father?" Laura asked.

"Tomorrow I expect. Just for a short while. He gets very tired."

"Where will we spend Christmas?"

"With Wal and Miriam," and she added, "they've made you a lovely room."

"Do they have a garden?"

"Yes, they do."

"If they have a garden why couldn't Miffin have come with us?"

"It's a small garden. Miffin needs a lot of space so she's better off at home. You'll see her when we get back."

"When will that be?"

Natasha hesitated. "I'm not too sure."

"Will it be when Father dies?"

Natasha swerved. This conversation was becoming something of a minefield. "Yes," she finally answered. What else could she say?

Laura was persistent. "Why can't the doctors make him better?"

"I'm afraid there are some diseases the doctors can't cure?"

"Could I get this disease?"

"No," she said quickly, "you couldn't get this one."

"Why couldn't I?"

Natasha began to wilt under the relentless interrogation, "because only grown-ups get this disease."

Laura considered this before asking, "Will Father go to heaven?"

She hesitated. "Yes, I think so."

"Euan says he doesn't believe in heaven or God." Natasha yanked at the gears. Euan should learn to keep his bloody mouth shut. Laura went on, "I don't suppose Clive will go to heaven now that he's a burglar. And B says Jocky's a 'wrong-un', so he won't go to heaven either." She paused. "Do dogs go to heaven?"

Natasha replied with as much patience as she could muster, "None of us know for sure what happens after we die Laura, but we like to think we go to a place where everyone is happy. So if it's such a lovely place, dogs are bound to be there."

Laura seemed satisfied with this. Natasha glanced at her and saw she still had on her thinking face so she waited for the next question.

"Do you think Father would like me to play my 'cello to him?"

Natasha hadn't considered this, although they had brought Laura's 'cello with them. "He might like that very much. Let's wait and see." It seemed a good time to try a diversionary tactic. "Why don't you look at the number plates on all the cars and pick out the letters that belong to your name?"

This kept Laura occupied for quite a while and then, to Natasha's great relief, she drifted off to sleep.

She drove on, alone with her confused thoughts about Euan and Hilary.

Euan, having watched Natasha drive past the lodge at speed, returned a little puzzled, to see what she had left for him. He removed the paper from the bottle and smiled as he saw the Tomatin label, but as he went to replace it on his desk the smile faded. He saw the card from Hilary and knew at once she must have seen it. It would explain her hasty departure.

"Damn!" he said out loud, "Damn! Damn! Damn!"

He tore up the card and threw it into the waste-paper basket. This was going to take a lot of explaining if anything was to be salvaged from the situation. Natasha wasn't stupid. She would know exactly what that message from Hilary meant. He sat for a long while trying to figure out his best course of action. At last he reached for the bottle and poured himself a large drink. It was probably best not to mention it at all but try and pick up the pieces once she returned.

CHAPTER THIRTEEN

"Of course," Miriam remarked, sitting on the side of the bed dabbing Chanel skin food onto her face, "Dolly is quite right. That child does seem to have an exceptional talent and thankfully at the moment seems quite unspoiled by it. I do so loathe precocious children."

Wal who had been gently drifting off now rolled over, looked at his wife and gave a sigh. She was obviously wide-awake and in a talkative mood. Sleep would be out of the question at least for the foreseeable future, which meant she would be expecting some sort of a response. He thought about Laura. "There is a sort of 'je ne sais quoi' about her" he agreed. "And my mother is right about something else, she's right about Laura looking like Celia at that age. I know the colouring is different because she gets those dark looks from Gerry..."

"Let's hope that's the only thing she's inherited from him." Miriam broke in sarcastically.

Wal couldn't let that pass. "To be fair we really know very little about Gerry. He could have many hidden talents."

Miriam was unrepentant, "I think we know quite enough about his hidden talents thank you very much. Look where they've landed him."

Wal was a little shocked, "Miri, the man is dying." He lay back and closed his eyes and for a moment there was a blessed silence. Then he heard her chuckling.

"Don't you think the French language is quite ridiculous Wal? I mean, just now you said 'je ne sais quoi', which in direct translation means 'I not know what' which is a terribly clumsy way of saying something so simple. It's absolutely typical of the French!"

Wal didn't really feel up to putting the Gallic case, but in any case was spared this because his wife had instantly moved on to another topic. "I was rather touched by Laura's reaction to the old nursery. She seemed genuinely excited."

"I should think so. It's like Aladdin's cave up there. I've never seen so much junk crammed into one room."

"It's not junk Wal" she said indignantly, "some of those toys are quite valuable. The rocking horse is a real antique."

Wal closed his eyes hoping this might be the moment to drift off. Miriam climbed in beside him and lay on her back.

A minute passed and then she gave him a poke, "Wal?"

He opened his eyes and said wearily, "Yes?"

"I thought we might give a party?"

"What sort of party?" he ventured nervously.

"A Christmas drinks party. I know it's only a week till Christmas but I'm sure we can rustle up a few people by Friday. That would give us five days to prepare it."

Wal tried to ignore the 'us' and said, "What sort of people were you thinking of rustling up?"

Miriam sat up, "Well, for a start it might be a good opportunity to have your mother and Tinker over to stay. Then of course, there's Belinda and Nigel and I thought we could invite Thaddeus Smith and there's that doctor Natasha goes on about. And it would be kind to have Henry round. We haven't seen him in a long time." She saw Wal's bewildered expression, "Oh Wal, you know who I mean, the one I call 'poor Henry'."

He was alarmed and said severely, "I trust you're not trying to match-make for Natasha. She has quite enough problems already."

"Of course I'm not," she sounded indignant, "I was just trying to be kind. Henry's always struck me as something of a lost cause. He's lonely in spite of all those silly girlfriends he keeps dangling around." She broke off. "I trust you won't insist on inviting Euan."

"Well of course I won't." Wal sounded exasperated. "Apart from anything else he's stuck in Norfolk." He paused, "I also get the distinct impression that all is not entirely happy on that front. Relations appear to be definitely strained between him and Natasha."

Miriam lay back again. "Does that mean the affair is coming to an end at last?"

"I wouldn't count on it," Wal said gloomily, "That affair is set to run and run, disastrous though it be for both of them."

Miriam ignored this. Her mind had gone back to the party. "It might be a good opportunity for Ben to bring over his new girlfriend."

"Well, as long as he doesn't bring along any of his awful City cronies." Wal frowned, "What's the name of this girlfriend? I can never keep up."

"Sapphire," she told him.

"Good God! What sort of name is that?"

Miriam didn't answer but went on, "It's such a pity Alex is up north and can't get back. Otherwise we could have had a real family gathering."

Wal winced at the thought of his eldest son, who at this moment was cavorting around the stage in pantomime costume. It was such a waste of a good brain and yet Miriam didn't seem to mind his thespian antics at all. He rolled away from her onto his side. His eyelids felt like lead. If only she would go to sleep.

"We really ought to find some friends for Laura," she murmured. There was silence. At last Wal thought she has finally drifted off, but she suddenly shouted "Got it," so loudly he jumped. "Darling, what is the name of that nice barrister friend of yours? They live quite near us. We went to a party at their house last summer..."

"The Reid's," Wal said, "Jeremy and Annie Reid."

"That's them," she sounded triumphant. "I remember they have a lot of children. There was one who must have been about Laura's age. Do you have their address? Or better still their telephone number? I could ring your secretary in the morning. Wal? "

But Wal was finally asleep. Reluctantly Miriam turned off the light.

Getting Laura ready for the hospital the following day proved an uphill task. She had wanted to go in jeans and wellington boots and it was only after a great deal of persuasion involving tears, bribery and coaxing, that she finally agreed to a blouse and skirt. A further compromise was then reached allowing her to wear her old duffle coat if she wore shoes and not wellies. It was out of character for her to be quite so difficult and Natasha presumed it was Laura's way of showing her nervousness. It was understandable. She hadn't seen Gerry for nearly four years. It was bound to be an ordeal quite apart from the fact that the man was in hospital and the child knew he was dying. Her worries about the wisdom of the visit were further increased by Laura's silence in the car. She glanced across and saw that she looked solemn and rather pale. It was going to be a pity if she clammed up altogether. She did so want Gerry to see his daughter at her best.

In the event it was actually Kenny who saved the day. The moment they stepped out of the lift he called out, "Hello Laura. We've been waiting for you to arrive." His funny clown face was wreathed in smiles. "I'm everso pleased to meet you. I was telling your mum. I have a kid sister who's just your age."

Laura immediately lost her shyness. "What's her name?" she asked.

"Karen," he told her. "We all had names beginning with K. My younger brother's Keith and I have an older sister called Kathy, silly really." He patted the seat of a chair. "Now, why don't you come and sit by me and then you can meet everybody. Your mum's been teaching us to paint. We've got everso many pictures to show her."

"I can paint." Laura said.

"Well of course you can. You're probably much better than us love. We're a pretty hopeless lot in here I can tell you."

There were gales of laughter at this. Natasha noticed that Bill in the wheelchair was missing. As they started to show her their paintings she said, "Can I leave Laura with you for a minute Kenny? I just want to have a word with the doctor."

She knocked on the office door and went in. "I'm sorry to bother you Dr Sternfeld. I wanted to let you know I've brought Gerry's daughter Laura in to see him. Will that be all right?"

He looked up and smiled. "Welcome back. Gerry's been expecting both of you. And please call me Michael, everybody else does." He turned to Sister. "Has Gerry had his medication yet?"

She nodded, "About half an hour ago."

"Gerry had a rather restless night," he explained, "so we've given him something to ease the pain. It acts as a sedative and might have the effect of making him drowsy, but he should be all right for Laura's visit."

Natasha felt she was becoming used to the hospital euphemisms. 'Rather restless' meant that he was in terrible pain and a 'bad turn' meant that he'd almost died.

Michael stood up. "Where's Laura now? I'd like to meet her."

"I left her with Kenny," she said, then asked, "Where's Bill? I didn't see him today."

A quick look passed between the Sister and Michael. "I'm afraid we lost him, it's the way it can happen. All these patients are suffering from at least one life-threatening illness and any sudden deterioration usually proves fatal." Natasha was looking shocked so he added, "I constantly have to remind myself I am working with terminal patients because they can appear so normal. However, they're all living on borrowed time. In Bill's case the disease had gone to his brain. We knew he didn't have long." He hesitated and then said, "It doesn't help to get too attached to the patients."

It was a warning and she knew it.

They walked down the corridor where they could hear gales of laughter coming from the direction of the Recreations Area. Kenny caught sight of them and called out, "Oh Natasha, your Laura's a scream! She's had us in stitches, telling us all about her dog and his misdemeanours in the shit-hole."

Natasha murmured, "Oh Lord," and Laura looked anxiously at her mother. "I was only explaining about the shit-hole because they asked me about Miffin and I said she had rolled in it and got right pongy." There was more laughter.

Sometimes, Natasha thought, a country childhood had its drawbacks, but all she said was, "Laura, I want you to meet Michael. He's the doctor."

Laura stood up, walked over and eyed him solemnly. "Can't you make my father better?" she asked.

Michael looked at Natasha who said quickly, "I've explained about that already Laura. Michael is doing everything he can. Now say goodbye to Kenny."

Laura turned and waved.

"See you later," Kenny called after her, adding laconically, "I'm not going anywhere."

Laura now seemed to have lost all her nervousness and didn't seem worried by the sight of Gerry and all the tubes. She walked straight over to his bed and without any hesitation held out her hand and said, "Hello Father."

He smiled and took it. "Hello Laura." His pale filmy eyes tried to focus on her. "My goodness, how you've grown, you were quite small when I last saw you."

There was a lump in Natasha's throat. She knew he could see very little.

Laura said, "I'm seven now."

"Seven. That's a good age to be."

Natasha pulled up a chair so that Laura could sit down near the bed. "You can take your duffle coat off Laura. It's quite warm in here." This took some time as she struggled with the toggles, refusing any help, then she hitched herself up onto the chair.

Gerry asked, "How do you like being in London?"

Laura thought about this. "I do like it and I have a big room with lots of toys and books," she paused, "but I am missing Miffin."

Gerry looked towards where Natasha was standing. "Miffin?" he queried.

She explained. "Miffin is her dog, a very large English sheepdog."

Laura leaned forward and whispered, "She's always in trouble 'cos she gets so dirty with all the mud and she's pongy from the..."

Natasha intervened, fearing yet another description of the shithole. "Tell your father about the Christmas concert Laura."

The child looked surprised. This didn't seem a very interesting topic compared with Miffin's exploits, but she knew she was on her best behaviour so obeyed. "At my school we had a Christmas concert and I played a carol on my 'cello..."

Gerry interrupted. "I didn't know you played the 'cello. Do you know, the 'cello is my favourite musical instrument?"

"I could bring it in and play it to you if you like." Laura said.

"Well I would like that very much but it might be rather difficult to bring your 'cello in here."

Laura looked at Natasha who said, "It is not a full sized 'cello. I don't see why we couldn't manage it."

Laura added, "I could play you the carol I did for the concert."

Natasha laughed. "That was the all right bit. Tell your father what happened when you were the shepherd."

Laura made a funny face and gave a wicked grin. "I dropped the sheep I was holding and it rolled down the steps, bump, bump, bump and we all began to laugh."

Gerry laughed too, "Oh dear, what a calamity."

"It was a calamity." She struggled with the word. "And the teacher was cross with me afterwards. I don't think I will be allowed to be a shepherd next year."

"Never mind," said Gerry, "you just stick to playing the 'cello."

There was a moment of silence which Natasha was just about to break when Laura said in her clear, childish tones, "I'm sorry they can't make you better Father."

Natasha stood frozen with horror, but Gerry gave a ghost of a smile, "I'm sorry too because it means I won't be able to see you grow up."

Laura said almost cheerfully, "but Mama says you will go to heaven."

"That's very generous of her," he said drily.

Laura was now unstoppable. "And I think there is a heaven, even if Euan says there isn't one, because Miffin is going to go to heaven."

Gerry's eyebrows went up at the mention of Euan but all he said was, "I think you're absolutely right Laura. I think there is a heaven too."

Natasha stepped forward. "Your father should rest now Laura. You can come back tomorrow. Perhaps we will bring your 'cello with us."

Laura eased herself carefully off the chair and carried it with difficulty back to the window. She picked up her duffle coat and began the long process of doing up the toggles. As she did so she said, "When I get back Miriam says I can help her with the Christmas tree and

Wal and Miriam are giving a party on Friday and I'm going to meet a new friend."

"That sounds fun," Gerry said. "Do you have a party frock?"

Laura looked anxiously at her mother then shook her head. "I have a summer party frock but not a winter party frock. Mrs B was making me one but it was a horrid pink colour and it was too tight and it scratched. I wouldn't wear it."

She sounded so fierce that Gerry laughed. "I will ask your mother to buy you a frock that you like from me."

"Thank you Father," she said, going towards the door. "Goodbye, I will see you tomorrow." She waved cheerfully.

Natasha went to follow her. Glancing back she could see Gerry's face was racked with pain. It had been a supreme effort.

"How was your father?" Kenny asked as Laura skipped towards him.

"He was very pleased to see me," she said, "and he's going to buy me a party frock."

"Oh my, who's the lucky girl?"

Natasha said quickly, "Kenny, can I leave Laura with you again for a minute? I just want to go back to Gerry."

She let herself into his room quietly and was alarmed to see tears running down his face. "Oh Gerry I'm sorry. She's upset you. She does have a way of saying things..."

He shook his head vehemently and his words came out in little gasps. "It's not that. I just wish I could see her better. I wish I could see the face that matches that character and spirit..." He broke off in a violent fit of coughing and Natasha waited for him to recover. "Will you buy her a frock from me?" He waved his hand in the direction of the locker by his bed, "I have a cheque book in there..."

"Don't worry about that now," she said and then not wishing to hurt his feelings added, "We can settle up later when we've bought the dress. You're tired now, so I'm going to go, but we'll come back tomorrow."

As she reached the door he called out with all the strength he could muster, "Natasha, is Euan part of your life again?"

She sighed and returned to the foot of his bed. "Not really Gerry. He came back from America about a year ago in order to write a book. He's renting the lodge at the Dower House that's all."

His voice was getting feebler but he pressed on with almost fevered determination. "I know I have no right to give you advice but I would be very distressed to think you had renewed your relationship with Euan. He's no good for you Natasha. My earnest wish is for you to find a man with whom you can share your life and one who will be a good father to Laura. I know deep in my heart that Euan Mackay is not that man."

"I understand," she said quietly and once more turned to go.

He gasped out, "What is the subject of Euan's book?"

"The Antichrist," she said.

The next day they went shopping and after a long and exhaustive process, found Laura a party frock they both liked. It was dark green corduroy with a white broderie-anglaise smock and it suited her Kate Greenaway looks. She danced round the shop "Do you think Father will like it?

"I'm sure he will."

"Kenny said I'd be the bell of a ball."

"Belle of the ball," Natasha said, "belle is the French for beautiful. It means you will be the most beautiful person at the party."

Laura wrinkled her face. "Kenny is funny," she said.

They didn't take the 'cello in that afternoon but showed Gerry the party frock instead. Natasha knew he couldn't see much, so took great care to describe it. Laura waited anxiously for his approval.

"You will be the belle of the ball," he said.

Laura laughed. "That's what everybody says Father."

They met Michael on the way out. "I've been asked to a drinks party on Friday, at Walbrook Grove."

Natasha was a little surprised but pleased they'd invited him. "I hope you can come. Thaddeus is going to be there."

Michael smiled, "I know, he told me. I will do my best to get away but it will depend on what's happening here. We tend to get a bit short staffed over Christmas." He turned to Laura, "Your father tells me you play the 'cello."

Laura nodded and Natasha said, "We were thinking of bringing it in so she could play for Gerry."

Michael said to Laura, "I used to play the double bass, which is like a 'cello only much bigger. I do hope you will let me hear you play."

"Kenny wants me to play for him too," she said.

"That sounds a great idea." He turned back to Natasha. "Thaddeus suggested Gerry might visit him on Christmas afternoon."

Natasha looked very surprised. "Is that possible? Isn't he too ill to move?"

"We'd have to make careful arrangements and I'm afraid you'll have to pay for a private ambulance, but I think it should be feasible. The change would do him good."

"Then please go ahead with whatever you can arrange and don't worry about the expense."

CHAPTER FOURTEEN

Friday arrived and Wal watched his wife as she darted round the room putting the finishing touches to the party preparations. She was decked in a new dress of cream brocade, only broken by a large white belt at her waist. Privately he thought she resembled a rather large meringue but decided it would be better not to comment on her appearance. If he were critical she would get upset and if he tried to pay her a compliment she'd either be suspicious or take it wrong. So instead he said, "I had a strange visitor in my office today."

Miriam stuck her finger in one of the dips and said vaguely, "Oh yes, who was that?"

"Euan Mackay."

She spun round to face him. "Oh God, does Natasha know?"

"No, that's the odd thing. He particularly asked me not to say anything to her about his being in London."

Miriam was unimpressed. "I'm glad to see he's showing a bit of sensitivity at last. Natasha hardly needs him in her life at this particular moment. So what did he want?"

"He brought Christmas presents for Natasha and Laura. He also brought a very good bottle of cognac for me... for us."

"Well, I'll be fascinated to see what he's given Natasha," and she added with a hint of envy, "no doubt something very expensive."

Natasha approached the evening's activities with a certain amount of apprehension. She'd never been over-fond of parties and in the last few years had done her best to avoid them. The recent harrowing events at the hospital had done nothing to increase her enthusiasm for the social scene. She now sat on the bed putting off her descent downstairs and allowed her thoughts to wander. As usual they went straight to Euan. In spite of the image of him with Hilary Waters which had been haunting her since her return to London, she found she missed him desperately. It was the paradox of her life, especially in recent weeks, that when she was with Euan she wanted to get away, but when she was away, she longed to be with him again. It was an impossible situation and as Florence had pointed out, almost certainly unhealthy. Gerry obviously thought so and she suspected Wal and Miriam did as well. She sighed. What could she do? She wasn't ready to give him up. At night, as she lay in the empty bed, her physical longing for him was almost unbearable. Did he miss her like this? She presumed he loved her otherwise he would have given up and left. But was he as obsessive as she was? She just couldn't answer this, but whatever Euan felt, she still couldn't agree with him that it was a mistake for her to be with Gerry, or to let Laura see him. If that meant putting their relationship in jeopardy, so be it.

With this defiant thought she stood up. She really did have to get ready for this bloody party. After all, it had been difficult to ignore the enormous trouble that had been taken in organising the evening. Since breakfast Miriam had been behaving like a whirling dervish. All offers of help had been refused and this had at least given her the chance to brave the wilds of Knightsbridge and do her Christmas shopping. She looked at the packages in the corner of the room. It had been difficult deciding on something for Gerry, after all what could one give a dying man? In the end she'd opted for a large scented candle. It might at least help blot out the awful anti-sceptic smell in his room.

Now, as she zipped herself into a new dress of pale blue silk, she thought of the strange contrast between the affluence of Walbrook Grove and the suffering in the hospital ward. Life could sometimes be very odd.

The doorbell rang. No avoiding it now. She threw a shawl round her shoulders and made her way down the stairs.

Dolly and Tinker were the first to arrive.

"Oh my darlings," Dolly wailed, "we've had the most ghastly

journey. It took us hours to get here."

Wal took her coat. "Well if you will drive that ancient vehicle Mother, what can you expect?"

"Nonsense!" she said indignantly, "there's nothing wrong with my old car. It was just the traffic and Tinker's directions." She went into the room keeping up a running commentary. "How wonderful it all looks. Hello Natasha darling. Miriam you must have worked so hard. Oh there you are Laura, give Tinker a kiss. And what a beautiful tree..."

Laura stood on one leg. "I did that with Miriam."

"What a clever girl you are." Dolly flopped into a large armchair. "Oh, that's better. Now Laura come over here where I can see you." Laura went and obediently stood in front of her. Dolly made an examination. "That's a lovely dress you are wearing."

"Father gave it to me."

"Did he indeed?" and she added drily, "What very good taste he has."

Natasha turned to Tinker who stood silent beside her. "You must be exhausted Tinker. Would you like to be revived with a cup of tea?" He nodded gratefully and followed Natasha into the kitchen.

Dolly declared, "Well I'm certainly in no need of tea. A very large gin and tonic for me and don't stint. I am not getting into that car again today."

The doorbell rang again and within half an hour the room was full. The Reid's arrived with their daughter Millie and Laura immediately dragged her upstairs to her room. Natasha was introduced to someone called Henry, a contemporary of Wal's at Cambridge.

"Henry is one of a very select band of my friends who has held out against the married state," Wal told her.

Henry gave a bellow of laughter. "It's been a damn close run thing. I've been engaged three times." He gave another bellow.

"Now Henry," Wal said in mock seriousness, "I'm leaving you with Natasha on condition you behave, she's family."

Henry saluted. "Over and understood sir!"

Natasha made a study of him. He had the air of a country gentleman, but time and over-indulgence she suspected had done its worst.

His face was florid and his shape portly. She learned that he was in property and had offices in Belgravia and at the moment was between girlfriends. She was just beginning to feel they had reached the end of his small talk, when she was rescued by the arrival of Thaddeus, resplendent in emerald green waistcoat and red bow tie, blending in well with the Christmas tree she thought. As he approached them he cried, "Henry Turnbull by Jove!"

"Thaddeus Smith," thundered Henry, "I haven't seen you for years."

Natasha took the opportunity to escape and leaving the men to their reunion she wandered over to the window. Suddenly a powerful image of Euan standing by the garden seat overwhelmed her. It was a vision so strong it stayed for several seconds. A shiver went through her and she turned back. This house and the garden held so many memories. It was in this very room and at a similar party that she'd re-met Euan all those years ago and it was in the garden she had said goodbye just before she married Gerry.

Miriam called across the room, "Natasha, your doctor has arrived."

She went into the hall to meet him.

"It was really good of you to come," she said suddenly feeling shy. He looked different out of his white coat.

He smiled. "It was Thaddeus who insisted I made it. He worries I have no social life."

"I don't suppose you have time for one." She took his coat.

"That's true and I won't be able to stay long tonight." He looked at her and added, "If I'm perfectly honest, I've never been a very social animal."

"Me neither," and she added, "When I first went up to Norfolk I didn't see anyone for nearly a year. It was wonderful, but my family panicked, convinced I had become a recluse."

"It's good to find a kindred spirit," he said and peered into the room. "Is Thaddeus here?"

She nodded. "He is, but he's bumped into an old friend and I doubt you'll be able to get a word in edgeways for the moment."

"Good, then I have every excuse to stay and talk to you."

They walked over to get a drink and he told her he'd made all the arrangements for Christmas day. It would only be for a couple of hours and Gerry might not even last that long but he was convinced it would do him good.

They talked on and were immediately noticed by Dolly whose searching eyes had picked them out. She summoned over her daughter-in-law. "Who is that man talking so earnestly to Natasha?"

Miriam looked across the room. "Oh, that's Gerry's doctor," she explained.

Dolly sighed. "How do they do it, those Maddington women? They bowl men over like nine-pins. Natasha's grand-mother Audrey, who God rest her soul was no oil painting, had a permanent coterie of young men flocking around her. Celia was a great beauty so I suppose the effect she had was hardly surprising and now Natasha is the same. Mind you, she's looking particularly lovely tonight in that pale blue. Laura will be the same, mark my words. That Maddington strain is lethal. I mean just look at the poor man. He's totally besotted already."

Miriam laughed, "You're wrong there Dolly. From what I can gather he's a dedicated and single-minded doctor who has little time for anything apart from his patients, not even Natasha."

Dolly was unconvinced. "Believe me I know what I'm talking about. I have made a study of it over the years. It's something to do with a fragile quality they all have..."

But further thoughts on the subject were forestalled by the entrance of Lady Fay Stanhope.

"My God," Dolly exclaimed. "Can you believe it Tinker? There's Fay Stanhope looking like something out of 'Aida'."

"I presume you don't mean one of the elephants?" Tinker murmured.

She looked reprovingly at him and then burst out laughing. "You are a wicked old thing Tinker darling."

At this point Laura rushed into the room. "Mama, Millie's asked me to go over to her house. Can I go? Can I?"

Natasha looked at Laura's flushed face and decided calming methods were called for. "Well of course you can, but not tonight. It's already quite late."

Laura tugged at Natasha's hand. "Can you come and talk to her mother?"

Natasha looked apologetically at Michael. "I'm so sorry I think I'd better go."

He smiled. "I don't think you have much choice."

Fay, her entrance sabotaged, stared after the retreating child and said to Miriam, "I presume that human bombshell is the famous Laura? I'd been told she was a rather quiet child."

"She usually is," Miriam laughed. "I think there have just been too many excitements today, including meeting a new friend."

Michael had a quick word with Thaddeus and then took the opportunity to slip away and soon the other guests began to depart.

As Natasha turned out Laura's light she reflected that the party hadn't been quite the ordeal she'd been expecting. In fact she had enjoyed it.

The next morning, Christmas Eve, she deposited Laura early at Millie's house. She then saw Dolly and Tinker off in their battered old jalopy and rang Thaddeus to tell him about the arrangements for Christmas afternoon.

"I asked Henry as well," he said, "I hope you don't mind, but he was going to be on his own."

"Gerry won't be able to stay long" she said, "and we'll all leave after he goes."

Thaddeus gave a laugh. "Without wishing to be rude my dear, that is probably just as well. It is a rather busy weekend for me, what with Christmas Day landing on a Sunday this year."

"Are you absolutely sure it's not going to be too much?"

"No, no," he was quick to reassure her. "Michael is going to accompany Gerry and see him back to the hospital."

"It's so good of him," Natasha said. "I'm sorry that will rather ruin his Christmas."

Thaddeus chuckled. "He's Jewish my dear, he doesn't have a Christmas."

*

An hour later she put the 'cello in the car and set off to collect Laura from Millie's house.

"I've bought a candle for you to give to your father," she told her.

The child thought for a moment. "Can I give one to Kenny as well?"

"All right, if I see a shop, I'll stop and buy one."

"A red candle, he likes bright colours."

Natasha said, "It won't be as special as the one for your father. His candle smells of jasmine, which is a lovely flower."

"Kenny won't mind," Laura assured her.

As they stepped out of the lift Kenny, catching sight of the 'cello, called out, "Hello Laura, are you going to give us a tune?"

They walked over to join him and Natasha said, "While you take the 'cello out of its case Laura, I'll go and see if your father is ready for us."

By the time she returned everybody was singing 'Away in a Manger' and quite a crowd had gathered, with nurses, porters and visitors all grouped round the small child and her 'cello.

When she finished Brian said, "That was so lovely, I feel quite choked."

Someone said "Give us another one Laura," and she looked a bit worried, "I only know 'Silent Night' but I sometimes go a bit wrong on the last two lines."

Kenny laughed, "Don't you worry about that love, we'll sing extra loud." He then broke into a fit of coughing. Natasha watched him as he tried to recover and felt anxious. He definitely didn't look so good today and there were dark rings under his eyes. Michael came and stood beside her and at the end of the two verses everybody clapped. Laura looked a little bewildered at this. She stood up and said, "I'm going to go and play for my father now."

Natasha carried the 'cello and the three of them walked down the corridor with Laura skipping ahead. "If she can get a sound like that out of that size 'cello," Michael observed, "just think what she will do when she reaches the full size."

They opened the door to find Gerry smiling. "I heard you playing Laura. Are you going to play a carol for me?"

She shook her head. "No, because I've made up a special tune for you Father."

This was news to Natasha and she just hoped it wouldn't be too gloomy. Laura's compositions had a tendency to be rather melancholic. But in the event it wasn't, and there was nothing enigmatic or indefinite about it either. It was broad and melodic, and although quite simple it had a strange and beautiful theme. She played it through twice and then, unusually for her, she sat without moving. There was a good minute before anyone spoke and then Gerry said huskily, "Did you write that tune yourself Laura?"

"Yes," she said, "I wrote it for you."

Gerry struggled to overcome his emotion but finally said, "Thank you darling. It was wonderful." He turned his eyes away from Laura and said with a bleak smile, "I think I have just seen a glimpse of your heaven Natasha."

Michael turned and without a word left the room.

Laura put her 'cello down and gave Gerry his candles. He insisted on lighting them at once so Natasha went off in search of matches. When she came back Laura was explaining that her candle smelled of a flower but she couldn't remember the flower's name.

"Jasmine," Natasha told her.

The flame flickered into life and Gerry made an effort to sit up. "I can see the flame," he said, excitement in his voice. "What would Christmas be without carols and candlelight?" but the effort of speaking was too much for him and he sank back on the pillows. His voice was now very faint. "You have given me carols and candlelight and I thank you. I thank you both from the bottom of my heart."

He closed his eyes and for the first time Natasha thought that his face had lost a little of its strain and he looked at peace. She glanced at Laura, put her finger to her lips and picking up the 'cello they tiptoed out of the room.

CHAPTER FIFTEEN

That night Natasha's sleep was filled with strange and savage dreams. She slowly emerged from them feeling panicked and disturbed. It was strange how dreams could be so familiar and yet so unreal. The images still remained with her even after waking. Euan had been in there somewhere and he had been kicking a heap of rags that on close observation had a look of Gerry. She shivered and blinked herself fully awake, slowly focusing on familiar objects in the room. There was a full moon and it was almost light as day but when she switched on the light and picked up her clock she saw it wasn't yet six.

It was Christmas Day and this year it would be a strange one, unlike any other. She just hoped the afternoon at Thaddeus wouldn't prove too much of an ordeal for any of them. Wrapping herself in her kimono she tiptoed into Laura's room. The child was still sleeping soundly, strands of black hair strewn untidily against the white pillow. Her stocking at the foot of the bed remained untouched. Natasha's eye caught the silhouette of a very large package standing on its own. There didn't appear to be a label on it so she presumed it was from Wal and Miriam. She returned to her own room and climbed back into bed, but as she was about to turn off the light she caught sight of another small parcel behind the lamp which she hadn't noticed before. Again, there was no label. Taking off the outer wrapping she pulled out a red Cartier box. Gingerly she opened the lid. Inside was a large, oval, silver watch, with a heavy silver bracelet strap. There was no label or message. She took it out and ran her hands over the smooth surface. Then she turned it over. There was a short inscription, 'Natasha from Euan'. She put it on her wrist, clicked the clasp and sat staring at it.

How clever of Euan, there was no love or endearment, just something that would be a permanent reminder of him.

The door burst open and Laura entered carrying her stocking. "There's a big parcel at the end of my bed. I couldn't carry it. Can you bring it in here?"

Abandoning the idea of further sleep Natasha fetched it from Laura's room. Half an hour later the bed was covered in wrapping paper, string, tangerines, toys and sweets. The large parcel turned out to be an antique music stand, again from Euan. Natasha felt a mixture of gratitude and irritation. It was so perverse, first to refuse to take an interest in the child's music and then take the trouble to find her the perfect present. He was just impossible.

When they had shared the tangerine and Laura had eaten several chocolate snowmen, Natasha packed her off to get dressed and sent her on down to breakfast. She then went onto the landing, sat by the telephone and dialled Euan's number at the lodge.

He answered almost immediately.

"Happy Christmas," she said. "Thank you for our wonderful presents. It was really generous of you."

"Glad you liked them."

She sighed. Euan's telephone manner was always so clipped and detached. She longed for him to say something affectionate or kind, but knew this was very unlikely, especially in the present circumstances.

"Are you going to the hospital today?" he asked.

She answered quite truthfully, "No, not today," and didn't elaborate about the visit to Thaddeus. Instead she said in cool tones, "When do you go over to the Walters' house?"

He said dismissively, "Not until noon and I won't be staying long. I've still a lot of work to do on my proofs."

There was silence for a moment and then curiosity got the better of her. "How did you manage to get the presents to us?"

"I have my ways," he said enigmatically. It was obvious he wasn't going to enlarge on this. She was just about to ring off when he said quietly, "Tash if you need me, just ring. I'm always here."

After putting down the receiver she sat for a few minutes thinking.

It hadn't exactly been a satisfactory call, but then it hadn't been totally unsatisfactory either. On the whole she was glad she had made contact.

They arrived at Thaddeus a little early. Laura, in her new dress her face flushed with excitement, showed no signs of tiring. He led them into the drawing room, a room she hadn't seen before. The walls were dark green, the curtains heavy brocade and the velvet sofas and chairs were covered in tapestry cushions. It was almost grand but the formality was broken by the untidy scattering of books and newspapers. She sat down and warmed her hands at yet another log fire. Thaddeus gave her a guilty look and said, "I keep my sins to a minimum with just one fire in the house. No fire in my study today."

She smiled and then glanced towards the grand piano. "Do you play?"

Thaddeus sighed, "Very little I'm afraid, but it's such a beautiful instrument, I can't bear to get rid of it. It comes into its own when visitors play, Michael for instance."

"Michael?" she was surprised, "I thought he played the double bass."

"Oh he may do that as well but he's an outstanding pianist. I remember going to many school concerts and he was always the soloist. The dear boy is quite brilliant. We'll get him to play something when he arrives."

Laura was dancing round and round the room, for no particular reason, just from sheer happiness. "Keep still Laura," Natasha said, "you're making us all dizzy."

Thaddeus smiled indulgently. "I have a present for Laura and it might be a good move to give it to her now. I'm a great believer in occupational therapy."

It turned out to be a large illustrated book of fairy tales and Laura immediately became immersed.

"How clever you are," Natasha said, "that should keep her happy for hours."

Thaddeus beamed like a small boy who'd been told he'd done well in his exams. They lit the many candles and Natasha told him that Gerry would love them because his sight was just good enough to make out the flicker of the flames. Henry arrived, red-faced and cheerful, bearing gifts of champagne, wine and chocolates. When they all had a drink Thaddeus put on some carols and they sat round the fire.

It was into this gentle peace of carols and candlelight with a child quietly reading, that Michael wheeled in Gerry half an hour later. Laura immediately went to sit at Gerry's feet and told him about her Christmas, "but I'm wearing my best Christmas present Father," she told him. Natasha was touched by this unexpected tact and it obviously pleased Gerry, who although silent was smiling. As the carols finished Natasha turned to Michael, "Thaddeus tells me you play the piano. Would you play something for us?"

Michael stood up. "Of course, but first I have a surprise for Laura." He sat at the piano and started to play. It turned out to be a piano arrangement of the piece Laura had composed for Gerry. Natasha didn't recognise it at first but Laura said at once, "That's the tune I wrote for Father."

Gerry nodded and said in frail tones, "It is indeed. It is so good to hear it again."

When Michael finished he said, "It was such a beautiful melody it stuck in my head. I hope you don't mind Laura."

She shook her head and said solemnly, "No, I don't mind."

Natasha looked at Michael and felt an overwhelming gratitude. It was such a kind gesture to have done that, not only for Laura but for Gerry as well. She was also relieved it hadn't been one of Laura's melancholic tunes. This one was different and Michael had made it sound beautiful and somehow noble.

Henry dabbed at his eyes and Laura looked at him curiously, "Why is that man crying?"

Thaddeus saved Henry the embarrassment of explaining. "Henry has been in and out of the 'vale of tears' for as long as I can remember. Anything can set him off." He patted Henry affectionately, "There's nothing wrong in the display of emotion dear Henry. We should all give vent to our feelings it's very good for us." He turned to Laura,

"Now young lady, you come with me and help bring in the tea things."

There was silence in the room for a moment. Then, with a great effort, Gerry said, "Would you play something else Michael, for Natasha? Her mother was a fine pianist and I know how much she missed her playing."

Natasha was touched. "Thank you Gerry," she said quietly.

Michael played a Chopin prelude she knew very well. It was full of wistful beauty and sadness, a mood that suited the day. Natasha watched him as he played and she marvelled that Michael's large hands could produce such a delicate touch. It brought a lump to her throat and tears once more coursed down Henry's cheeks.

During tea, as the sky darkened and there was only the light from the candles and the fire, Thaddeus put on the carols again. Laura said, "There you are Father, candles and carols. You said you liked candles and carols at Christmas."

His voice faced almost to a whisper, "Indeed I do Laura. It has been the perfect Christmas." A spasm of pain crossed his face. "It's time to go," he said.

With great speed Michael wheeled him from the room. Gerry gave a feeble wave and the door closed.

"Why did Father go so soon?" Laura asked.

"He was tired," Natasha answered, wondering whether she should go after them. Thaddeus forestalled her, "I'll go and help them into the ambulance car. Michael only allowed for an hour."

He left the room and Laura went back to her book. Natasha started to clear up the tea things. As Henry handed her his cup he said in a gruff voice, "Such bravery in the face of so much pain. It puts everything into perspective somehow. I feel very humbled. I know I moan on about my life being a mess, but witnessing that just now..." He raised his hands in a helpless gesture and sank back sodden and crumpled into the armchair.

Natasha put the tea cup on the trolley and decided on a change of subject. "I wish I could play the piano. It's one of the great regrets I have about my life."

"You could always start learning now," Henry said encouragingly.

She smiled. "I could, but I probably won't and to be honest I don't think I have any talent for it."

"You know," Henry said, "I think after today, my priorities will change and I will try and make better use of my time."

Later that evening, after Laura had gone to bed, Natasha rang Michael to thank him for his help and to inquire after Gerry.

He sounded grave, "Not good I'm afraid, and he's developed a liver problem."

"Is it serious?"

"Yes, it is. Basically his liver has ceased to function. He has bouts of vomiting and almost constant diarrhoea."

"Maybe it was a bad idea to move him today," she said sadly.

"Absolutely not," Michael sounded firm. "It was very important for him to see Laura today," he paused, "especially as it will be the last time."

She was panicked, "What do you mean the last time? Is he going to die tonight? Should I come over to the hospital now?"

He was quick to reassure her. "No, no, there's no immediate danger, although he can't last much longer. It's just that Gerry doesn't want Laura to come to the hospital again. He quite rightly doesn't want the child alarmed. He gets taken ill very suddenly and this could frighten her, quite apart from it being undignified for him."

Natasha said quietly, "I understand, although I will have to think up some explanation for her."

"There's something else," Michael said. "It's Kenny. He collapsed yesterday. He may not last through the night."

"Oh God," Natasha said miserably, "Laura will be upset about that as well. They had formed quite a friendship."

"Perhaps you could tell her he loved the candle she gave him. It's lit all the time now." He paused again. "I'm sorry to be the bearer of so much bad news."

"It's hardly your fault," she said angrily, "It's this bloody disease. Anyway, thank you for all you did today."

She rang off and joined Wal and Miriam.

"We're having a glass of Euan's cognac," Wal said. He handed her a glass and she smiled at him wanly. Miriam gave her an anxious look. "Darling, you look all in. Why don't you give the hospital a miss tomorrow? Belinda and Nigel are coming over. We could all go for a walk in Richmond Park. Laura would like that. They're bringing Waffles, their new dog."

Wal shuddered, "It really is the most ghastly specimen with absolutely no bladder control."

"She's only a puppy darling..." Miriam started to protest.

Natasha interrupted them. "Actually I have a problem and I'd greatly value your advice." She explained about the telephone conversation with Michael.

Miriam sat for a moment in thought and then went into practical mode. "I do have a solution. If you remember, Dolly and Tinker take a house in Cornwall right after Christmas and they always ask us to join them. We haven't done so since the children left home but the invitation is always there. Why don't I go this year and take Laura with me? I know she'd love it and I could do with a break myself."

Natasha turned the plan over in her mind. Would Laura mind being wrenched away from London just as she had settled in? Added to which would she mind being alone with just adults, none of whom she knew very well?

Reading her mind Miriam said, "Why don't we suggest taking Millie down as well to be company for Laura? They appear to be great friends already and two children are no more trouble than one. If anything they are less."

Laura was told about this plan the following day and immediately became excited, especially at the thought of being with Millie. She didn't mention Gerry and probably thought she would be seeing him on her return. Natasha was a little surprised that Millie had become such an instant friend. She was the total opposite to Laura, large for her age, fair and placid, but from the first moment they'd become inseparable. It made the Cornwall suggestion so much easier. The harassed Annie Reid was only too happy to relinquish one of her children. She also suggested that Laura could perhaps join Millie at her school for a term. Natasha greeted this suggestion with relief. She had been wrestling with the problem of Laura's schooling. Term was due to start in a week and it would have been difficult taking Laura back to Norfolk at this time.

"Will I be able to get her into the school at such short notice?" she asked.

"I'm sure it won't be a problem," Annie assured her. "The headmistress is a friend and when she hears about your situation I am sure she will understand."

After seeing off the Cornwall party, Natasha turned to Wal, "I cannot thank you enough. You've both been so terribly kind, solving all my problems. I just don't know how I'd have managed…"

Wal put an arm around her. "It's the least we could do," he said gruffly. "To tell you the truth, having to concentrate on your problems has been an absolute tonic for Miri. She's almost back to her old self." He gave a chuckle. "As for the holiday in Cornwall, I'm really pleased she's gone. It's me that hasn't wanted to go down there in recent years and I know how much she has missed it."

Natasha still felt anxious. "What about your meals? It looks as if I'm going to be spending most of my time in the hospital."

Wal was dismissive. "Don't worry about that. You just concentrate on whatever you have to do." He added almost cheerfully, "I can always join Henry at his Club if I get desperate."

The next few days fell into a routine. Natasha would get to the hospital early and spend most of the day with Gerry, breaking only for the odd meal or a walk. Sometimes she would read to him, sometimes they talked, but their conversation was limited because he would tire so quickly. Mostly he slept. When he needed cleaning or changing she would call the nurses and take herself off to the Recreations Area. It was a strange sort of limbo time.

On the fourth day Michael sought her out to tell her that Kenny had died in the night. It shouldn't have been a shock, but it was and left her feeling desperately sad. It was absurd really because she had known him for so short a time.

The rest of the day proved difficult. She made an effort to sound normal as she read 'The Pilgrim's Progress' to Gerry. She reached the passage where Mr Valiant-for-Truth starts to cross the river. Her voice began to falter and she struggled as she read, 'and so they passed over and all the Trumpets sounded for them on the other side. And all the Bells of Heaven did ring for joy'. It was too much. She mumbled to Gerry that she would be back in a minute and ran down the corridor to the cloakroom. Locking herself in, she put her head in her hands and started to sob. It took some minutes for the bout of weeping to subside. Wearily she got to her feet and vaguely tried to repair her blotched face. On her return to Gerry's room she saw Michael coming towards her talking to a nurse. She looked away but it was too late. He abruptly left the nurse, took her by the arm and led her to the window.

"What's happened?"

"I don't know," she gulped. "It was just everything, Kenny and..." She looked at him. "I kept seeing his little clown face and hearing that cheerful voice," breaking off she dived for her handkerchief. "Oh God, this is hopeless. I'm so sorry."

"You need a break," he said firmly, "and as a doctor I'm prescribing one. I have a rare evening off tonight. Another doctor is covering for me. So you will come back and have supper with me and that's an order. It won't help Gerry if you become tired and emotional will it?"

She gave him a bleak smile. "You're right. I accept and thank you."

Back at Gerry's bedside she found he was dozing so she didn't disturb him. The room was so warm her eyes closed and she drifted off to sleep. Sometime later she was woken by a weird noise. Gerry was moving restlessly and muttering some sort of strange gibberish. She leaned over him but he looked wild and his eyes were rolling. Feeling alarmed she called to him two or three times but he didn't seem to recognise her voice and his mutterings only became more frantic. Suddenly he began to thrash about violently. One minute he would pull himself up into a foetal position, the next throw himself out full length. She was so frightened he would fall out of bed she rang the bell for the nurse. Sister arrived with another nurse and taking one look at Gerry sent the nurse to find Michael. He arrived quickly and while the two nurses held down Gerry's flailing arms he gave him an injection.

"He'll calm down now," he told Natasha. "Wait outside and I'll be with you in a minute."

Feeling shaken she went out into the corridor. Michael joined her. "He's sleeping now but I'm afraid you can expect more of this. The problem is that he's had so much morphine he's experiencing morphine-induced hallucinations."

"My God," Natasha said wearily, "is there no end to the agonies these people must endure? It's positively medieval. And where does he get his strength from? He's only skin and bone. I know it sounds callous but why doesn't he just let go."

Michael looked at her. "I did warn you, this can often happen. These patients won't let go until they are ready. I often think it's as if they want to clear the decks of one life before embarking on another." He paused. "There could also be something troubling Gerry. It might help if you tried to talk to him when he wakes up. He'll be more lucid after his sleep."

"I'll try," she said.

She wandered down to the Recreations Area, where the atmosphere was unusually quiet and subdued. Brian looked up and said, "I suppose you heard about Kenny."

Natasha nodded, "Yes I did, I'm so sorry."

"We're going to miss him," Brian gave a sniff, "he was always so cheerful was Kenny, kept us all going. Always ready with a joke. He used to make us laugh, make us forget..." His voice petered out.

She sat beside him and held his hand. "I know," she said feeling helpless and inadequate.

The pile of paint boxes stood stacked in the corner. Usually someone was using them but today they were left abandoned, maybe as a mark of respect. She sat on with Brian talking quietly, until the nurse came to wheel him back to his room. She looked in on Gerry but he was still in a deep sleep.

On a sudden impulse she left the hospital and went round to see Thaddeus.

"Is it very bad?" he asked, as he let her in.

"Yes it's miserable." She followed him into his study and sat by the fire. "One of the patients died last night. He was called Kenny and he was younger than me, in his early twenties. What a waste, what a bloody awful waste." She was near to tears. "I feel so helpless. I don't know how Michael can stand it."

Thaddeus said quietly, "I think the only way he can stand it is to try and find a cure."

Natasha was silent for a moment then she said, "I don't quite know how to put this but I think there is something troubling Gerry. He is very restless and disturbed. Michael says he's suffering from hallucinations brought on by the morphine but I think it's more than that."

Thaddeus considered this. "You feel he won't let go until he has resolved whatever it is that is troubling him?"

She was grateful for his understanding. "It's something like that. I know it sounds callous but I don't want him to hang on now. His suffering is terrible. It's not a life. I would just like to help ease him out of this existence."

Thaddeus made no comment but went to his bookcase and pulled out a slim volume and handed it to her. It was 'The Dream of Gerontius'. She was curious, "I've heard the music but I haven't read it. I do remember it being rather frightening. Isn't it very Roman Catholic and gloomy?"

Thaddeus smiled. "It does smack a little of incense but I gave it to Gerry to read in South Africa when he was at his darkest and most despairing. He wrote and told me afterwards that one passage had helped him greatly. It might be a good idea if you reminded him of it again. I'll mark it for you."

Armed with her spiritual remedy she returned to the hospital. Gerry dozed fitfully but didn't really wake properly again. At some point he opened his eyes and said in an almost normal voice, "Hello Natasha, are you still here? Then he closed his eyes and went back into a deep sleep.

*

At seven Michael collected her and drove her to his flat. It was in a large block, smartly appointed with a porter and lifts. He said apologetically, "I know it's very characterless but it suits my life style. I spend little time here so I just need everything convenient and on hand. My great extravagance is to have a housekeeper who is also an excellent cook. I have no time to cook myself."

The flat was much larger that she expected with windows giving panoramic views over the London skyline. The living room was stylish, with minimum furniture, a grand piano and just one picture. She peered at the signature and gasped, "My God, is that an original Picasso?"

Michael nodded and said with a smile, "It is actually, left to me by my father."

Natasha remembered Thaddeus telling her that Michael's father had been an art dealer. Even so, an original Picasso! She sat down feeling a little awed as Michael handed her a glass of wine. "Supper's been organised, so we can eat whenever you want."

Over the meal he asked her about Gerry.

"Is that out of professional interest?" she asked giving him a quizzical look.

"Well no, but I'm curious." He hesitated. "To be honest I didn't expect Gerry to have a wife and certainly not a wife like you. "

She sighed. "It's a rather complicated saga and will take some time if you really want to hear it."

"For once I'm in no hurry," he said, "so take as long as you like."

So she told him, starting with Euan and her mother, moving on through the car crash, Euan coming back into her life, moving into Garrick Square, their stormy affair, the splitting up, marrying Gerry on the rebound, finding out he was gay, leaving him and moving up to Norfolk. She finished with the return of Euan and with Gerry getting AIDS. She leaned back exhausted.

Michael looked at her, "That's quite a story."

The candles had almost gutted and were flickering erratically. He blew them out. "Let's move into the other room. We can finish the wine in there."

Once settled he asked, "So what happens now?"

She took time to answer. "I honestly don't know. I feel I'm in limbo and can't really see beyond Gerry dying, but I have a feeling this experience will have changed me somehow."

After a moment Michael asked, "Will you go back to Euan?" He had taken his glasses off and the sea-green eyes were regarding her with a strange intensity.

She recognised that look. Euan looked at her in a similar way sometimes. It was just not something she could cope with at this moment so she turned away from his gaze. "If I'm honest," she said slowly, "I just don't know. Euan is very angry with me at the moment. He was totally against my being with Gerry and hasn't stopped telling me so. I'm fairly angry with him myself..." She broke off. "Do you mind? I don't think I can talk about it right now?"

Michael nodded and put his glasses back on, as if to underline his acceptance that the conversation had ended.

She picked up her glass of wine. "Tell me about your work. How did you come to be involved with AIDS?"

"I was in New York doing research on immunology," he told her, "it was 1985 and AIDS had just hit the news. Rock Hudson died and suddenly, far too late, the world woke up to the monumental catastrophe they were facing. I don't want to bore you with statistics but by that time in the States alone, 36,000 Americans had been diagnosed with the disease and 20,000 had died. With the death of each new celebrity the panic increased."

He leaned forward, "My involvement came through a friend of my mothers who was working in an AIDS baby unit. He asked me to join him and I set aside my research to do so." He gave a wry smile. "This move didn't please my parents who felt I was sacrificing my career. I tried telling them there was also research work to be done on the AIDS virus but they were never comfortable with my change of direction." He sighed. "There is so much fear and ignorance about this disease."

"Why did you return to London?" she asked.

"My father became ill with cancer so I came back to be with him. After he died, a vacancy came up in the ward I'm in now." He shrugged, "I was seen as a suitable candidate and more or less bullied into it. I try to combine the clinical work with research but it's becoming increasingly difficult to give adequate time to both. I will probably go back to full time research if they can find a replacement for me." He added with a wry smile, "It's not a job that everyone wants."

"I should think not." Natasha retorted. "I don't know how you keep your sanity working there. At least in the other wards you have a chance of curing the patients and sending them home. With the AIDS ward there is no hope at all and most of them die very young."

Michael said quietly, "I think our best aim at the moment is to ease the pain and give a sense of dignity in death, as far as we can. The frustration with this virus is that it is potentially a curable disease."

"It is? Then are you closer to finding a cure?" Natasha asked.

He smiled and said, "Well ironically there is a cure in existence. If the human race would stick to safe sex with one partner and didn't share injection equipment and all blood was tested, then there would be no spread of the HIV virus." He smiled. "But I'm a realist and I know we'll never change the habits of mankind. At least in the West people have started to take care, no doubt prompted by the bombardment of advertisements that first came out describing the dangers of the illness. But memories are short and as soon as the disease slips out of the news complacency sets in again. Sadly the alarm bells only start to ring when another famous person dies of it." He shrugged and said wearily, "The only answer is to find a cure. It is a horrifying fact, but by the year 2000 it is thought there will be 40 million HIV sufferers in the world and most of these will be in the developing countries."

Natasha looked shocked. "Surely something will have happened by then?"

Michael poured out the wine. "I hope so, but we are up against the most extraordinary virus, quite different from any we have encountered before. It is fiendishly clever and doesn't behave like other viruses. Just as you think you are near to a break-through, it changes. And it hides. Someone can be sick for a very long time without knowing they have HIV and all the time they are infecting others." He made a gesture of frustration. "After years of work we still know almost nothing about it. So far it has defeated us, but somewhere, somehow there has to be an answer. We just have to understand its cunning games and learn how to destroy them."

"You make it sound almost human," she said.

He smiled. "In a way it is, well, an evil human anyway."

"The Antichrist," she murmured, then seeing his startled expression she added hastily, "it's the subject of a book Euan's writing."

They were silent for a moment. Then he looked at her, "I really am sorry. I have talked for far too long."

"Don't apologise please," she said quickly. "I really do find it fascinating."

He sighed. "At the moment my greatest fear is that AIDS fatigue has set in again with the public. The dramatic impact of the illness has worn off, consequently funding is getting less just at the very moment it should be increasing."

He stood up and smiled, "and that is quite enough for one evening. I'm going to make you some coffee and then organise a taxi."

Natasha had been concentrating so hard on what he had been telling her she didn't realise how desperately tired she was. Now in the silence of the room her eyelids felt like lead. She leaned back and sank into the cushions. What an interesting evening it had been with Michael talking so passionately about his work. He was such a clever man and such a good doctor. He was a wonderful pianist too. Hadn't he played her favourite Chopin prelude? How could he have known it was her favourite? He was such a clever man...

Her eyes closed. She decided Michael was a bit like a younger version of that funny American actor, what was his name? Walter something, Walter Matthau, that was it. Her thoughts felt very muddled. Was she a little bit drunk? She did feel a bit...

Moments later Michael returned with the coffee and found her fast asleep. He put down the tray and gently laid her full length on the sofa, putting a cushion under her head. Covering her with a blanket he watched her for a minute, then turned out the light and quietly left the room.

CHAPTER SIXTEEN

Natasha was woken by the sound of wind and rain lashing against the window. Blinking herself out of oblivion she stumbled across the room and looked down at the road below. The trees either side were almost doubled over by the force of the gale. Looking at her watch she saw it was eight o'clock. She had slept for nine hours.

"Terrible storm in the night," Michael said as he came into the room. "I'm glad it didn't wake you earlier. It's been making the most terrible racket."

She smiled, "I don't think anything would have woken me. I'm sorry to have crashed out on you. It must have been all that good wine and food..."

"And all the talking," Michael looked apologetic. "I'm the one who ought to apologise. I obviously wore you out."

Natasha shook her head, "No, it was just what I needed."

He suddenly looked a little shy and said almost abruptly, "We ought to be leaving for the hospital in half an hour. Does that give you enough time to get ready? There's everything you need in the bathroom."

When they were in the car she asked if there was any further news of Gerry.

"He's had a quiet night. There's little change." He turned his windscreen wipers on to full. "This weather is awful, 1995 is certainly going out with a bang."

"Of course, it's New Year's Eve," Natasha said, "I'd quite lost track of what day it was." She was quiet for a moment and then murmured, "It would be good somehow if Gerry made it into 1996."

They stopped at some traffic lights and Michael glanced at her, then cleared his throat. "I'm beginning to feel like the Greek messenger, always the bearer of bad news." Natasha's eyes widened. The traffic started to move again. "I'm afraid the Press are on to Gerry, the fact that he has AIDS. Apparently there are several reporters outside the hospital."

"They're like vultures," Natasha said angrily, "just hanging around waiting for him to die."

"It's abhorrent I agree but we have no power to stop them. It's happened before when we've had celebrities who have died in the ward. I've no idea how they get their information but they always turn up. I know it's distressing and I really am sorry."

She shrugged and said flatly, "Gerry warned me that something like this might happen. He was worried, not for himself, but for me and Laura. I was hoping…" Her voice trailed away.

Michael drove on in silence. There was little he could say to comfort her and he desperately wanted to. Throughout the ordeal she had faced each new problem with her own peculiar blend of practicality and courage. She did so now. "I suppose, given Gerry's appearances as a TV vicar, it was only to be expected. I had hoped, as he's not worked in television for a few years they might have forgotten him, but I know there have been some repeats of his programmes lately. Laura saw one of them." She sighed. "There has been so much in the news lately about the Church and sex scandals. Gerry's death from AIDS must seem the perfect story."

Michael momentarily put his hand on hers. "With a bit of luck they won't make too much of it. Anyway, this morning we'll park at the back, so you won't have to see them."

Natasha walked into Gerry's room and stared down at his inert body. He's like a shrivelled animal, she thought, not a human being at all. The raspy breathing was proof that he was still alive but otherwise he just looked like a carcase. She idly wondered if she would have been able to face this scene if it had been Euan lying there and she knew she probably wouldn't. What everyone saw as her bravery was only possible because of the emotional detachment she felt. She had compassion and sympathy for Gerry, even admiration for the way he had faced his illness, but sadly she realised that it didn't amount to love. It was a curious fact but she had felt more emotionally distressed over the death of Kenny than she did for this dying man. At the back of her mind there still hovered a reminder of those awful London years when his cruelty had almost destroyed her. Yet she was moved by his reaction to Laura and relieved too, that Gerry had at last found someone he could genuinely love. This illness had brought a change in him. He was a humbler, kinder, more compassionate man. She smiled to herself. Surely Thaddeus would remind her that he was the proverbial lost sheep who had gone astray, but who now was found.

After a while he opened his eyes.

"Hello Gerry," she took his hand, "I'm sorry you've had such a bad time. Michael says it was the effects of the drugs." He nodded but didn't speak, so she went on. "I spoke to Thaddeus yesterday. He wanted me to read you this." She took the slim volume out of her bag. "It's from 'The Dream of Gerontius'. Shall I do as he suggests?" Again Gerry nodded. She wasn't quite sure how much he was taking in but decided to read it all the same. She took a deep breath. "This is the section he says you liked, where the SOUL says,

> 'Dear Angel, say,
> Why I have now no fear at meeting Him?
> Along my earthly life, the thought of death
> And judgement was to me most terrible
> I had it aye before me, and I saw
> The Judge severe even in the crucifix
> Now that the hour is come, my fear is fled,
> And at the balance of my destiny,
> Now close upon me, I can forward look
> With a serenest joy.'
>
> Then the ANGEL answers,
> 'It is because
> Then thou didst fear, that now thou does not fear.

Thou hast forestalled the agony and so
For thee the bitterness of death is past."

She closed the book. Gerry still said nothing. She wondered if he'd gone back to sleep and replaced the book in her bag. A minute or two went by. Then Gerry said in a surprisingly strong voice, "I should like to see Thaddeus. Will you ask him to come over now?"

She stood up ready to go but he gestured for her to sit down again. A look of desperation crept across his face. "What is it Gerry? Are you in pain?"

He shook his head then rasped out, "I want your forgiveness."

She felt shocked, "There is no need...really..."

He said it again with even more urgency and then gasped out, "Do I have it?"

"You have it," she said and added, "If you will also forgive me."

It was his turn to look surprised. She held up her hand to stop him talking. "We were both at fault Gerry. I shouldn't have married you. In that I was just as wrong." She paused. "But something good did come out of it. We do have Laura."

He closed his eyes and a tear trickled down his cheek. "Oh yes," he murmured, "We do have Laura."

"I'll go and ring Thaddeus," she told him but again he started to speak. The effort now was unbearable to watch, the words coming out in short gasps. "Please...I want you to tell Laura...I want her to know... how proud I am of her...how very proud..."

He could say no more.

Natasha said gently, "Of course I will tell her Gerry. I promise."

Thaddeus came straight over and stayed with Gerry for about an hour. "He'll slip away now," he told Natasha, "He seems to be at peace."

"Thank you for your help," she said, giving him back 'The Dream of Gerontius'.

He looked at her, "No, thank you for your's. Call me."

She watched the little bustling figure make his way to the lifts, then turned and slowly went back into the room. Gerry was sleeping but she noticed his breathing was getting shallower. The nurses came in every hour to do what they could but for the rest of the day he drifted in and out of consciousness. She was brought cups of tea, then supper on a tray but she felt little like food. She wondered where Gerry's mind had strayed to. Was his spirit already travelling into some unknown distant land? It was strange, watching the human spirit die. She had never been near death before but somehow it wasn't as frightening as she had anticipated. There was a feeling of great calm in the room and a gentle peace. When it was dark she lit Laura's candle, then twiddled with the radio knobs and found some music. It was Bach, the double violin concerto. She sat back listening and waited.

Just before midnight Michael looked in. "Come with me," he whispered, "Gerry will be all right for a moment." He led her to Sister's office. "It may seem inappropriate," he said, "but life has to go on, so we are going to drink a glass of champagne to welcome in the year 1996." The night Sister and two nurses were already sipping from paper cups. The radio was on and they listened to the chimes of Big Ben. "Happy New Year," Michael said and they all hugged. For some reason, Natasha felt closer to tears at that moment than she had done all day.

She returned to Gerry. Some while later he opened his eyes and said in quite a clear voice, "It's strange but I have no pain." Then he closed his eyes again. His breathing was now so weak she had to strain to hear it. At about two o'clock she could put off sleep no longer. When she awoke, there were two nurses in the room. One of them, seeing she was no longer asleep, came over to her.

"He's gone Natasha," she said.

Natasha stood up and walked over to the bed. She stared down at him, feeling nothing but a great wave of relief. He looked at peace.

"What happens now?" she asked.

"It's probably best if you leave," the nurse told her, adding kindly, "go and sit in Sister's office. They'll give you a cup of tea."

Natasha sat in the office and waited. Looking at her watch she saw it was just before seven. She felt very alone, strange and disorientated.

Sister came in with a cup of tea. "I've brought you Gerry's belongings. I'll get you to sign for them later." She bustled out again. Natasha stared down at the little pile of objects. There was his wedding ring, a gold watch, his reading glasses and his wallet. It was a large wallet of black crocodile and had been smart once, a reminder of Gerry's more successful days. Now it looked worn and shabby. She opened it. Inside was a cheque book, a few pound notes and two dog-eared photographs. One was of her taken just after they were married and the other a fairly recent picture of Laura. There was something almost unbearably poignant about them. They were all that remained as a reminder of Gerry's earthly life and it wasn't much. Wal told her he had completely sold up before he'd left South Africa. Now, except for these few possessions it was as if he'd never been. Feeling desperately sad, she put them in her bag and went out to call Thaddeus.

"I know it's a terrible cliché," he told her, "but you must look on it as a merciful release. His suffering was terrible and now he is at peace. Go home and get some well-deserved rest."

"What about the funeral?" she asked.

He paused. "There is sometimes a few days delay when releasing the body of patients who died from AIDS. I will ask Michael about it. Today is Sunday, but a week tomorrow sounds quite possible. There is no rush, we can discuss details later. I must be off to church now. There I will offer up prayers for Gerry and of course for you. God bless you my dear."

Michael was waiting for her in the office. She wanted him to take her in his arms and say something comforting. She thought he wanted that too, but somehow he seemed unable to. So they stood staring at each other. After a moment he said, "I'm afraid I can't leave the ward at the moment. Will you be all right?"

"Yes. I think Thaddeus will want to talk to you about the funeral."

He nodded. "I'll do that," and added with a gentle awkwardness, "Go and get some rest Natasha and that's an order."

She gave him a wan smile. "Yes doctor."

*

She had completely forgotten Michael's warnings of the day before, about the press, so the reception party of reporters and camera men waiting for her at the front of the hospital came as a terrible shock. Questions were fired at her from all sides.

"Mrs Masterson, did you know your husband was gay?"

"How do you feel about the Church and Homosexuality?"

"How do you react to your husband dying of AIDS?"

She found herself responding to the last question, "It's a shocking way for anyone to die." Then she pushed past them saying "I have nothing more to say."

She reached home to find Wal waiting for her and fell into his arms. "I'm so sorry," he said.

She looked at him, her eyes brimming with tears. "The Press knows."

He nodded. "I heard it on the lunchtime news."

"What did they say?"

"They just said that the death had been announced of the Reverend Gerald Masterson, familiar to many for his broadcasting and TV appearances."

Natasha broke away, "Did they mention AIDS as the cause of his death?"

Wal looked uncomfortable. "I'm afraid they did. At least they said that he had died from complications after suffering from AIDS."

She sat down and put her head in her hands. When she looked up she said, "I feel I have failed him. I should have somehow prevented it from leaking out."

Wal shook his head sadly. "There was nothing you could do. Gerry was known to millions. It was inevitable the story would break."

Natasha stood up in panic. "I must tell Laura."

"It's all right I've already spoken to Miriam." Wal's tones were soothing. "If you agree she will tell Laura. It's better than you breaking the news over the telephone. They are driving back tomorrow and you can explain it more to Laura then. Now go and get some rest. You can do no more for the moment."

*

The next day Wal sat in his office studying the papers. They did not make happy reading and the tabloids in particular were pretty lurid. He stared at the headlines, 'Secret Life of TV Vicar' 'Gay Vicar dies of AIDS' 'TV Gerry's Gay Secret'. Several had pictures of Natasha leaving the hospital and one was headed, 'Shock of Gay Vicar's Wife – Exclusive.' Wal read on with sinking heart, 'Standing in tears moments after the death of the Reverend Gerald Masterson known to millions as the TV Vicar, his beautiful wife revealed the shock she felt over his dying of AIDS.' Wal sighed and turned to the broadsheets. In general they only made brief references to Gerry's death. Two of them carried short obituaries mentioning his time in religious broadcasting, his television programmes and his work in the South African Townships. These he cut out. They might be of some consolation to Natasha and she might even want to keep them for Laura. The rest he threw away.

What a mess he thought. What a bloody awful mess.

In Norfolk Euan was thinking the same thing. He stared at the pictures of Natasha and murmured angrily to himself, "you bloody little fool; you could have avoided all this."

George Roxby Smith and his wife Inga were having morning coffee in their spacious living room overlooking the Alps. George was flicking through the English papers that arrived once a week. He picked up one of the tabloids and let out a sharp "Oh my God!" and Inga looked up. He handed her the paper. She gave a look of disgust and said coldly, "So Gerry died of AIDS. What a terrible man, no wonder your daughter left him." She handed it back and he stared at the picture of Natasha leaving the hospital. She may have left Gerry and with good reason, but she had also been with him at the end and that must have taken considerable courage. George was left once again, puzzling over this daughter who had never loved him and that he had never understood. She remained as great an enigma to him as his wife Celia had been. It was a permanent source of bitterness.

*

After a fitful sleep Natasha decided to ring Euan. "I expect you've seen the papers?"

"Yes." He sounded grim but didn't elaborate.

"The funeral will probably be next week."

He showed no interest but asked, "Are you coming back after that?"

"Yes." There was a pause and then she said "Has there been any local reaction?"

Euan said grimly, "Yes, shock horror. What did you expect?"

He rang off abruptly and she reflected sadly that he hadn't even asked her how she was.

Ten days later, during the drive home in the peace and quiet of her own company; she had time to ponder on recent events, especially the day of Gerry's funeral. She and Thaddeus had arranged a simple service with only two hymns, 'Amazing Grace' chosen by Thaddeus, perhaps for the line 'I once was lost but now I'm found' and 'The King of Love my Shepherd is', chosen by Laura because she had sung it at school. In his short sermon Thaddeus praised Gerry for his great gift of communication both in his media work and in South Africa. He also paid tribute to the fortitude and courage with which he had faced his last illness. He finished by saying, "All human life is a journey and all of us make this journey in different ways. In the latter part of Gerry's life, his journey took him through misery, stormy sorrows and sharp affliction, but he found redemption and peace at the last, drawing strength from those he loved most." Thaddeus had looked at her when he said this and she had been moved and grateful to him for these words of comfort.

Laura remained solemn and unquestioning throughout the ceremony. Indeed she had said little on the subject since hearing the news of Gerry's death. There was one night when she had been tearful and on being asked what was worrying her, she'd replied she was missing Miffin. On the whole she had felt it best to leave Laura to decide for herself how she wanted to grieve. She was also relieved she hadn't asked about the cremation, although she looked pathetically bewildered as the coffin made its way down the aisle.

It was after the service, when a few people had returned to Walbrook Grove that for the first time Natasha felt the strain to be almost unbearable. Henry, who had sobbed all the way through the funeral, now became incapable of even finishing a sentence. "I just wanted to say...words fail me on these occasions...I do hope I can...it all seems so...you have my condolences." At which point Natasha thanked him, kissed him on the cheek and left him searching for his handkerchief.

The most difficult moment had been when she came to say goodbye to Michael. They'd stood in the roadway in the cold afternoon air. He'd taken off his glasses and she'd looked again into those sea-green eyes.

"I will miss you," he'd said awkwardly. "Will you keep in touch?"

"Of course," she'd said finding it hard to keep her emotions in check. "Try not to work too hard."

He'd started to walk to his car and then had suddenly turned back, taken her in his arms and whispered in her ear, "Please come back Natasha." That was all. Then he'd gone.

She slowed down to drive through a village.

I can't think about Michael now she told herself, it would have to wait until later when she would have time to properly think through her feelings about him, which at the moment were confused. Instead she thought about her remaining days in Walbrook Grove sorting out the many problems. Apart from organising the funeral, there had been settling Laura into her new school, the reading of Gerry's Will and the decision of what was to be done with his ashes. In the event, all had gone comparatively smoothly.

She'd had great misgivings about leaving Laura in London, but to her relief she appeared to have settled happily, especially after the promise of seeing Miffin for half-term. Laura had luckily formed a great attachment to Miriam, who in her turn seem to dote on the child. She had promised Laura she would visit every fortnight, so this term would involve a lot of travelling to and from Norfolk, but by Easter things should have returned to normal.

As Wal had predicted, the Will had been straight-forward and dear old Thaddeus had solved the dilemma over the ashes. He'd pondered for a while and then suggested the River Thames. He explained that a tidal river was a good place to have your ashes scattered, flowing as it did into the sea. It embraced the wider universe and he'd added that he would say a blessing for Gerry as he scattered them.

So all in all, thanks to the kindness and help of a great many people, her ordeal seemed to be over. She was glad she had made the decision to be with Gerry at the end and was convinced it had been the right one. In a strange way, however harrowing the experience, it had been enriching as well.

Now, as she neared home she realised how emotionally drained she was, with little or no reserves left. However why should that matter? Once back in her house she would have plenty of time to recover and she felt a surge of excitement at the thought of seeing Euan. It would be such a relief for her life to return to normal again.

As she drove past the lodge she hooted and Euan immediately walked up the drive to meet her. He didn't look very welcoming and without a word followed her inside.

Once settled by the fire he said rather coldly, "I imagine it was pretty awful."

She was surprised he sounded so hostile, but said, "Yes it was, but I couldn't help feeling how much worse it would have been if I had loved Gerry. I think it would be almost unbearable to watch a death like that if there were any real attachment."

Euan looked at her curiously. "So what did you feel?"

"I don't know, a mixture of things." She shrugged, "sadness, regret, helplessness, inadequacy. In the end I admired him for his bravery and I was thankful that after all the horrors he had gone through, he died peacefully in his sleep."

Euan said grimly, "Leaving you to clear up all the mess."

She frowned. "Actually Wal did most of that, especially dealing with the press. Luckily there were more important news items like the Wales's divorce, so it all died down after a day or two." She added, "There were two quite good obituaries…"

"I saw them," Euan said curtly, his tone implying it was more than Gerry deserved.

Natasha said almost defensively, "The church was full too. Apparently there are still devoted followers of Gerry, in spite of everything."

Euan gave a snort. "Well not up here there aren't. You should be prepared for a pretty frosty reception in the village."

She felt shocked by his callous tones but all she said was, "I'm hardly likely to be affected by that, I never took much part in village life. However, I am now relieved I made the decision to leave Laura in London."

At the mention of Laura Euan looked a little guilty. "Oh yes, I wondered why she wasn't with you."

Natasha thought sadly that he obviously hadn't even noticed Laura's absence. It was significant somehow. "Well, the school term started before Gerry's funeral," she explained, "so it would have meant a lot of travelling up and down to London if I had brought her back. In view of what you say it seems I made the right decision."

She was given an immediate idea of what Euan meant by a 'frosty reception' when Mrs B came in and inquired whether Mr Mackay would be staying for supper. The tone was distinctly disapproving and there was no mention of 'welcome back,' or 'sorry for your loss,' or even an inquiry about Laura. It was as if everyone to do with her was now tainted and labelled as 'undesirable'. Even poor Miffin skulked around like some leper. Euan told her over supper he'd given up going to the pub since the news had broken, because he got so bored with the only topic of conversation - Gerry.

Natasha sighed. Euan still seemed full of resentment and anger towards her. Conversation was strained and at the end of the meal she pleaded exhaustion and went to bed alone.

It had been a strange home-coming and far from the one she'd been expecting. The normality she had so longed for seemed a very distant prospect.

The next day she started to tackle the mountain of mail. There were some comforting letters from people she didn't know and some from those she did, including Fay Stanhope. There were also a few unpleasant and insulting letters which she put straight in the bin. She picked up one envelope without a postmark that must have been hand delivered. It was typed and it read,

Mrs Masterson.

We do not want your sort round here.

As a parent at the school I do not want my kid to have to mix with your kid. So the sooner you clear off the better it will be for the rest of us.

A Resident of Lower Roxby

She sat feeling shocked and shaken. How could people be so stupid and ignorant? After a moment she started to read it again and then the telephone rang. It was Livvy and she sounded flustered.

"I'm very relieved you're back, I thought you ought to hear the news about Florence at once."

Natasha felt panicked. "What's happened?"

"She's in hospital, a heart attack two days ago. Although no longer in intensive care she's still very ill. I know another hospital visit is the last thing you need but Florence is asking to see you."

"Give me the details Livvy," Natasha said wearily, "I'll go over and see her tomorrow."

Later in the day she went down to the Post Office and on the way met Jocky. The path was narrow and there was no way they could avoid each other. He shifted uneasily from one leg to the other. "Sorry to hear about your misfortune," he gave her a curt nod and moved quickly on. Misfortune! Well that was one way of putting it.

The Post Office was full of chattering women but as she entered they all stopped their talking and stared at her. Feeling the colour mounting in her cheeks she made her way to the counter and asked for some stamps. Nobody spoke a word until she left. Then she could hear the babble break out again even louder than before. Close to tears she walked briskly home.

There was another letter waiting for her, again obviously hand-delivered. This time it was from the Headmistress of the school.

Dear Mrs Masterson,

I was sorry to hear of your loss, especially in such very difficult circumstances.

Thank you for informing us that Laura will not be returning to the school for this term.

I think it would be sensible for you to consider making this a permanent arrangement.

I deeply regret having to say this but feelings among several of the parents are being strongly expressed, both to the Governors and to me personally. In the circumstances they do not want Laura to be allowed to mix with their children.

However misguided their views, this is a situation we feel we have to take seriously.

Our main worry is that Laura might find herself bullied by children who have overheard their parents discussing the situation. I know you will agree this would be very upsetting for the child.

We have greatly enjoyed having Laura at the school and send you both our very good wishes for the future.

Yours sincerely,

Faith Green

Headmistress, Lower Roxby Primary School.

She put down the letter. Suddenly the awfulness of her return and the injustice of it all hit her and she burst into angry sobs. She was still crying when Euan found her a short while afterwards.

"What is it now?" He sounded more exasperated than sympathetic.

She showed him the two letters. "I don't understand how they can all be so stupid."

He shrugged. "The headmistress's letter is really quite reasonable. They're just frightened. Don't you understand? They're afraid their precious wee bairns will pick up the bloody disease from Laura."

Natasha felt angry. "For God's sake, haven't they watched Princess Di visit patients suffering from AIDS and holding their hands? It's ludicrous to suggest Laura could give it to them."

"They don't know that do they?" Euan shouted back at her. "And in all honestly, Gerry *could* have infected both of you. It was only by a lucky fluke that he didn't." She looked so stricken his anger abated. "I did try to warn you. I did tell you to keep away from the whole ugly business."

She said obstinately, "My being with Gerry when he died made absolutely no difference. They still would have reacted this way once they knew I was his wife."

"Well it didn't help matters having your picture plastered all over the fucking papers did it?"

They were silent for a moment and then she said, "There is still no reason for them to think they could catch it..."

Irritation got the better of him. "We may know that but they don't. This isn't London you know. We're out in the Styx here. They haven't moved out of the bloody Dark Ages."

"There's no need to keep swearing," she said tearfully. "And I don't understand why there is all this moral indignation. It's not as if Gerry is the first man to die from AIDS..."

"Oh for God's sake Natasha, grow up! Quite frankly I sympathise with them. For years Gerry was on his religious soap box, ramming it down their throats on how to lead good, pure, moral lives and all the time he was living a lie himself. That's what sticks in the gullet."

"And you're a saint I suppose."

"Don't drag me into this. It wasn't my face that was plastered all over their television screens."

They were silent for a moment and then she said, "You're just angry because you didn't want me to be with Gerry while he was dying."

"No I didn't want you to be with Gerry while he was dying because I knew what would bloody happen and I didn't think the man was worth it. For that matter, I still don't."

She said defiantly, "I tried to explain to you why I needed to be with him. It was for Laura's sake as well as mine. Why can't you understand that? Everyone else does."

Euan started pacing up and down the room, "Well, I'm not everyone else." Then he stopped. "Who is this 'everyone else' anyway?"

She wanted to tell him about Thaddeus and Michael but in his present mood she didn't dare risk it, so she just shrugged and said,

"Oh, I don't know, friends, the family..."

That did it. Sarcastically Euan turned on her, "Of course, I might have known you'd mention the fucking family. I might have known you'd drag them into it. Laura and the family, the family and Laura, it's all I ever hear. Do you know you're going to turn that child into a bloody icon? I mean, just look at this room. It's covered in photographs of Laura and the family. There's no escaping them..." His voice rose to a crescendo and his temper finally snapped. In one grand gesture he swept his arm across the table of photographs sending the frames clattering to the floor, splintered glass flying out in every direction. Without another word he turned, walked out of the room, slamming the door behind him.

Natasha stood rooted to the spot. Then she fell to her knees, too shocked to cry. After a while she began picking up the pieces of glass bit by bit, stacking the broken frames in a neat pile. She came to a large silver frame that contained the photograph of the three of them; Euan, her mother and her in Iona. She stared at it. The frame was badly dented but the glass, although broken, hadn't fallen out. The cracks obscured the picture. At one time this picture had been one of her most treasured possessions. Now she couldn't bear to look at it. How could she and Euan possibly live together after this? She tried to remember the last time they had laughed together, or even been happy, and found she couldn't. Instead there had been resentment, anger and hate.

Turning the frame over, she held it above the metal bin. As she tapped it, the smashed glass fell into the void with a strange tinkling sound. For some time she just sat, the picture on her lap. Then she took the photograph out of the frame, tore it up and let the shredded pieces follow the glass into the bin.

CHAPTER SEVENTEEN

By the time Euan was halfway through his second glass of whisky his anger had begun to subside. He regretted having lost his temper but for God's sake wasn't it understandable? His relationship with Natasha had been going on for nearly ten years and he was still waiting for her to agree to live with him. No wonder his patience was wearing thin. Since his return to England he had done his damndest to be on his best behaviour. Indeed, he had only fallen off his perch once or twice, the most serious lapse being the dismal Livvy dinner party. It had introduced him to 'that woman' and now he was treading on eggshells waiting for the moment when the dreaded subject of Hilary Walters was tossed into the arena. It was unlikely Natasha would have forgotten about it and the consequences of that particular little peccadillo could be dire.

Euan drained his glass, poured himself another and thought about his visit to the Walters on Christmas Day. It had been a nightmare scene of almost Edward Albee proportions. By the time he arrived they were both in foul moods resulting from an incident earlier. Hilary had massaged Barry's feet with luxurious scented oils, her Christmas present to him. Forgetting the oils were still on his feet Barry had slipped while going to the shower and seriously hurt his back. The rest of the day was spent moaning about the pain and hobbling around on a stick. He'd apparently called Hilary a stupid tart for giving him such a dangerous present and she'd taken immediate umbrage. The atmosphere remained distinctly frosty throughout lunch and wasn't helped by Hilary's obvious flirting with him and veiled intimate references. He didn't stay long and after the Christmas fiasco he'd quickly put a stop to Hilary's troublesome attentions. It had been a damaging episode and one he greatly regretted.

Now, with Gerry gone, it was time for him to snatch the initiative again and make a plan. The first move was to get Natasha away from the house and sever all Roxby connections. In view of recent developments with all the unpleasantness in the village this shouldn't be a problem. He felt almost Machiavellian in his new power of scheming. Could it be that at last events were finally going his way? In the last few weeks an American publisher had taken on his Antichrist book and sent him a handsome advance. He raised his glass in a silent toast. Thank God for the Americans because the English publishers wouldn't touch it. In addition he'd been asked to work on a new television series for the BBC and even old Otto in LA had been in touch saying he had a lucrative project for him. It was a sudden embarrassment of riches. Now all he needed was for Natasha to agree to go with him. It didn't matter where, the world was their oyster.

He gave a sudden frown. Of course Laura might pose a problem and that would call for careful handling, but he was sure everything could be resolved once Natasha had agreed to go with him.

Draining his glass he decided it would be sensible to go and make his peace straight away. Apologies would be needed. He was quite prepared to grovel and tell her he was genuinely sorry to have lost his temper. He would even offer to buy her some new photo frames.

Without bothering to put on a coat he set out for the house but he hadn't gone far when a car swept past him and stopped outside the front door. Euan stood still, swaying slightly, and peered into the darkness. It was Livvy.

"Damnation" he muttered under his breath. There was no point in joining in on a family reunion, so he turned round and made his way back to the Lodge.

Reaching for the bottle he decided he might as well make a night of it.

*

Natasha had decided to do the same. As soon as Livvy arrived she opened a bottle of wine.

"I've got stacks of the stuff," she said waving her hand at the wine rack. "I asked Euan to order for me and he was a little over zealous. Anyway, I feel like getting drunk tonight. Will you join me?"

Livvy laughed. "Well Edmund's out at some medical conference so I see no reason not to."

They sat by the fire and Natasha glowered into her glass. "A toast," she said, "here's to us and damnation to all men."

They both drank and Livvy regarded her anxiously. "You sounded awful on the phone. Is this to do with Gerry? We read about it in the papers. It is so unfair they should have dragged you into it."

"Oh stuff that," Natasha said, "my state has nothing to do with Gerry. That's all history." Catching sight of Livvy's shocked face she checked herself. "Well of course it was awful but my main feeling now is relief that at last it's over. Gerry was immensely brave but his suffering was terrible." She paused. "It's the unpleasant aftermath that has been upsetting." She showed Livvy the letters and told her of her ordeal at the Post Office. "I now know how lepers feel," she said gloomily, "all I need is a bell and I can walk around yelling 'unclean', 'unclean'. Even Mrs B has been treating me like some sort of alien."

Livvy put down the letters. "That's awful. I can see why you're upset."

Natasha refilled their glasses, "Worst of all, I had a truly terrible row with Euan."

"What was that about?"

She shrugged. "I don't honestly know. It blew up out of nothing. He's still very angry with me for going to London to be with Gerry and he's fed up with the problems here. Anyway he just lost his temper and smashed up all my photo frames."

Livvy looked shocked. "Why on earth did he do that?"

"He hates all this," Natasha swept her hand vaguely round the room, "the house, the Roxby connections, the family, all that sort of thing."

"He's just jealous," Livvy said, but Natasha shook her head. "I don't think it's just that. He wants me for himself, uncluttered by my past with all the baggage and trappings. He wants to get me away from what he calls this conventional life which he so despises. Oh God, I don't know any more. He's been absolutely awful ever since I got back."

She paused in thought and then suddenly sat bolt upright. "I'll tell you something I've decided. I'm going to sell the Dower House."

Livvy protested. "But you love this house..."

Natasha shook her head. "I did, but not any more, not after all this Gerry business. It's not that they're driving *me* out. I could take on the old bats in the village any day. No, it's because of Laura. The headmistress was actually right. I couldn't possibly risk it."

Livvy sat for a moment lost in thought. "Are you really sure? You've made this house so beautiful."

"Well I'll buy another house in London and make that beautiful."

"London?" Livvy looked surprised. "Won't you miss the country?"

Natasha shook her head. "Not really, I was never a proper country person like you. I will try for a compromise, a house with a large garden and somewhere near a park or common so Miffin can exercise." She laughed. "I couldn't possibly face Laura if I didn't include Miffin in our plans."

She emptied the bottle and Livvy looked guilty, "I'm beginning to feel rather drunk."

"Good," said Natasha, "I'm happy to lead you astray."

Livvy gave a laugh. "It's actually quite odd. You're moving away from the country just as Edmund and I have decided to move into it."

"You're moving?"

"Yes, Edmund has at last agreed." She paused and sipped her wine thoughtfully. "I had become really depressed lately, you know the childless thing and the fact that Edmund was always working. Last year I gave up my work because I wasn't enjoying it, but that left me with a lot of time on my hands. I began to feel miserable, as if life were passing me by. Anyway, Edmund must have noticed my gloom because quite suddenly he suggested we sold our Norwich house and buy somewhere in the country, not too far from the hospital of course. He even suggested I should keep horses." She gave a laugh. "Bless him, he hates horses."

Natasha stood up. "Doesn't this stuff go down easily? Let's have another bottle to celebrate our new lives."

Livvy also stood up. "I'd better leave Edmund a message to say I'm staying the night. I can't possibly drive back now."

Once they had settled again Natasha asked, "Have you found anywhere yet?"

Livvy shook her head. "We've looked at one or two places but they didn't seem quite right. We actually thought about Florence's farm now that she is giving up, but the estate needed to keep it as a working farm and we wouldn't want that."

Natasha threw another log on the fire and they sat in silence sipping their wine. Suddenly she leapt to her feet and shouted, "I've got it!" She shouted so loudly Livvy jumped. "I have the perfect solution. You and Edmund must take over the Dower House. It would be ideal, near enough to the hospital for Edmund but enough in the country for you. There's even room for horses. It's the answer to both our problems."

Livvy thought about it and then said cautiously, "I'd like to say yes because you're right, it would be perfect. But won't you want a lot of money for it? We might not be able to afford it."

"Oh that isn't a problem." Natasha sounded scornful. "I'm sure we can easily come to an agreement and I honestly don't think it would fetch that much. People don't want draughty old houses these days, especially out in the Styx as Euan would say. Anyway, I'd much rather you had it than sell it to a stranger. After all you are a Roxby. Let's keep it in the family." And she smiled to herself, thinking how annoyed Euan would have been by this conversation.

Next morning found them both feeling rather fragile. Natasha plopped the alka-seltzers into two glasses and they stared at the fizzing liquid.

"I am definitely in pain," Livvy admitted.

Natasha nodded. "Never mind, it was worth it and did us both good," and she gave a sigh "I met Mrs B removing the bottles this morning and received yet another reproving look. My black marks are coming in thick and fast."

As if to underline the point Mrs B entered with a pot of coffee. She banged it down and the door closed behind her with rather more force than necessary and Natasha burst out laughing. "Did you see her face? It's enough to turn the milk sour. Thank goodness the B's have given me a month's notice. It saves me the unpleasant task of doing it myself."

Livvy poured out the coffee. "You didn't tell me they were going."

"Quite honestly, compared to all the other disasters that hit me yesterday, the B's departure seemed very minor. Mrs B informed me they wanted to move out of the area because of the problems with their nephew Clive. There was a local scandal when he was caught stealing. This may have been part of the reason, but poor old B looked embarrassed and unhappy. I am sure he didn't want to leave. The beautiful vegetable garden, which you will inherit, is entirely B's creation. However, Mrs B's mind was made up. She is one of those women either totally for you, or totally against. Before the Gerry scandal she was the most loyal person you could find. Afterwards, well those damned papers changed all that and it's Mrs B who lays down the law in that household. No, in the circumstance it's worked out rather well. You and Edmund won't need them."

Livvy shot her a look. "You're still serious then? About selling the house?"

"Of course I am why shouldn't I be?"

"Well we'd both had quite a lot to drink…"

Natasha laughed. "I know but I was very serious, in 'vino veritas' and all that. What about you? Are you still as keen on the idea?"

Livvy said quickly, "Oh yes absolutely, the more I think about it, the more ideal it seems. I was trying not to get too excited in case you changed your mind."

"Well I haven't." Natasha said firmly, "You'll just have to behave like Mrs B and put your foot down. Tell Edmund it's a fait accompli. If he's uncertain you should add that it has family links, he can't argue with that. Anyway I am presuming our plan will work out and I shall ring Miriam to tell her to start looking for London houses at once."

Livvy looked at her admiringly, "You don't waste any time do you?"

Natasha gave a shrug. "These last few months have rather changed my outlook on life. It's made me realise we can't waste our lives in dithering." She paused. "I'll tell you something else I've decided Livvy. Once I'm settled in London I'm going to find a job," and she added quickly, "It's nothing to do with needing money, Gerry has left us well provided for. It's just something I want to do. I'm actually thinking of going back to the hospital to work with AIDS patients."

Livvy looked astonished. "I would have thought that was the last thing you wanted to be involved in right now."

Natasha shook her head. "On the contrary, I really want to help and I think I could. There's a great need for people to form Support Groups. I'm going to ring Michael Sternfeld once I'm settled in London and get his advice." She added, "If you remember Michael was Gerry's doctor. He's a brilliant man and runs that AIDS unit almost single-handedly."

Livvy noted the change of tone when Natasha mentioned Michael. She gave her cousin a long look. "Don't tell me you're falling for him?"

"Good lord no, it's nothing like that," Natasha said almost too quickly. "I just admire him. He's a great doctor, totally selfless and dedicated."

They were quiet for a moment. Then Livvy asked, "So what are you going to do about Euan?"

Natasha looked uneasy. "Honestly Livvy? I just don't know. I need to give him a cooling off period I suppose and then take it from there. He hasn't heard my new plans yet. We'll see how he reacts to those."

Euan didn't have a chance to react that day because in the afternoon Natasha made the trip to the hospital to see Florence.

When she arrived the nurse said severely, "Don't stay long. She's only just out of intensive care." This sounded serious, so it was with some relief that Natasha found Florence sitting up in bed looking very alert, her white hair fluffed out like some exotic bird.

"I'm so glad you could come," she said as Natasha bent down to kiss her. "I needed to see you."

Natasha sat beside her. "I was intending to visit you anyway but didn't expect to find you in here. Are you feeling better?"

Florence made an impatient gesture as if her illness was the last thing she wanted to talk about. "Yes, it was nothing, just a mild heart attack. Everyone is making an unnecessary fuss. I've told the doctors to let me out by the end of the week." She gave a chuckle. "I'm such an appalling patient they may well do just that."

Natasha gave a frown. "I don't think you ought to think of going back to the farm too soon."

"Well I'm not going back to the farm," Florence declared. "The fact is the old ticker has been playing up for some time, so I had already arranged to leave the farm and go to somewhere more suitable. I shall go straight from here to my new residence, a perfectly decent nursing home. That's why I needed to see you. There's something I want you to have. It's at the farm and you will have to go over and collect it." She opened her locker and took out a piece of paper. "This is the name and number of the man who holds the keys to the house. Get in touch with him and he will let you in. In the hallway you will find two pictures that were painted by your grandmother. I wanted you to have them because I remember you saying how Bernard left all Audrey's paintings to that dreadful woman. What was her name?"

"Gemma Woods."

"That's the one. Isn't it odd how you can never remember the names of people you dislike? Anyway, those pictures are yours. I always loved them and know you will too. Your grandmother was such a talented artist."

Natasha was both touched and delighted, but Florence cut short her thanks with a wave of the arm, indicating the subject was closed. "The rest of my things are being packed up and sold at Auction and will eventually go into my Estate. Dear old Wal is dealing with all that."

This made Natasha smile. "I sometimes wonder if Wal has time for any other work outside family matters. He was really wonderful over the whole Gerry business."

Florence looked at her. "That must have been an ordeal. You ought to give yourself time to recover. It must be a great relief to be home."

Natasha made a face and shook her head. "I only returned to Norfolk a few days ago and it's been pretty awful since then." She didn't mention Euan but told Florence of her frosty reception in the village and the letter from the school.

Florence sighed. "I sometimes lose all patience with my fellow man. The older I get, the more crassly stupid I find the majority of human beings. Animals are so much more agreeable." She fixed her sharp eyes on Natasha. "So what happens now?"

Natasha hesitated. "I think I am going to sell up and move back to London. I can't bring Laura back to the village after what's happened," she paused, "actually, I'm hoping Livvy and Edmund might take over the Dower House when I leave. Livvy seemed very keen on the idea when I suggested it and I think it would be perfect for her."

"That's marvellous news." Florence's face lit up with a smile. "It's about time Edmund understood Livvy's needs. She's a country girl at heart." She regarded Natasha with some concern. "And will you be happy leaving the country and going back to town?"

Natasha nodded. "Yes I will. I was never as countrified as Livvy. I know it is the right place for me now and also I'll have plenty of choice of schools for Laura. I also want to find her a 'cello teacher. I hope I don't sound like a doting mother because I'm really not, but she definitely has a talent and best of all she loves playing without any pushing from me." Florence smiled at this and Natasha added, "I left Laura behind in London while I sort things here. She is staying with Wal and Miriam." The blue eyes looked questioningly at Natasha who said quickly, "I have been really surprised by Miriam. I remember her as strict and controlling with her own children, but with Laura she's completely different. If anything she's almost too indulgent and Laura loves being with her."

Florence said drily, "Gracious me, she must have changed. I used to feel sorry for Belinda, Alex and Ben. Having no children of my own

I became very fond of them and was worried by their cold, cheerless upbringing. Of course they had everything money could buy, but they were emotionally starved. Wal bless his heart was hardly ever at home and when he was he didn't seem able to relate to them somehow. It's probably why Belinda married an older man. What's that husband's name?" Natasha told her it was Nigel and she said, "That's him, such a boring fellow."

Natasha thought of the opera evening and Nigel fussing over Belinda, calling her his 'child bride'. "They are slightly tiresome together," she said with a sigh.

Florence was more forthright. "I find them maddening but Belinda now has all the affection she could ever crave for." She chuckled, "If my old fellow had behaved like that I'd have cheerfully strangled him. Any sign of children?"

Natasha shook her head. "Not yet. They're very besotted with their new puppy."

Florence sighed and murmured, "How depressing," but made no further comment. Instead she looked at Natasha. "If you are moving to London what happens to Euan?"

Did this woman forget nothing?

"I think," Natasha said slowly, suddenly voicing her thoughts out loud, "I think Euan and I may have reached the end of the road. It will make me very unhappy but somehow I have to be brave enough to accept this and finish it once and for all."

Florence took her hand and spoke kindly but firmly. "Yes, my dear that is indeed what you have to do. I have heard enough to know that your relationship with Euan cannot survive. You have a great deal of courage. Go and make a new life for yourself. It may seem like the end of the world for a while but I know you will be fine." She removed her hand. "In fact I am sure of it. You see, you are like me at your age and I have a strong feeling there will be someone else for you, just like my dear old boy turning up for me."

She closed her eyes as if that speech had taken her last bit of strength. Natasha stood up and kissed her on the forehead. "Please be sensible and do as the doctors say. I shall come and see you again soon, if not here then in your new residence." She squeezed Florence's frail hand. "Thank you so much for the pictures. They will always remind me of you."

Florence smiled a sweet contented smile.

She died two days later, a massive heart attack in her sleep.

"I think she knew it was going to happen," Livvy said. "She had spent the last few months putting her affairs in order. I'm really going to miss her. She was such a wise old bird."

"Not old," Natasha said, "Florence had the gift of eternal youth."

The next day she was walking towards the vegetable garden when she saw Euan coming up the drive towards her. Her heart began to thump uncomfortably. She wasn't sure she yet had the stomach for a final confrontation.

"Hello stranger," he said.

The rangy charm was still there but she was determined not to be thrown by it.

"Hello," she said, with just a touch of hostility.

"Oh dear, I see I'm still in disgrace." He smiled and held out a package. "I've brought you a present, by way of saying I am sorry about what happened. I went 'gang agley' as my father would have said."

"What does that mean?"

He smiled. "It means to go off the rails."

She removed the brown paper and took out three antique silver frames. They were beautiful but she thought miserably it changed nothing. His deep down anger with her remained and it was that anger that had made him break the frames in the first place.

"Thank you," she said. There was an awkward silence. She looked up at the sky. "Isn't it odd weather, so sunny and mild? It's more like spring than winter."

He smiled at her disarmingly. "What a very Jane Austen observation." She remembered he had made that comment once before in rather similar circumstances and it increased her misery. He looked at her. "Does Miss Austen think it is warm enough to sit outside?"

They moved across the lawn to the garden bench. B was working in the distance and the church clock chimed midday. It was a peaceful scene. She didn't really want to shatter it. After a long silence she said, "I've decided to sell the Dower House and move back to London."

Euan looked at her shocked. "Isn't that a rather sudden decision?"

"I don't think so. After everything that's recently happened here it seemed the logical thing to do." She stared straight ahead, not wanting to meet his eye. "In fact, it has worked out well. Livvy and Edmund are going to take over the house."

Before he could stop himself he said, "How convenient, keeping it in the family eh?"

She gave a sigh. "I thought you'd make comment like that. I'm actually very relieved. There'll be no complications with Estate Agents and the whole deal can go through quickly, which is just the way I want it." She had a defiant look on her face.

Euan was silent and then said, "Have you definitely made up your mind to go to London?"

"Yes."

He made a study of her. She was different somehow and it left him unsure how to proceed. This certainly wasn't going the way he had anticipated.

After a moment he said quietly, "I was actually going to ask you to come away with me." Her heart began to pound but she said nothing. He went on, "At last we finally have a chance of making a life together. I've been waiting for nearly ten years to ask you. Gerry has died and that part of your life is over. We could both make a fresh start." He paused to see how she was taking it but couldn't tell. Her face had an impassive expression. He decided to continue. "I've just done a good publishing deal and there's more work on offer, so finance is no problem. It doesn't tie me to any particular place so we could go almost anywhere." He hesitated. "I don't actually think London is the best idea for us. There would be no chance of getting away from the old life. There are too many old memories in London, too many people..."

"Too many members of my family." she said pointedly.

He didn't answer straight away, sensing danger. Finally he gave a sigh. "I just don't think we stand a chance if we are in close proximity to your old life. I want you with me Tash, I want you badly, but you must give us a chance to make it work."

He sat back, lit a cigarette and waited for a response.

At last she said slowly, "When you say 'us', does that include Laura?"

Euan looked a little uncomfortable, "Well, yes, of course."

The lack of enthusiasm in his voice confirmed her worst fears. With a sinking heart she said, "You have to understand Euan, things have changed. It's not just you and me any longer. I now have to think of Laura as well. However much you say she is included, I know that it's only because you know you can't have me without her." She turned to him with tears in her eyes. "Don't you see? That's just not good enough. She can't just be dragged along as a sort of," she searched for the word, "as a sort of appendage. She's just been through a traumatic experience. It wouldn't be fair to uproot her to somewhere strange after all the upheaval she's gone through recently." Euan was still silent and Natasha added, "It's why London will be best for us. It will give her a period of stability among the people she knows and loves."

"Meaning your family," he was unable to keep the scorn out of his voice.

Something in Natasha snapped. "Oh for goodness sake Euan, you are obsessed with this family thing. I'm beginning to think something dreadful must have happened in your childhood" She paused. "If it did, isn't it time you sorted it out and got over it? Otherwise this 'family' thing will haunt you forever. Laura has less family than anyone I know. She has no grandparents to speak of, because you can't include my father who we never see. She has no father, no brothers or sisters. I am all the actual family she has. However, she does have people she's grown attached to and yes, some of them are related to me in some way, Miriam, Wal, Dolly, Tinker and Livvy. Why should that matter? They happen to be people who are part of our lives. You can't expect me to cut myself off from everyone I know and love just because you want me too. I am hoping once we're in London we'll make new friends…"

"Friends?" he cut in, "Or are you looking for a new man in your life, someone who will give you a conventional marriage and be a father to Laura?"

She said impatiently, "I'm not looking for anyone Euan. I just want to try and make the best life I can for Laura and myself." She got up and walked away from him. He watched her and felt annoyed for having badly misjudged the situation. He realised too late he should have included Laura from the start.

Natasha didn't turn round. She tried hard get control of herself because it would be all too easy to cry. Finally summoning all her strength she turned to face him and blurted out, "You and I can't make a life together Euan. It is time we both faced it. God knows I've wanted us to be together for so long I'm worn out with longing. But I know it won't work. Each time we've tried it has gone terribly wrong. There's just too much in our past that causes problems, too many skeletons." She held his gaze, her voice calmer now. "You know it. I know it. And this isn't something that can just be blamed on Laura. All right, I agree she has made a difference, but the reasons are the same as they were ten years ago. Somehow no matter how much we love each other, we always end up fighting. We go round in circles and always finish at the same point. You complain about me living in my past but I feel I am living with yours as well in some way. I know you will reject that but it's true." He stubbed out his cigarette but still said nothing. She made a helpless gesture. "Maybe the real reason is that I can't be the sort of person you want me to be."

He sounded impatient. "What on earth is that supposed to mean?"

She shrugged and said miserably, "I don't have your way with words and I'm no good explaining how I feel. I only know that everything is fine between us as long as I do what you expect of me and hide what I really want or think is right."

Euan snapped, "That simply isn't true..."

"It is Euan," she retorted. "You're always telling me what I have to do, how I have to think, how I have to feel. I am always being swayed away from decisions that I know deep down are right, and then, f I don't agree with you, you get angry and annoyed. Look how angry you were with my decision over Gerry. How long would I have had to live with that anger? Would you ever let it go? Even now you're laying down the law telling me I have to cut myself off from everyone I love and go right away. Did it ever occur to you that this is not what I would want? Did it ever occur to you that I might not entirely agree with the way you live and do things?"

"What sort of things? Be more specific."

She shrugged. "Well to be honest, I find your moods difficult to cope with. I don't like it when you go out on your benders. It upsets me when you sneer at people I like. It upsets me when you show contempt for things that I believe in. I feel stressed when I am put under pressure to reverse decisions I know in my heart are right. I feel I can't be my own person..." She paused then said quietly, "It actually upsets me that you had an affair with Hilary Walters."

"Oh for God's sake, that wasn't an affair."

"Are you denying you slept with her?"

"No but it was nothing. It meant nothing."

"It did to me," she said sadly and he could see she meant it. "It's nothing to do with approval or disapproval. It was to do with trust. Suddenly I didn't trust you anymore and I felt betrayed."

He burst out angrily," If you hadn't left me to do your Florence Nightingale act, it wouldn't have happened. It was out of anger and frustration. I got drunk and she was there, simple as that. Good God, you ask me to understand *you*. Why can't you understand *me*? It has been ten years of waiting and I've tried my damndest to be patient, but Christ, you'd try the patience of a saint and I am no saint."

She gave a bleak smile. "I don't think either of us is a candidate for canonization" She sat down beside him again. "Please, I don't want this to turn into a series of recriminations. I really regret what hell I've put you through, the hell I've put us both through. I only hung on because I know I will never love anyone else in the way I love you. But I also know this has to stop now and we shouldn't prolong the agony."

He sensed defeat. Looking directly at her he said, "Is this it then?"

"Don't you see it has to be?" Her courage was almost out. She gave a mirthless laugh. "You'll be all right Euan. In the end what matters to you is your writing. I'm not saying you didn't love me..."

"Do," he corrected her.

She smiled, "All right, do, but you still have writing to fill your life. You don't really need me."

He shook his head. "That's not true, but if that's what you want to think I probably can't change your mind."

They were silent again. At last she stood up and said hesitantly, "I think I need to find something to fill my life as well. I'm going to find a job when I get to London."

He looked startled, "What sort of a job? Will you go back to painting?"

"No, not that," she hesitated, "I've decided to work with AIDS patients."

His reaction was hostile as she knew it would be. "Doing what for heaven's sake?"

"I'm not sure yet, some sort of counselling. I'll start off by joining one of their Support Groups."

He groaned. "Oh God, you're going to turn yourself into one of those terrible middle-class do-gooders."

She said angrily, her eyes blazing. "You see? That's exactly what I mean. That exactly illustrates what I have been saying. You sneer at everything and I can't live with that continual contempt."

He stood up. "You know you're very beautiful when you're angry." Holding out his arms he said, "Come here."

She went to him and they stood motionless for a while, clinging on to each other.

"We've been here before," he whispered in her ear. She nodded, too miserable to speak. "I hear everything you say Tash, only this time it has to be final. I shall go right away. If I leave now the break will be permanent. Do you understand that?" She nodded again. "God help me," he burst out, "It wouldn't be so bad if I didn't love you so damnably."

He kissed her almost roughly then pushed her away.

She watched him as he walked away across the lawn and out of her life.

*

For the next two days she walked about in a dreamlike state. She felt numb. She didn't even cry. Maybe she had no tears left. There were moments before he finally left when she was tempted to run down the drive, fling herself into his arms and tell him that she hadn't meant any of it. But each time somehow she managed to stop herself. At night she would stare at his empty pillow, remembering the way he'd looked at her, the sound of his voice and the feel of his touch. Why on earth had she thrown all that away? Nobody could ever make her feel like that again. At these times the memories would overwhelm her with an almost physical pain.

A week after his departure she received a letter and a cheque. It merely said,

Herewith money for two month's rent. A van will collect my things next week and put them in store. I have no immediate plans but may travel for a while. Be well and happy, my love, always, Euan.

On the last day at the Dower House she sat in her bolt-hole staring out onto the garden. Zack was cutting the coppice and she could hear the sound of chopping from her window. It was like the last act of the Cherry Orchard. It had all happened so quickly. Wal had organised the transfer of the house to Livvy and Edmund with speed and efficiency. Miriam had thrown herself into the task of finding them a London house and it only needed her now to make a decision. The packing cases were in the hall. The B's were taking care of Miffin until their departure at the end of the month. After that Livvy would take over until she had her London house ready.

She neither felt excited or depressed at the thought of the new life ahead. Her only wish was that the terrible ache in her heart would finally disappear.

Maybe in time it would.

She looked down at her watch and sighed. As long as she wore his watch there would be a constant reminder. But it really made no difference. Euan would always be part of her. Even if the pain eventually did leave, the memories of him would always remain.

EPILOGUE
OCTOBER 1996

Six months passed. Euan spent the first four in exile, wandering Byron-like round Europe. Eventually he made his way to Greece but there the Isles of Greece made him homesick for Scotland and so he returned. He stayed with his brother Cal for a few days and met his wife and two nephews for the first time. One night he and Cal had stayed up into the small hours hitting the whisky bottle and talking over their childhood. It went some way to purging the damage their father had done to them and it gave him a moment of wry amusement to think he had finally done something that would have met with Natasha's approval. He had never talked to her about his own childhood skeletons, but instinctively she had known he had them. Stupidly he had left taking action too late for her and regret and sadness swept over him. He knew how much she would have enjoyed meeting Cal and his family as well.

It was while staying with Cal that he heard about the house on Mull. From its description it sounded exactly the sort of place he wanted and he travelled across the water to see it. The house was situated on the Ross of Mull, and looked out over the Sound towards Iona. The owner wanted a quick sale. With no hesitation Euan put in a cash offer and to his surprise it was accepted low as it was. However, getting his furniture and books out of store and installed at Fintra had been a complicated business. They'd had to be brought up from London to Oban, loaded onto the ferry to Craigmure and then driven across the island. Now he had been installed for nearly two months and he felt he had finally come home.

The house stood in isolated ground a few miles from the village. It was built of solid grey stone but the interior was white and in every room there were great open fireplaces for the peat. As a rule his only companions were the seagulls that wheeled and mewed above him. On a clear day, when the skies were blue, he could see Iona Abbey and the white sand of the beaches. On grey days the mist swirled in from the sea and the birds huddled together on the telephone wires looking wet and bedraggled. He didn't mind this weather. It was good for writing, or so he hoped.

His life took on a kind of routine. He spent most of the day working, with occasional breaks for walking. In the evening he'd go down to the local hostelry where he would find good company and food. When he didn't feel like cooking a local girl Meg came in to cook and clean for him. Quite early on she'd taken to crawling into his bed some nights as well. He hadn't thrown her out. She was pleasing enough and gave him some relief from the memories that interrupted his waking hours and most of his sleeping ones as well. Damn Natasha! Would he never be able to rid himself of her?

Occasionally, as he glanced across the Sound towards Iona and saw the McBain Ferry coming in, he would remember the three of them, standing on the quay all those years ago. So vivid was the memory he could almost see the tall, beautiful Celia and the leggy child with her mass of chestnut curls, playing ducks and drakes at the water's edge.

Otherwise his memories were all of Natasha. He recalled the first moment of seeing her grown up; a skinny waif dressed all in black but still with those chestnut curls. He remembered her at Fay Stanhope's party when she arrived clutching a bunch of lilies, an entrance that made everyone in the room gasp. She had such a strange mixture of beauty and innocence and yet she never seemed to be aware of the effect she had on people. As he stared out of the window he would remember the most poignant memory of all. It was on her wedding day, when she had been a vision in white with flowers like stars in her hair, but on her face had been a terrible look of anguish as she realised the terrible mistake she had just made. Oh God, if only he hadn't been such a fool and stopped her from going to Gerry.

The fleeting memories were almost the worst... the odd expression, the husky voice, her scent, her touch... It was at these times he reached for the bottle and drowned his sorrows. He told himself it would have been easier if she'd died. There would have been some solace in bereavement. He could then have grieved for her properly with the memories belonging to him alone. Instead he was tortured with the thought that she might yet be someone else's to enjoy and cherish. That was too much to bear. He couldn't concentrate on anything. Each writing project he started was quickly abandoned. His restless mind could stick at nothing.

One night the mist turned to driving rain and he sat listening to it beating down on the roof. The peat in the fire gave out a gentle, sweet smell. He lit a cigarette and turned on the radio. It was the slow movement of the Schubert Quintet. Euan shivered as the ghosts returned once more. The last time he'd heard that music had been in Garrick Square. Natasha had been on the sofa, her head in his lap and he had stroked her hair while they had listened together. Neither of them had spoken. Afterwards they went up to bed and there... and there...

The movement came to an end. He could bear it no longer. He stood up and switched off the music. Suddenly his mind was made up. Throwing some clothes into a case he drove the car to the village and informed Meg he would be away for a few days. Then he took the ferry to Oban and caught the next night train to London.

There was no disguising the uneasiness in Wal's voice. "Are you in London Euan?"

"For a few days," came the clipped reply.

"Are you on business?"

Euan smiled knowing full well the reason for Wal's questioning. He was terrified he was in London to see Natasha. "Yes Wal, I'm here on business."

"Oh right," Wal sounded relieved. "Do I get to see you?"

"I'd like that."

They arranged a meeting for the following day.

Wal decided not to mention this conversation to Miriam. It would only worry her and he didn't want to jeopardise what seemed to him like her complete recovery.

*

He looked rather enviously at Euan as he entered his office the next day. The man looked fit with a faded suntan that had obviously not been acquired in England. This year the summer had been a washout.

"I see you've been away," he said.

Euan sat down. "Very good Sherlock! I travelled for a while and finished up in Greece. I've not been back long."

"Back where?" Wal again sounded nervous.

Euan took his cigarettes out of his pocket. "Do you mind?"

Wal shook his head and handed over the client ashtray. Euan blew out the smoke slowly. "I've bought a house in Scotland, on the Ross of Mull."

"Is that Mull the island?"

"That's the one."

"And you're writing?"

"I've been trying to," Euan said drily. "Just lately I've been suffering from writer's block but I hope when I embark on my new project I shall soon become unblocked."

"Am I allowed to know what the new project is?" Wal asked.

Euan smiled. "No" he said and stubbed out his cigarette.

After a moment he looked directly at Wal. "How is Natasha?"

Wal said cautiously, "She's well I think. I haven't seen her for a while. She's been busy with her new house." He paused. "Is that why you're here, to see Natasha?"

Euan shook his head. "No we won't be seeing each other again. We decided it would be better to make the break permanent."

Wal tried to disguise his relief. "That was probably a wise decision."

Euan said savagely, "For whom?"

There was silence in the room and then he said more calmly. "Is she seeing anyone?"

Wal looked uncomfortable. "I am the last person to know these things but I think she has formed a friendship with Gerry's doctor." He added quickly, "It's to do with the work she is doing at the hospital. I don't think it's in any way a romantic attachment."

Euan said grimly, "I think you'll find it probably is, or at least will be." He looked at Wal's anxious expression. "I could never have given

Natasha what she wanted. I hope she can find someone without all the baggage we carried. She rightly said there were too many skeletons for us to deal with. She has gone through enough. I only wish her happiness now."

He stood up and handed Wal a card. "I came to give you this. It is my new address and telephone number in Scotland. If anything happens to Natasha I want you to let me know."

Wal began to feel a nervous tick in his eye. What sort of thing was Euan envisaging? He stared down at the card. "What if something happens to you? Do you want me to tell Natasha?" It was like some complicated opera plot.

Euan looked at him quizzically. "Has Natasha asked you to tell her?"

"Well, no she hasn't."

"Then don't."

Really, Wal thought crossly, they are the most impossible pair. They can't live with each other and they can't live without each other and I'm the one always caught in the cross-fire. He hadn't actually heard Natasha mention Euan once since coming to London, but just occasionally he caught her with a sad expression and wondered if that was because of Euan. Dear God, they couldn't both be miserable for the rest of their lives could they? Surely the wounds would heal in time? Miriam was convinced there was already something between Natasha and the doctor. He wasn't so sure. Natasha had been through the kind of affair that didn't just die away overnight. She would need more time. It would be a relief if the doctor was prepared to give it, because he seemed a good man. Whatever happened in the future he hoped he could stay out of it and not be asked for advice ever again.

As Euan moved towards the door Wal said, "How long are you going to be in London? Do you have time to come round to Walbrook Grove for a meal? I'm sure Miriam would love to see you."

Euan threw back his head and laughed. "Wal you are a hopeless liar. You know perfectly well Miriam wouldn't want that at all."

Wal looked sheepish and suddenly totally out of character Euan crossed the room and gave him a great hug. "You've been a wonderful friend Wal and I'm grateful for all your help. I know how difficult it has been for you." He turned at the door and gave a smile, "And now I'm off to see a shrink."

Wal looked amazed. "I thought you'd be the last person in need of a shrink."

Euan smiled. "It's purely for research. I'm seeing a man called Strutter."

Wal gave a start. "Wait a minute. Didn't Celia have a psychiatrist called Strutter?"

"Indeed she did. You have a good memory."

Wal frowned. "Celia died nearly sixteen years ago. He must be quite old by now."

Euan shrugged. "Middle sixties I should imagine. He's still practising at the same address in Wimpole Street." His parting words were, "Don't tell Natasha you've seen me. She knows she has my love."

The next day Euan arrived at Wimpole Street at the allotted time and asked the receptionist for Dr Strutter.

"You can go straight in Mr Mackay" she said. "He is expecting you."

Dr Strutter was at his desk but as Euan entered he stood up and went to meet him. "How good of you to be punctual," he said shaking Euan's hand. "So many people regard punctuality as an optional extra these days, which I find most annoying." He indicated for Euan to sit in one of the large leather armchairs and he sat down opposite him in the other.

Euan studied him and was surprised how little he had changed over the years. He was just as he remembered, a neat, dapper little man.

He said, "I think I should tell you at once that I haven't come to see you as a patient."

Dr Strutter stroked the knees of his trousers. "I rather presumed not. My secretary tells me you want to collect Celia Roxby Smith's notebook, is that correct?"

Euan nodded. "I wasn't sure whether you'd still have it after all this time. It is sixteen years since Celia had the car accident."

"Is it really that long?" Dr Strutter crossed the room and opened a cupboard. "We never seem to throw anything away here, although we shall run out of storage space soon. Here it is." He handed the slim black book to Euan.

"I'm very relieved you found it," Euan told him. "You see it is Celia's account of her sessions with you and I need it as research for a book I'm writing."

Dr Strutter looked quizzical, "About Celia?"

Euan nodded, "About both of them actually."

A strange look crossed Euan's face and it was a look that didn't escape Dr Strutter's notice. He waited for further enlightenment. Euan spoke in clipped tones, "I have been having a love affair with Celia's daughter Natasha on and off for the last ten years. It only ended recently."

"I see," Dr Strutter again stroked his knees. He said no more but privately thought it was an interesting situation. First this man had lost the mother and now evidently he'd lost the daughter as well.

Euan said suddenly, "Do you remember Celia's 'Parallel Lines Theory'? How the events in certain people's lives seemed to run in parallels?"

"Indeed I do."

"Well I think she might have been on to something. It could form the basis of a book."

Dr Strutter was again silent. After a moment he asked, "Forgive me for being curious, but is Natasha like her mother?"

"In some ways yes," Euan replied. "It's not so much a physical resemblance. Celia was taller and had different colouring. No, it's more the similarity in their expressions and gestures." He paused. "In other ways Natasha is completely different. She is more centred than Celia was and more confident. Although still young, she is a woman of great courage and integrity." He added quietly, "I find her quite impossible to forget."

Dr Strutter remained lost in thought. There was only the sound of the ticking clock on the mantelpiece. "I have certainly never forgotten her mother," he murmured at last.

Euan regarded the good doctor thoughtfully, suddenly struck by something that had never occurred to him before. Dr Strutter had been in love with Celia. Wasn't that rather odd? It was usually the patient that fell for the shrink not the other way round. He wondered if Celia knew.

Dr Strutter interrupted his thoughts and said with a smile, "So is the plan to write these two women out of your system?"

Euan gave a mirthless laugh. "Something like that, or at least, it is what I am hoping." He stood up. "I won't take up any more of your time Dr Strutter."

Dr Strutter shook his hand. "I wish you good luck with your book Mr Mackay."

As Euan reached the door he said, "Would you be kind enough to send me a copy when it is published? I should like to read it."

A few days later Euan was back on Mull.

He installed himself at his desk and with calm deliberation opened a new writing pad. Staring out of the window for a while he seemed lost in thought. Then he picked up the antique pen that Natasha had given him.

'Write something beautiful with it,' she had told him.

Well he would. He would write the story of their three lives. He would write about Celia, and Natasha, and how he was inextricably bound to them both.

For a moment he held the pen poised above the blank page. Then in a neat hand he printed out the title at the top,

PARALLEL LINES.

Printed in Great Britain
by Amazon